A MILLION MIRACLES

USA TODAY BEST SELLING AUTHOR
ROBERTA KAGAN

Copyright © 2024 by Roberta Kagan

All rights reserved.

No part of this book may be reproduced in any form or by any electronic or mechanical means, including information storage and retrieval systems, without written permission from the author, except for the use of brief quotations in a book review.

ISBN (ebook): 978-1-957207-85-8
ISBN (Paperback): 978-1-957207-86-5
ISBN (Hardcover): 978-1-957207-87-2

Title Production by The BookWhisperer

PROLOGUE

In a small town about forty miles outside of Krakau, Poland a little boy with golden curls that have been kissed by the sun, sits in the plush green grass in front of a two-story brick house. His skin glows in the sunlight as he plays with the toy gun his father gave him as a gift for his fifth birthday. "Liam, there is a war going on," his father explains as he uses his hands to show his son how to hold the gun properly with his finger on the trigger.

At first, the child looked at the gun skeptically, not knowing what to do with it.

His father seemed perplexed by the boy's response. "Liam, you must never be afraid of guns, or of war. You must realize, even at your tender age, that you have an advantage because you are a superior man—a German—a pure Aryan. And you will grow up to rule the world. This is your destiny."

Liam wasn't sure what any of this meant exactly, but he knew his father was smiling, and his mother was too. His father rarely smiled at him. He wasn't one to smile easily. So, even though Liam didn't understand what his father was trying to convey, he was happy to have his approval.

"These are the flags of the enemy," his father said as he revealed a poster to Liam. On it were the photos of three flags. "Now, stand up like a man, aim at these flags and then shoot them."

Liam looked up at his father, confusion written across his face. He didn't know how to shoot a gun, but he didn't want to disappoint his father. Liam's gaze dropped to the ground, and he began shaking his head. He was trying hard not to cry. He knew his father hated weakness, and he longed for his approval. Liam shuddered as his father stared at him.

"Ahh, I suppose, I can give you a little leeway. After all, you are only five years old, and I can't expect you to know how to fire a gun." His father said as he stood up and straightened his SS officer's uniform. "So, I will teach you."

Liam was relieved when his father ruffled his hair as he picked up the toy gun. "Now watch me carefully, because some day very soon you will be using a real gun." The older man said as he pointed the weapon at the picture of the red, white, and blue flag on the poster, then he took perfect aim and pretended to shoot. "I fired my gun at the American flag and that means that I just killed an American." Liam's father smiled. "Now, my son, it's your turn. You aim at the Russian flag." He said, pointing to the second flag on the poster. Liam took the gun. His little hands were trembling as he took aim.

I hope I do it right. I don't want Daddy to be angry with me. I don't want him to hurt me again. Liam thought nervously. He had endured his father's anger and, on some occasions, had suffered beatings at his father's hand. *I wish he wasn't going to be home all night. I wish he had to leave and go to work.*

"Shoot the gun, boy," his father was losing patience.

Liam pulled the trigger as he'd seen his father do only a few minutes earlier.

"Good boy," his father nodded.

Liam smiled proudly.

Later that afternoon, while Liam's father was at work, he felt more at ease shooting at the poster of the American, Russian, and British flags. He pretended that the enemy soldiers were advancing, and he alone was holding them back. After all, he repeated the words his father had told him—he was a German, a superior Aryan man.

Liam's babysitter, who had recently turned twelve, came walking out of the house. She was carrying a cup for him that contained *Himbeersirup* — raspberry syrup — mixed with cold water. "It's really rather hot out here," she said, "I thought you might be thirsty."

Liam nodded. "I am," he said as he laid the toy gun down in the grass and drank heartily. "Look, it's snowing again, but it's so hot?" Liam said, confused as he lifted his hands up to feel the white flakes as they fluttered down from the sky.

"That's not snow, Liam. Those are ashes," the babysitter said as she raised her hands up in the air.

"Ashes? Who told you that?"

"My father," Liam's babysitter said. "But it's a secret, no one is supposed to know."

"Then why did you tell me?"

"I don't know," she said. "Just don't tell anyone else, all right?"

"All right. I won't tell anyone." Liam said. "If we're keeping secrets, then can we play the American game you taught me? Ring Around the Rosy."

"Of course, we can, but you must keep that a secret too." The young girl said, taking the cup from Liam and setting it on a table that was out of the way. Then she took Liam's hands, and they began to walk clockwise in a circle. "Come on, sing with me."

Liam giggled. Then they both began to sing, "Ring around the rosy, pocket full of posies, ashes, ashes, we all fall down." Liam and his babysitter ran around singing the little tune until they both fell to the ground laughing.

MEANWHILE, just across the way, just out of sight, a hungry and disheveled young woman stood imprisoned behind a fence of electrical barbed wire. She dare not touch the wire. One touch meant certain death by electrocution. A few feet away, above her head was a sign that read "**_Arbeit Macht Frei_**"—"Work makes you free." But of course, she knew this was a lie, unless you could consider the turning of a human body into ashes a form of freedom.

PART ONE

CHAPTER ONE

Pitor Barr felt a chill run through him as he glanced over at Horst. Horst stood smiling beside his wife Gretchen. But Pitor could see behind the smile, and he knew Horst was only pretending to be his friend. It was almost funny to Pitor, because he too was living a lie, pretending to be Konrad Hoffmann, an SS officer. Heidi, who was Konrad's fiancée and Gretchen's best friend, did not seem to notice any of it. She was too excited as she stood beside Konrad, smiling broadly. Her hands trembled as she held the small bouquet of sunflowers—the official flower of the Reich—that were wrapped together with a white ribbon.

"We're really getting married. I can hardly believe it," Heidi whispered to Pitor as she reached over and took his hand in hers, gently squeezing it. "I'm so happy. Oh Konrad, I am going to be the best hausfrau. I went for German wife training, and I promise I will not disappoint you. I know what is expected of me."

Pitor glanced over at Heidi and returned her smile. He knew he should tell her he was happy too, but this was a lie he couldn't bring himself to say, at least not right now. He had been up all night fighting painful memories, knowing that he was about to enter into a marriage that was a complete falsehood.

When Pitor looked at Heidi, it was clear to him that he could never love her, his heart still belonged to his wife, Mila. He hated everything about Heidi, especially her dedication to the Nazi party. Pitor hated the Nazis—they had taken everything he cherished away from him. They had murdered Mila and stolen Jakup, his only child. His precious son. And it was because of them that he stood here today, beside this woman, forced to live this lie. Because, although Mila was gone, he had made a vow to find his son, and Heidi was the only one who knew where little Jakup had been taken. *Mila, Mila.* He closed his eyes and saw her beautiful face in his mind. She was his *bashert*; the one person he believed God had created for him. And now she was gone. If it had not been for their son, Pitor would have taken his own life. But he had promised Mila before she died that he would find Jakup. So, he could not leave this earth before he found him and made sure his little boy was safe.

Pitor had not been listening. He had been lost in thought. Heidi nudged him, jarring him back to reality.

"I do," Heidi said. Then she looked at Pitor, waiting for him to respond.

"I do," he answered.

"I now pronounce you man and wife."

Robotically, Pitor bent down and kissed her. Gretchen and Horst clapped. But as Pitor looked up, he caught that strange look in Horst's emotionless, pale blue eyes again, that told him to beware.

As previously planned, the two couples walked to a tavern not far away for lunch to celebrate the marriage. Heidi was beaming as they sat down at a table in the corner. She laid her bouquet down on the table beside her. Pitor managed to smile at her, and when she looked back at him, her eyes were filled with admiration, and her face was glowing. Her maple brown eyes sparkled, and although Pitor had never found her to be even remotely attractive, he had to admit that today, she was almost pretty. They placed their order for steaks and beer. When the beer arrived, they toasted the newlyweds, and Heidi began to tell a funny story about how she never thought someone as handsome as Konrad might find her even remotely interesting. Pitor smiled at her indulgently, but he had other things on his mind. Now that they were married, the marriage would have to be consummated, and he would have to have intercourse with her more than once over the time they would spend together. This was a concern because he had to be very careful. How was he going to ensure that she never saw him naked? Pitor felt a bead of sweat run down the back of his neck into his SS uniform jacket. He was hiding a dangerous secret. If he was not very careful and she saw his manhood, she would know that he had been circumcised. And then she would know the truth. Pitor was sure that Heidi adored him, but he could not trust her not to turn him into the Gestapo. The Germans had been carefully trained to turn anyone in who they felt was an enemy of the Reich. And because he was circumcised, she would know that Pitor was Jewish, and that he was not the pure German SS officer by the name of Konrad Hoffmann, who he had led everyone to believe he was.

CHAPTER TWO

That night when they returned to their apartment, Heidi was giddy. She had drunk far more beer than she normally did, and she was excited to make love to her new husband. "I'm going to take a bath and put something on that I bought for tonight. It's a surprise. I think you'll like it," she said, smiling at him. "I can hardly wait to lie in your arms as der Mann, Hoffmann."

Pitor smiled at her. "I'll be here waiting, Frau Hoffmann. Take your time."

After she disappeared into the bathroom, he sat down in a chair in front of the window on the east side of his bedroom. He gazed out at the stars and began talking to Mila in his mind, as if she could hear his thoughts. *I owe you some explanations. I have done some things that I know you would find distasteful. But I promised you I would find our little boy. And now I have found a way to keep that promise. I married Heidi because she works at the Lebensborn, the place where they took Jakup. He has been adopted by an SS officer and his wife. It was strictly against the rules for Heidi to tell me where he had been taken. She could have lost her job, and from what I understand, it's a very good job. I knew I had to offer something she really wanted if I was going to get her to risk losing it. The only way I could convince her to tell me the name and address of the couple who had Jakup was to make her think I was in love with her, and even that wasn't enough. So, I had to marry her. I know this was devious and against everything I believe to be right. But when it comes to our son, I would do anything. Don't worry, she doesn't know that Jakup is my son. I told her I was obsessed with the child because he reminded me of my younger brother, who died. I know this sounds crazy, but somehow it worked.* He thought back to the day Jakup went missing and recalled that a young woman in the ghetto who lived not far from Pitor and Mila, said she saw a Nazi officer take Jakup. Pitor would have done anything to find his little boy, but at the time, he was imprisoned in the ghetto and had no idea of how he could even look for his son. So, he decided he had to find a way to get out. That was when he had joined a group who were organizing an uprising. *Mila, my love, I was so proud of you, you were so brave during the uprising. And although we didn't win, it was as successful as we could have hoped for. We were just a handful of Jews with only a handful of weapons, but we sure scared the hell out of Hitler's army.*

Hot tears ran down his cheeks. *But, I lost you.* Pitor inhaled deeply. *My darling, my Mila, my one and only true bashert. I will never get over losing you. When I laid beside your body in the forest, I wanted to die too. And my life has been empty since you have been gone. If I hadn't been discovered by that group of partizans I don't know if I would ever have found the strength to go on. But then I was captured by* Sturmscharführer *Konrad Hoffmann, a Nazi SS Officer. At first, Konrad thought I was a deserter from the German army, and he planned to turn me in. But as we made our way through the forest, I befriended Konrad, convincing him I was not a deserter, but that I was a German soldier who had been left alive after my entire platoon was killed in battle. Hoffmann and I looked so much alike that we could have been brothers.*

Konrad began to brag about his future. He said he was on his way to a gala that was going to take place high on a mountain at Hitler's retreat called the Eagle's Nest. And it was at this party that Konrad was to be promoted. He had been told that he had been selected to be one of the Führer's personal bodyguards.

That was when I started making a plan.

Pitor opened his eyes for a moment and glanced at the door to the bathroom. He could hear Heidi singing softly. Then he gazed back out at the stars and began to talk to Mila again. *I listened and learned everything I could about the life of Konrad Hoffmann. And I decided it would be helpful to infiltrate the Nazi party to find out where and why a Nazi might have taken our son. So, one night as we slept, I murdered Konrad. I took everything he owned, including his papers, and assumed his identity. And because of our uncanny resemblance, I knew that unless someone had been a close friend of Konrad's, they would never suspect that I was an imposter. I attended the dinner at the Eagle's nest where I assumed Konrad's new job and infiltrated the Nazi party.*

Pitor could hear Heidi moving around in the bathroom. She was still softly singing to herself. But he was fairly sure she was about to enter the bedroom. *What a challenge.* He thought. *How am I ever going to keep up this façade long enough to find out what I need to know from her?* He took a long swig from a bottle of schnapps that he had sitting on the table beside his bed. The bitter liquid burned his throat. And he felt his skin crawl in anticipation of the night to come. But he reminded himself that she knew where to find Jakup. And she had already told him a great deal. She had revealed a secret that made him livid. *Mila,* he thought, *Heidi told me it was Horst who had stolen Jakup. Heidi said that Horst had been instructed by his superior officer to go into Warsaw and find Polish children that looked as Aryan as possible. This was because the Germans, even with the home for the Lebensborn, could not produce enough blond haired, blue-eyed children to populate their new Germany, which the Third Reich was sure was going to rule the world for the next thousand years. Heidi was working at the Lebensborn when Horst brought Jakup in. However, she wasn't blonde hair and blue-eyed, so as a little brown sister she served the Reich by caring for the Lebensborn children.*

I guess I should tell you what the home for the Lebensborn is. It's a very disturbing program that comprises beautiful homes that had been set up all over Germany and Norway where women of pure Aryan blood are mated like prize mares with SS officers to produce perfect Aryan children. Once the children are born, they are taken from their mothers and put into the Lebensborn nursery. One year or so later, Himmler goes to the home and names these children in a naming ceremony. Once they are named, they become eligible for adoption by a married SS officer. However, the Lebensborn homes weren't able to give the Nazis as many children as they had hoped for, and so the Germans had been forced to steal Polish children from their families and Germanize them. But try as he might to steal a Polish child, Horst had been unable to fulfill his mission. Heidi said that he walked the streets of Warsaw searching for a child. But he had been unable to find a one who fit the desired criteria. It seemed the Polish families had grown wise, and they were keeping their children inside. And so, one day after a confrontation with his superior officer that left him in desperation, Horst broke the law and stole our son. He told Gretchen, his girlfriend, and Gretchen told Heidi in confidence that Horst had done the unthinkable. He had gone into the ghetto where he had taken a Jewish child that looked so Aryan no one would ever suspect that the little boy was a Jew. When Horst arrived with Jakup at Heim Hochland, he registered Jakup as a Polish child taken from Polish parents in Warsaw. No one questioned him.

CHAPTER THREE

Heidi was dabbing perfume and talcum powder all over her body. She lifted a black lace nightgown out of a box and let it fall over her head. Then she glanced in the mirror. *I am not beautiful.* She thought, *but I am so very fortunate. Konrad loves me.*

Never in her wildest dreams had Heidi thought that a man of Konrad Hoffmann's caliber would be interested in her. Each day, handsome SS officers came and went from the home for the Lebensborn where she worked, and when they married, they chose women who had blonde hair and blue eyes—Aryan goddesses. Heidi thought back to when Gretchen and Horst met. *I know Horst was not handsome nor successful, but when he showed an interest in Gretchen, I was genuinely happy for her.* Heidi's best friend, Gretchen, was initially grateful to have Horst. And after they were engaged, he felt he could confide in her, so he told her his secret. He revealed that he'd stolen a Jewish child to fill his quota. And although Heidi was jealous that Gretchen had found a husband, she loved her friend too much to turn Horst in. And so all was well, until Heidi had a different fate. When Konrad Hoffmann appeared—a blond, blue-eyed war hero, brutally handsome and holding a high-ranking post—Heidi was swept off her feet. And this changed things between Heidi and Gretchen. *Gretchen was oozing with jealousy tonight at the ceremony. I could see it written all over her face.*

CHAPTER FOUR

"Heidi, are you okay in there?" Pitor called out.

"Yes, my love. Just a few more minutes." She replied.

Pitor looked out at the stars. *I met Heidi at the gala where I was receiving Konrad's promotion, and Heidi and Gretchen were presenting the children. When Heidi and Gretchen brought the beautiful blond Lebensborn children out to display them for the adults to see how well Himmler's Lebensborn program was progressing, I saw Jakup. But I had to remain calm. From my seat on the side of the room, I watched our son playing with the other children, all the while I kept an eye on the women who were caring for him. I could feel my heart beating out of my chest, and I knew I must find a way to get close to him. And so, when I saw Horst plant a kiss on Gretchen's lips, I decided I would warm up to Heidi.*

Just then, Heidi came out of the bathroom wearing her silk negligee. "I love you," she said, looking into his deep blue eyes.

Pitor nodded. "Yes, I love you too."

That night he made sure Heidi did not touch him and discover his secret, and Pitor closed his eyes and pretended Mila lay beneath him. It was quick, but Heidi did not mind. She was so grateful to lie with her husband. "My husband," she said to him, cuddling deeper into his arms. "There isn't anything I wouldn't do for you."

"My wife," the words stung his tongue as they left his mouth, but he knew they were exactly what he needed to say for his plan to work.

CHAPTER FIVE

Poland, Auschwitz-Birkenau

Steffi Seidel stood outside sweating as the hot sun began to rise. She was in a lineup of prisoners, all of them terrified as they awaited roll call. Roll call, or *Appellplatz*, took place twice a day. But sometimes, if the guard in charge felt exceptionally cruel, the prisoners would be forced to remain standing outside for several hours regardless of the weather. Steffi looked around her and her heart ached with sadness and loss.

From the first time she saw the Nazi soldiers, she had known they would not be good for Germany. And then when they came into her neighborhood and rounded up all the Jews, she had been faced with a terrible dilemma. Her neighbors' children, Asher and Zita—two Jewish children—had come to her for help. She knew the risks, but she was born and raised a Christian and she couldn't turn her back on them. So, Steffi took them in.

After the Nazis came to power, things changed in her village— food was rationed, and everyone was hungry. Turning Jews in to the Gestapo would bring a reward of food. People would often trade their neighbors for a loaf of bread, but she could never have betrayed anyone. She would rather have starved to death. However, she understood that sometimes people were weak when they were hungry and needy. In fact, one of her friends, a young mother, who lived just a few farms away from Steffi's family farm had turned a Jewish family in. When Steffi asked her how she could do that, the woman responded, "My child was hungry. I couldn't bear to look into his eyes and see him starving. I did it for my child, Steffi." And so, although Steffi could never have done that, she forgave her. Steffi had grown up going to church every week. Before her mother got sick, she'd taught Steffi to love everyone. Once, when she wanted to know more about the life of Jesus, her mother told her that Jesus was a Jew and that the Jewish people were the chosen people, and since that day she had never felt any hatred towards them, and she could never understand why some of her friends did.

Now with the sun beating down on her head, Steffi looked around the roll call line, and realized she was alone. Her mother was dead, and she had no friends left. As she was being arrested and taken away, she pleaded with the Nazis, and the German girls she had gone to school with turned their backs and shunned her. Sometimes, when the loneliness became overwhelming, and the cruelty she witnessed was more than she could bear, Steffi secretly wished they had killed her too, rather than arresting her and bringing her to this terrible place called Auschwitz-Birkenau. If she hadn't believed that suicide was a sin, she would have found a way to take her own life. But she had to believe that she was still alive because Jesus had another purpose in mind for her. And so, she put her trust in him. Even here, in this man-made hell, she often felt the gentle hand of Jesus on her shoulder, and His love in her heart. And this was enough to convince her that her work on earth was not yet finished, because if it was, she was sure Jesus would have taken her home to Heaven.

Finally, after what felt like hours standing in line, the *Oberaufseherin*—the head female overseer—arrived. She looked annoyed that she had to stand outside as the heat of the day began to descend upon Poland. But she took the clipboard from the guard and then began to call out the prisoner's numbers. Steffi answered when her number was called. When roll call ended, Steffi was sent into another line of women who were leaving the camp to go to work at the rubber factory. Her job was miserable. It consisted of eleven hours on her feet without a break while the noxious odor of rubber grew thicker in the air by the minute, making it almost impossible to breathe.

Thinking about her life at the camp was unbearable. So lately she had begun to turn her thoughts to the one memory from her past that still made her smile. For a split second, she closed her eyes and recalled the one night that she'd spent in the arms of a kind and gentle man. A man who had the blond hair and blue eyes that the Nazis coveted, but who was not one of them. No, not at all, this man was the most kind and understanding person she'd ever met. And she was grateful that during his travels he had come upon her farm one day. Pitor Barr was his name. She repeated it silently in her mind. The first time she saw him, she'd been afraid of him. He wore the uniform of an SS officer. But she later learned that he was a Jew, only posing as a Nazi so he could find his son. There was no doubt about it; Pitor was dangerously handsome. Her eyes were still closed, but a smile came over her face as she forgot about how long she had been standing in line waiting for the guard to escort her to the rubber factory. She remembered how she had pleaded with Pitor to make love to her, and she was glad she did. It had been her first time being intimate with a man, and although she had been planning to wait until marriage, the war had changed everything. Steffi realized that with the Nazis in power, she might not live that long. So, she explained to Pitor that she didn't want to die never having known what it was like to lie in the arms of a man. He considered her request for a moment, then he agreed. He'd been so gentle and so considerate that she could make believe that she was with a man who loved her.

"Let's go. *Mach Shnell.*" The loud guttural voice of one of the guards rang through the camp as Steffi and the other women who were in line began to march to the factory. As they walked up to the front gate, a sign above them read, *Arbeit Macht Frei*. "Work makes you free. Not here." One of the women whispered, "The only thing that can free you from this place is death."

Steffi turned away from her, and when she did, she recognized a man who she had once known in school. He now wore the uniform of a Nazi officer.

She shivered as he came rushing out of the gate and over to the guard who was escorting the women to the rubber factory. She was sure it was him. Oh yes, she remembered him well. His name was Reinhard Woolf, and he was a cruel boy who taunted other boys who were smaller and weaker than himself. She never liked him, and it came as no surprise to her to see him working at Auschwitz. *It suits him to work here.* She thought. He never liked her either, because she had always been one to defend those who were too weak to speak up for themselves. Steffi hoped he had not seen her. She quickly looked away. Now that he was in a position of authority, he would certainly enjoy using his power to get back at her for all the times when she had stood up for people he was treating badly. She had caused Reinhard a lot of trouble in school by reporting him to the teachers and the principal. And now, he held her fate in his hands. This made her tremble.

Reinhard stood beside the guard whispering something that Steffi could not hear. All she could see was that the guard was nodding. Then, to Steffi's dismay the guard walked over to her and pulled her out of the line. Reinhard smiled as he took her chin roughly in his hand and turned her face towards his own. "Hello, Steffi Seidel. I'm sure you must remember me?"

She nodded.

"I can't hear you," he said. "What did you say?"

"Yes, I remember you Reinhard."

"You do have some nerve, don't you? How dare to call me Reinhard? Who do you think you are that you can refer to me by my first name?" He shook his head. "You are such a little fool. But then again, you always were, weren't you?" He didn't wait for an answer, "from now on you will refer to me as Kommandant. You will never dare to use my name again. Now, say it. Come on say, 'yes, Kommandant.'"

She repeated it, "Yes, Kommandant."

He laughed and a wicked smile lingered on his face. "That's better." Then he turned to the guard. "Do you know why this prisoner is here?"

"Yes, Kommandant. I know that she is not a Jew," the guard said. "She is a stupid woman who has proven herself to be an enemy of the Reich. She was arrested for hiding Jews."

"Shame that her hair is shaved. She wasn't bad looking before she was bald."

"It's only hair, Kommandant. It will grow back," the guard said trying to appease Reinhard. But instead, it made him angry.

"Do you think I don't know that, you idiot? Don't speak to me again unless you have something intelligent to say. It shames us Germans when one of us is so stupid. You are proving yourself not to be a superior Aryan and for that you should be ashamed." Reinhard cleared his throat as if he were losing patience. Then he grabbed Steffi's arm. "This woman will do just fine for my purpose. I'll take her."

Steffi felt her heart begin to pound. *Take me where? Where are you taking me? Of all people to find me here, why did it have to be Reinhard Woolf. He was one of the cruelest men in our town.*

"Let's go. Move." Reinhard said as he let go of Steffi's arm and nudged her in the back with his pistol.

He led her to an office behind the administration building. Then he closed the door and sat down behind a large desk and lit a cigarette. But when she sat down in the chair across from him, he said, "Did I say you could sit? No, I did not. Stand up you sow."

Steffi nodded and quickly got on her feet. It was difficult to look at him. She was afraid that her disdain towards him was obvious, so she looked down at her shoes.

For a few moments, the only sound was the ticking of the large, circular, black clock that hung on the wall. But Steffi heard her heart beating in her ears. She wanted to run, or to scream, but she didn't move or speak. She had no idea what Reinhard had in store for her, but she knew how much he enjoyed being cruel, and that left her unnerved. "Now," he said with authority. "You may sit." He pointed to one of the chairs.

Steffi sat down and folded her hands in her lap. She cast her eyes down and did not look directly at him.

"So, once again you did something stupid. You made the most crucial mistake, didn't you?"

She had no idea what he meant, but she took a quick glance at him.

"You hid Jews? I've always known you to be too soft-hearted, but this is beyond stupid. Oh Steffi, what kind of fool are you? You had to know that you were flirting with disaster. But if my memory serves me correctly you were always collecting stray animals, birds with broken wings, that sort of thing. And so these *untermenschen*, these Jews fit right into the misfit category of things you have always been trying to rescue." He shook his head, then put the cigarette he was smoking down for a moment in a strange-looking ashtray. Reinhard caught her studying the ashtray. "Interesting ashtray, is it not?" he said, smiling.

It was an ugly, misshapen thing that looked like it was rotting. But she said nothing.

"Would you like to know what it is?" he asked, but he did not wait for an answer. He kept his gaze on her as he said, "This ashtray is the pelvis of a Jewess that our esteemed camp doctor Mengele removed after she died when some experiments went wrong on her."

Steffi felt bile rise in her throat. She looked away from him and the ashtray. Reinhard picked his cigarette back up, and put it to his lips. Then he let out a laugh. "It was a gift. A very special gift. Not everyone owns one, you know. Only very special SS officers," he smiled. "I like to collect such unique things from my time working at Buchenwald. In fact, in my home just outside the camp, I own a lampshade made from human skin, well, Jewish skin, so I am not sure that you can call it human. But we all know that, right?"

She didn't answer. But it didn't stop him; he went on talking. "And, all my pillows are nice and soft. Do you know why? Because they are stuffed with the hair that we shave from Jewesses when they first come to the camp." Then he looked at the tattoo on her arm. "Ahh, it's a shame you will have to wear those ugly numbers on your arm for the rest of your years on earth. That is of course if you have any years left," then he let out a laugh.

She had so many things she wanted to say to him, and she would have done so, but she was so sick to her stomach that she could hardly speak.

"Are you sorry, Steffi?" he asked in a condescending tone. "Do you regret going against your own government? Your own people? Or do you still feel justified? You look like you have been through hell. You're skinny, and you look old. Very old. So, tell me the truth. Aren't you just a little bit sorry? Or are you just sorry that I, your old enemy, am in control of all these prisoners...you included?"

"I'm not sorry," she said boldly, but her knees were trembling, and inside she was terrified.

"We will have to see about that. We will have to see if I can't make you sorry." He smiled, and a chill ran through her. "I wonder if you still remember what you did to me?"

There was a moment of silence. *Of course I remember,* she thought, looking away from him. For a moment, in her mind's eye, she flashed back in time to when they were in school—there was a boy by the name of Seigbert who was born with one leg that was very short and twisted. But despite this, he bravely attended school. And although he could not stand up straight, Seigbert had found a way to walk. Many of the other children poked fun at poor Seigbert, but Steffi, who had always been sensitive, could see how painful and difficult even the smallest tasks were for him. And so, she'd always treated him with kindness. In fact, she had gone out of her way to help him every chance she could. Seigbert was a sweet boy who appreciated everything Steffi did for him. She was aware of his growing crush on her, but she was glad that he never acted on it, because although she was ashamed to admit it even to herself, she knew she could never be physically attracted to him.

One afternoon after the final school bell rang, students poured down the stairs towards the front door of the school. Seigbert was among them and unfortunately, so was Reinhard. As Steffi turned a corner towards the door, Seigbert saw her and waved as he called out to her, "Hello Steffi." She smiled and returned the greeting. He smiled broadly. But it took concentration for him to wave and walk at the same time. So, the action slowed him down even further than normal. Reinhard was behind him and in a hurry to leave the school. "Come on, you stupid cripple," Steffi heard Reinhard say. "You're blocking the stairs, and I have places that I have to be."

"I'm sorry," Seigbert tried to move more quickly. But his efforts were not fast enough for Reinhard, who was really annoyed.

"You shouldn't even be in school. You'll never amount to anything. You look like some kind of monster," Reinhard said. "You should be dead. If your parents had any sense they would have had you euthanized when you were born."

Steffi felt sick to her stomach. She couldn't remain silent; she had to say something. "Please try to be patient, Reinhard," she said. "He's doing his best."

This angered Reinhard even more. He turned and glared at Steffi. "Some of us have jobs, Steffi. Some of us are expected to be at work after school. We don't have time to be patient with cripples." He said as he pushed Seigbert out of the way. Seigbert lost his balance and fell down the stairs. As he tumbled down, Seigbert hit his temple on a sharp edge of the banister. He fell with a thud to the ground, and blood poured from his wound. Reinhard pushed his way through the crowd and out the front door without even looking down at Seigbert, who was clutching his head and struggling to get to his feet. Steffi ran over to the bleeding boy and helped him to stand up. Then she helped him walk all the way to her family's farm, where she cleaned his wound and gave him something to eat and drink before she let him go home. Steffi still remembered how upset she had been that day. She had been unable to sleep that night. All she could do was think of how hard life was for Seigbert. And how terribly Reinhard had treated him. She could have ignored it and minded her own business as so many of her friends did, but this was not Steffi's way. It would have haunted her if she had done nothing. And so, the following day she went to school early so she could go into the office. There, she told the principal what had happened between Reinhard and Seigbert. He responded by contacting Reinhard's father and then suspending the boy for his behavior.

"You might not have known this, Steffi, but after you caused me all that trouble that day in school over a lousy cripple who didn't deserve to live anyway, my father beat me for getting suspended," Reinhard stared hard into her eyes as he took a puff of his cigarette.

She shook her head. "No, I didn't know."

"It probably wouldn't have mattered to you even if you did know. You thought you were right in reporting me, didn't you?"

"You shouldn't have treated Seigbert that way." Then, even though her heart was pounding with fear, she said, "What gives you the right to decide who deserves to live. That is not your decision to make. That belongs to God."

"Oh Steffi, please. Everyone knows that the mentally and physically crippled are nothing but useless eaters. They contribute nothing to society. Nothing at all. They never did, and they never will. It would be best if they were to be eliminated completely from Germany."

"That's a horrible thing to say," she whispered.

"There you are," he laughed. "You are still the foolish idiot girl who I knew in school. Always going to church and talking about how good and kind Jesus was. Always instructing everyone about how Jesus would want us to behave. How would you know what Jesus would want? You don't even know if he ever really existed. You are a sheep who follows the messages from a book that is long out of date. I am talking about your bible, Steffi. The new bible is *Mein Kampf*, and it was written by a brilliant man who knows what we need to bring our country back to her rightful status as the one true world power."

She looked away from him. His words disturbed her because she knew that so many of Hitler's followers believed exactly as he did.

"Your self-righteousness is the reason you're here in Auschwitz. You are a pure Aryan by birth, and you don't belong here. But you took it upon yourself to go against the law and shelter the dirty Jews. And now look at you! Your religious beliefs are going to be your downfall. They are the reason you are here, and they are also the reason you thought it was your right to report me to the principal, all those years ago. Oh Steffi, you caused me a lot of trouble. And I never forgot it. But now, the tables have turned on you. And you can't do anything to hurt me. You have no one to report me to. You see, little Steffi, I am stronger than your God. Let's see if your Jesus can help you now." He began to laugh, a loud, hysterical laugh that made her cringe. Then he stopped laughing and was silent for a moment as he gathered his composure. In a low voice he growled, "It is nice to know that you are about to see that... I have the power to do as I wish with you. In fact, if I choose to do so, I could torture you mercilessly until I kill you and absolutely nothing would happen to me. No more principals for you to report me to. No more suspensions. I could cut you into little pieces and burn your body and then go home and take my wife out for a nice steak dinner."

She glared at him. She wished she were feeling brave, but she was truly afraid of him. He had always been cruel; however, when she stood up to him, he had been just a teenage boy. Now he was a man, an officer in the SS, and he had far too much power over the weak and helpless.

"I also have the power to make your life easier if I should choose to," he said, tapping his fingers on the desk in front of him. "Or," he smiled, "I can make your life a living hell." He laughed again, and she could see he was enjoying this. Bile rose in her throat, but she swallowed hard. "So, tell me Steffi, do you think you have it bad right now?"

She didn't answer.

"Answer me. How dare you not answer me when I ask you a question? Don't ever ignore me," he said, and he got up quickly and knocked the chair out from under her. She fell onto the floor and hit her elbow. A sharp pain shot through her. But she didn't make a sound.

Please help me Jesus. She prayed silently. *Give me the strength to say what must be said.* Then she began to speak. "I think the conditions in this place are barbaric. This atrocious treatment of the prisoners is disgusting. There I've said it," she said, waiting for the consequences.

He kicked her in the stomach. Pain shot through her entire body, and she couldn't catch her breath. He stood over her, watching her struggle. Then, wheezing, she drew quick breaths as an evil smile came over his face. "That was rather satisfying. When I first brought you here, I was planning to kill you, but I've changed my mind. Torturing you was so much more delightful. So, I have something new in mind."

CHAPTER SIX

Gretchen was sitting at the kitchen table in the small apartment she shared with Horst, her husband, when he returned from work that evening. She'd had a conversation with Heidi earlier that day, which had left her far too upset to prepare their evening meal. It was a conversation she knew she had to discuss with Horst. But she had been dreading it. Horst, exhausted as usual, walked into the apartment and locked the door behind him. "I'm going to wash up," he said, and she knew he expected his dinner to be waiting for him.

"No, don't go and wash up. Not yet. Sit down. We must talk."

"After dinner. I'm hungry."

"Horst, I've been waiting to speak to you all day. I can't wait until after dinner. We must talk now," Gretchen said, and something in her tone made him plop down in the chair across from her.

"What is it?" he asked impatiently.

"I made a terrible mistake. I did something that was very wrong. And I am very worried about it."

His eyes narrowed as he listened, waiting for her to speak.

She cleared her throat. "It happened a while ago. It was foolish gossip, I know. And I should never have done it. But at the time it seemed harmless. Now that Heidi is married to Konrad, Konrad wants to adopt Liam. It has become important, dangerously important."

"You're not making sense. I don't know what you are trying to tell me," Horst said.

"Well, when you took Liam from the Jewish ghetto in Warsaw, because you were unable to meet your quota of Polish children..." she paused, unable to say the words, "well... I accidently told Heidi."

There was a moment of silence. Then he stood up and slapped her hard across the face. Gretchen winced. She could see in his eyes that he was furious, and she was suddenly afraid of him.

"Why would you ever do such a stupid thing?" He growled. "I thought you had a little bit of intelligence. I was wrong. You're an idiot."

"Horst, I know it was wrong, and I am sorry. It happened a long time ago. In fact, I told her before we were even married. But it is driving me crazy."

"There is nothing we can do now. Let's hope she has forgotten about it. Hasn't that child been adopted?"

"Yes, that's right. And Heidi didn't pay much attention to it, until she became involved with Konrad. You see Konrad wanted to adopt Liam. He had some crazy obsession with the child. He said Liam looks like his little brother who died. Heidi said she tried to discourage him by telling him that Liam had already been adopted and that they could have children of their own or adopt a different child. But she said Konrad wasn't having it. He wants that little boy."

"That's insane," Horst said.

"Yes, it is. And as you know, it is against the rules for any of us to tell anyone where an adopted child was taken, so she refused to tell Konrad."

"All right," Horst seemed to be calming down, and Gretchen wished she did not have to tell him anything else.

But Gretchen knew she must tell Horst the complete story. So, she took a deep breath. "So, to discourage Konrad from wanting

Liam, Heidi was stupid enough to tell him that Liam has Jewish blood."

"She has never been a smart girl," he murmured.

"Konrad didn't believe her. So, to make her point, she told him how she knew. She told him that you had stolen Liam from the Jewish ghetto in Warsaw to fill your quota. And that was how she knew for sure that Liam was a Jew."

Horst let out a curse. Then he slammed his fist on the table. His face turned white as he stared at her. "Konrad Hoffmann is a Oberstrumführer. He is very high ranking in the party, and I have broken the law. Now we are in trouble—I have no doubt he is going to turn me in."

"But he isn't. He promised Heidi that he wouldn't do that. After all, both Heidi and I knew about it. Heidi and I would be implicated too. And, he is in love with her. Konrad would never want to hurt her. But he still plans to find a way to adopt Liam. Heidi says that if they adopt him, even though they knew the truth about him all along, then they would be as guilty as we are. And because of that, we could be sure Konrad would never say a word. What I am trying to tell you is that if they can adopt this child, it will keep our secret safe forever. I think we should try to help them."

"How?"

"I gave Heidi everything. I gave her the name and contact information. I'm sure Konrad will take it from here."

"That's all fine." He smiled at her, but his smile was cold and cruel. "But when he discovers that he cannot adopt that child he might just decide to report the whole thing and then we are doomed. We can't trust a man in his position," Horst shook his head. Then he stood up and began to pace. He reached into the cupboard and took out a half empty bottle of schnapps that they kept for special occasions. Taking a long swig, he wiped his mouth with the back of his hand and continued to pace around the room like a panther. Gretchen felt her neck growing hot, and she felt sure she was breaking out in a rash. For almost a full three long, pregnant minutes,

Horst did not speak. She was terrified of what he might do to her for her stupidity. At the time when she told Heidi, she hadn't thought much about it. Never in her wildest imagination would she have believed that this information would come back to haunt her.

"I think we are going to have to kill them both. I don't know what else to do," he said. "We can't trust them. And just one wrong word, one foolish word of gossip from your little friend could cost us our lives."

She nodded. *Horst has never hit me before. However, I can understand why he did. I've made a terrible mistake. Horst is angry, and rightfully so. So, I dare not argue with him. Besides, I hate to think of it, but he's right. Heidi and Konrad are a danger to us now. As long as they are alive, they have the power to ruin us. I don't know how Horst plans to carry this out, but if he says it must be done, then it must. It is the only way.* She felt sick to her stomach and dizzy. Gretchen and Heidi had been friends for many years, and although they had always been in a strange sort of competition with each other, they had shared so many moments and so many secrets. When Konrad came into their lives, it changed everything because, for the first time, Gretchen was not the better of the two. In the past she'd been the prettier one, the one who had a boyfriend, the one who was always chosen first for promotions. So, it had come as a shock to her when a man like Konrad Hoffmann had taken an interest in Heidi. And she had become terribly jealous knowing that Heidi had done better in life than she had. But even so, the idea of actually murdering Heidi gave Gretchen chills.

CHAPTER SEVEN

Uta Woolf climbed out of the backseat of the automobile and removed her white cashmere sweater. She turned to the driver and told him she no longer needed his services that day. It had been much cooler when she left that morning, but now it was hot outside. Uta draped the sweater across her arm. It had been a satisfying day. At least there had been no petty jabs at her from the other women. It was common for the wives of SS officers to treat each other with underlying contempt. They were all intent on proving that they were superior *hausfraus*. And sometimes she wished she could refuse their invitations, but her husband Reinhard expected her to attend the luncheons and house parties, and she dared not go against his wishes. Every social gathering was an opportunity for promotion. At least, that was what he told her.

The house was quiet when she entered through the front door. "Helga..." she called out.

No answer.

This was not uncommon. *I'm sure they are playing outside*, she thought as she laid her handbag and sweater down on the sofa. Then she walked back outside, and a light gust of wind caressed her skin.

At least there is a breeze, she thought as she went over to the side of the house to look for her son and his babysitter. She had been in such a hurry to get home when Lucas, their driver, had dropped her off she hadn't noticed the ashes falling down again. After Reinhard finally told her what the ashes were and why they were constantly raining down on them, she was disgusted. The idea of those filthy ashes falling on her and her son made her shiver. But here they were again, dropping from the sky. *I wish the Reich could find a better way to rid us of these disgusting Jews. Who knows what kind of diseases these ashes might carry.* She thought disdainfully. Then she saw her son and Helga, his babysitter, in the backyard. The two of them were playing in the ashes that were drifting down like snowflakes covering the lawn. The little blond boy was throwing his little hands up in the air, and they were filled with ashes. Revulsion came over her as bile rose in her throat. "Helga!" in an angry voice, Uta Woolf yelled at the babysitter. "Get in the house this instant."

"Yes, Frau Woolf." Helga said. She looked at Uta with fear in her eyes. "I'm sorry. I hope I haven't done anything wrong."

Once the three of them were inside, Uta glared at Helga, then said, "Take my son upstairs and give him a bath right this minute."

"Yes, mam."

"And make sure that you don't ever play in those ashes again," Uta shook her head and as she did, her blonde curls tossed about.

Helga quickly took the little boy upstairs. Once they were gone, Uta walked slowly into her husband's study and poured herself a glass of *bimber,* a black market liquor her husband had obtained from someone in the local town. She downed it quickly. But when she turned to leave the room, she saw Helga standing at the doorway staring at her. "What are you doing here? Did you leave my son alone in the bath?"

"No mam, I just wanted to talk to you before I bathed him."

"What is it that you want, girl?" Uta was frustrated.

"Please tell me why you are upset with me Frau Woolf. I didn't think I did anything wrong." Helga said, with tears in her eyes. "We didn't break anything. We were only playing. And they are only ashes."

"Do you know where those ashes come from? Do you know what they are?"

Helga shook her head. "No mam. All I know is that sometimes they just fall like rain from the big building with the chimneys that spit fire. My daddy says that the fire is magical, that it is going to be a guiding light that will save Germany."

"The fire? He told you that?" Uta knew Helga's father was a guard at Auschwitz, and she also knew that the bright orange flames that sometimes shot into the air were coming from the ovens.

"Please, don't be angry, Frau Woolf. I didn't think you would mind us playing outside. If I had known you would be upset with me, I would never have gone out."

"I don't mind you playing outside. But you must never go out when the ashes are falling. Do you understand me?"

"Yes, of course. And I am sorry. But can I ask why?"

"Ask your parents. It's not my place to tell you. Now go, you've bothered me enough for one day. Give my son a bath. Put his clothes in the laundry, and dress him in clean things, please." Uta said as she sank down into a chair in front of the window. Since Reinhard's promotion and their move to Auschwitz, Uta had hated to go outside. She even closed the windows sometimes, or played the Victrola to drown out the screams that echoed from the camp. Sometimes she even dreamed of the fire that shot out of the crematorium, and in her dreams it was the fires of hell. But of course, the children were too young to understand, and so they were unfazed by any of it. *They are blissfully ignorant,* Uta thought. But she could not be blissfully ignorant. She knew what was going on at the camp. And although she understood that the 'Jewish problem' had to be dealt with—that they had to be eliminated—she wished her husband had been given a different post, one that took them far from the stench and the sounds of Auschwitz. *Let someone else do this dirty work,* she thought.

Unlike some of the other husbands who tried to hide their work at the camps from their families, Reinhard had been honest with her from the beginning. He told her exactly what was going on at the camp. And since they never discussed it, she often wondered if any of the other wives were privy to such secret information. When he was first promoted, she argued with him, telling him she didn't want to leave her family in Germany and move to Poland. But he'd insisted. He told her it was their duty to serve the Führer and the Fatherland. When that hadn't convinced her, he'd promised her they would live in a beautiful home, with a sunken pool in the backyard. All of this would be provided for them by the Party for the very important work he would be doing. Reinhard promised his wife that they would have servants to take care of their every need. That she would have parties to attend, and lovely clothing and jewelry to wear. And he didn't lie. All of this had come true. However, even when they traveled home to Nuremburg to see her family, and she was far away from this place, somehow she felt that the smell traveled with her. It was as if it had seeped into her skin, her hair, her nose. And all the fancy perfumes and shampoos that Reinhard brought home for her could not get rid of it.

CHAPTER EIGHT

Reinhard Woolf sat in his office drumming his fingers on the desk as he thought about what he might do with Steffi. He remembered the day his teacher and the principal had come to his home and told his father that he had been suspended. After the teacher and principal left Reinhard's home, his father walked over to the park where Reinhard was playing football with a group of his friends. Several girls stood on the sidelines watching and cheering. One of the girls was Gretel Meyer, and at the time Reinhard thought she was the prettiest girl he'd ever seen. Because she was watching him, he was playing even harder than usual. He so wanted to impress her, hoping she might go for a soda with him. But his father didn't care that Reinhard's friends were watching. Oh no, Reinhard's father had a quick and powerful temper. He grabbed his son in front of all Reinhard's friends and then threw him on the ground. His father stood over him and took off his belt. "Your teacher and the school principal came to see me, and they said you have been suspended. You little louse, you good-for-nothing child! I am ashamed that you are mine!" Then, his father beat him. Tears formed at the corners of Reinhard's eyes, and try as he might, he couldn't stop them from running down his cheeks. He was so ashamed when he caught the look of horror in Gretel's eyes. The beating was physically painful; it left him bleeding and scared. But the emotional humiliation was worse.

"I'm not going to stop until you beg me to stop, you arrogant louse. You had better swear you will never get in trouble in school again," his father shouted at him loudly enough for everyone around to hear.

Reinhard was ashamed to beg. He saw Gretel turn away. But his father took no pity. The older man was relentless with the strap, and Reinhard could feel the shirt on his back shredding as the skin on his back tore. Blood seeped onto the football field. Finally, the pain was too much for Reinhard to bear, and even though he was red with shame, he begged. His father made him beg louder until all his friends stared at them in horror. Once his father saw that he'd broken Reinhard, he turned and left his son lying on the ground. Reinhard never played football again. In fact, he'd avoided the boys he played with. And whenever he saw Gretel, he turned and ran away. Three months later, he dropped out of school and joined the army to get away from home.

Everything that happened to me that day was Steffi's fault. If she had kept her lousy mouth shut, none of it would have happened. But it did. Once again, Reinhard considered what he might do to punish her. He decided he would not kill her, at least not yet. That would end his pleasure far too quickly. No, he was going to torture and humiliate her the way he'd been humiliated that day on the football field. The only difference was that he had the power to make her suffer even worse than he had.

"Guard!" he called out. "Guard! Come here now."

A young man in a neatly pressed uniform, with his dark hair slicked back away from his face, walked into the office

Reinhard pointed to Steffi. "Take this woman and lock her up, alone. Make sure she doesn't receive any food or water. She is not permitted to use the bathroom facilities. Let her rot in her own shit." He smiled at Steffi. "Until I decide what I want to do with her."

"Yes, Kommandant," the guard said, his eyes cold and emotionless.

"Take her now. It makes me sick to look at her."

Reinhard saw a look of fear pass over Steffi's face, and he smiled.

CHAPTER NINE

After he and Heidi were wed, it had taken a lot of effort for Pitor to consummate the marriage. He was not attracted to her at all. In fact, all he could think about was Mila. He constantly had to remind himself that the only reason he was doing any of this was to save his son. He was careful to make sure the lights were off each time he lay with Heidi so she could not see that he had been circumcised. And he repeated what he had already told her—that she must never touch his manhood. He said that this was a sexual fetish he had. She didn't argue since weird sexual preferences were common among the officers. In fact, many of the SS had fetishes far worse. But he didn't do this out of any sexual perversion. He did it because he did not want her to discover that he was a Jew. And even though he knew she was madly in love with him, he couldn't trust her not to turn him in. Wherever his son Jakup was, he needed his father, and so Pitor was going to find a way to get to him. No matter what.

"Do you have the information for me that I asked you to get?" Pitor spoke softly and gently to Heidi as he touched her cheek.

"You mean the information about Liam?"

"Yes," he said quietly. His heart was beating fast. He was

desperate for this information, and he had waited so long already. He was forcing himself to appear as patient as possible, but he wanted to scream.

"Yes, I have it. I have the name of the couple who adopted him, and the address where they are living."

He wanted to shake her, to make her get up and write down the information right now, but he took a deep breath and then, as calmly as he could, he asked, "So, where do they live?"

"It's far away. I don't think you are going to want to make the trip."

"Let me decide that," he said, and it came out a little more curtly than he'd hoped.

"You won't believe it, Konrad. They've taken Liam to Poland. I am sure you have heard about those camps where we send the Jews so we can keep an eye them. Well, that's where Liam's adopted father works. It's a place called Auschwitz. From what I've heard about it, it's rather awful. Dirty and disease ridden." She touched his hand. "You know I am still young, and we could have our own child."

Pitor ignored her. He repeated the word softly, "Auschwitz. Auschwitz in Poland." Then he asked. "And his name? What's the man's name?"

"You must make sure that no one finds out that I told you, or I will lose my job."

"Yes, I know. I promised you I would keep this a secret. And since you are my wife, you can trust me."

"So how are you going to do this? How are you going to convince this couple to let you adopt Liam?"

"I don't know yet," he said honestly.

"How will you tell them that you got their name and location. If anyone finds out that I told you I will be in a lot of trouble," she repeated this even stronger than before.

"I promised you I wouldn't tell anyone that it was you and I won't." He said, and the tone in his voice let her know he wanted an answer now, "So, Heidi, tell me, what is his name." He felt dizzy and a little sick to his stomach. *Somewhere in Poland is my little boy.* The very thought of it gave him chills. *And, even worse, what might happen to Jakup if these monsters ever found out that he is Jewish, and that Horst had stolen him from the Jewish ghetto in Warsaw?* He shivered as Heidi ran her fingers through his hair and whispered into his ear, "I will tell you everything. I love you."

CHAPTER TEN

Steffi spent what felt like days in the dark room with no food, water, or toilet facilities. Until finally one day the door opened, and a guard yelled at her. "Mach Schnell." The guard shoved his gun into Steffi's back as he forced her to walk to the medical building, where she was told to lie down on a table. Two male guards tied her down with a thick, dirty rope. She looked around frantically as they pulled her skirt up to her waist. *What are they going to do to me?* "Please, don't do this!" she begged.

But they ignored her.

"Please..."

Then, an exceptionally well groomed, dark-haired doctor walked into the room. He was very calm as he smiled at her. Steffi noticed a sizeable gap between his font teeth. "Hello," he said softly.

"Hello," she croaked. Her face was red and hot with embarrassment. She'd never been so exposed, and she wished her hands were free so she could pull her dress down to cover herself.

"I'm Dr. Mengele," he said. "And I am going to help you."

"I don't need a doctor. I'm fine. Can I please go?" Steffi begged him. Her whole body was shaking. What was about to happen to her was definitely Reinhard's doing. And she knew that because Reinhard had orchestrated it, it was going to be horrible.

Mengele didn't answer her. He turned away for a moment, and Steffi strained to see what he was doing. When he turned back, she gasped with fear. "No, please," she begged.

He ignored her. In his hand was a syringe with a long needle, which he slowly and calmly injected directly into her uterus. Pain shot through her entire body, and she began to shiver. The doctor's eyes glassed over, and when she looked into them, Steffi could see that he was enjoying every minute of her humiliation and torture. Never in her life had she felt such pain. Her entire body trembled with agony.

"I know it hurts," Mengele smiled. "But I've just glued your little uterus shut. Now, if all goes well, you shouldn't have to worry about getting pregnant."

Sweat poured down her face as Steffi reeled in agony, straining against the ropes as she twisted and turned. She couldn't speak. *Am I sterile now?* She thought. *What has this man done to me?*

Then Mengele threw the syringe into a bowl of dirty syringes, and he called for a guard. When a young male prisoner arrived, Mengele said, "Take her for a disinfection bath. Then have her tattooed, and after that take her to the sunlamp. She is so pale she looks anemic. Once that's finished, deliver her to block 24A."

"But please, I've already been tattooed!" Steffi couldn't stop shaking as she showed the doctor where a number had been written on her forearm.

"Not that tattoo," he said, smiling. "You are going to have another one. A very special tattoo." Then he turned to the guard and said, "Get her out of here. I can't stand to look at her."

STEFFI SAT down at a table across from a young man wearing a Star of David on his uniform. He apologized in a voice that was so soft that the guard who stood waiting for him to finish tattooing her could not hear him. He looked ashamed as he uncovered Steffi's chest with his dirty hands, careful to keep her breasts covered, out of respect for her modesty. Then he looked at the guard and turned back to Steffi. As gently as he could, he began to tattoo the words he'd been instructed to carve into the tender skin on her chest. 'Feld-Hure,' it meant 'Field Whore.'

Blood seeped from the sharp blade of the pen. And although she was in pain and horrified by the words she was going to wear on her chest for the rest of her life, Steffi refused to cry. She bit down on the inside of her cheek, willing herself to be strong. And finally, the tattooist was finished. He nodded to the guard, who had been watching. "You're finished," the guard said to Steffi. "Follow me."

Steffi stood up. She was aching all over but mostly within her heart. Blood trickled down the inside of her uniform. In her mind she whispered the words, Feld-Hure and she shivered. A single tear escaped her eye, which she quickly wiped away as she was led by the guard to a special block.

When she entered the new block, she saw several female prisoners, all of them young. And like her, not one of them was wearing a yellow star. That meant there were no Jewish prisoners in this block. Unlike the prisoners in the block where Steffi had been living previously, the heads of these girls were not shaved. She glanced around the room to see that they were not on work details; they were sitting huddled together and talking quietly. "This is where you will stay from now on," the guard said, then without another word, he left.

Steffi was trembling as she walked over to the group of young women who were still talking amongst themselves in whispers. "I'm Steffi Seidel," she said.

"Who cares," one of the women replied as she turned away from Steffi.

"Ignore her, she's a louse," one of the other girls said. "I'm Gerty and that mean one over there who just acted like she is better than the rest of us. That is Ursula." She said, pointing to the young woman who had just insulted Steffi.

"Where am I? What is this block? It's different from the other block where I was staying before," Steffi asked gingerly. She was afraid that she already knew the answer, and the very thought of it made her sick to her stomach. But she asked, because she had to be sure.

A young, pretty redhead pushed her wavy hair back from her face, and then in a sarcastic tone she said, "Welcome, my dear. This may look like Heaven, but it sure is not. You are one of the lucky ones, you've been selected for the brothel."

"Yes, but it's not that bad, so don't worry. We sometimes get extra food, and they don't shave our heads. And, most important, although we must do it with men we hate, at least we don't have to do it with Jews." Ursula said, smiling, "We just have to make the guards happy. And once in a while one of the officers comes in. If he has a fetish, he might beat you. But it won't be that bad. They usually come fast, or they kill the girl who can't get them off." She began laughing. It was a bitter, angry laugh.

"Yeah, and sometimes one of the officers sends us one of the male prisoners as a reward. That's usually for doing something that they want him to do, like squealing on a friend. You know? Anyway, we can get almost any type of visitor here. The only restriction is that we don't ever get Jews," the redhead said.

Steffi looked at each of the women, and she felt her stomach turn. She would much rather have continued to work in the rubber factory than face having her body violated every day by strangers.

"It's really not so bad here. I mean it could be much worse," a petite blonde with sad blue eyes looked at Steffi with pity. "The extra food helps. It will keep you strong."

"What an optimist," Ursula laughed. "Strong for what? Strong so we can live a day longer in this hell? Who would want to?"

Steffi nodded to the blonde. She knew the girl was trying to make this less traumatic for her, but it was a nightmare. The only man she'd ever made love to was Pitor. And if the war had not happened, she would have saved herself for marriage.

Making love with Pitor, who was a Jew, was breaking the law. Hiding two Jewish children was also breaking the law. Steffi knew she walked a tightrope each day, one misstep away from death, and every morning she woke with the thought that it might be her last. *Being a prostitute will not be easy for me. And I know this is why Reinhard sent me here.*

Steffi walked over to a cot on the other side of the room and sat down.

The little blonde with the sad eyes walked over to Steffi, and said, "My name is Hildegard, but you can call me Sigrid."

Steffi smiled.

"There's an open bed in the room that I share with several other girls. I'm sure that's where they'll put you."

Steffi nodded. "An open bed." She repeated mindlessly.

"Yes, we each have our own beds. That's a lot different from the other blocks where the prisoners are stuffed into beds together like sardines."

Ursula walked over to where Steffi and Sigrid were talking. "Yes, you will have your own bed. But just in case you were wondering, the girl who was sleeping there before you came down with typhoid and died. She died in that bed. But don't worry, it's been about a week since we found her dead, so you're probably safe," Ursula smiled and then winked.

Steffi stared at her. "Does it make you feel good to make me feel uncomfortable?" she asked.

Ursula just shrugged.

"Would you like to see the room we will probably be sharing. I mean, it's not much to see. But, well, come on let's get out of here. Ursula is in one of her moods today and it's best that we leave her alone. Follow me, I'll show you the room before the men start to arrive," Sigrid said, smiling wearily.

The room was small. Sigrid tried to keep her area neat and tidy, but the paint, which had once been white, was now dirty and gray. It was chipping, and there was a hole in one of the walls about the size of a baseball. "This is the bed," Sigrid pointed to a cot covered with a dirty graying sheet. Steffi sat down on the bed. It was nothing more than sawdust spread over wooden planks, and it was as hard as the floor. But Sigrid tried to smile and said, "You have to admit, it is better than the rest of the camp, no?"

"Yes," Steffi agreed with her. She knew Sigrid was trying to make things better for her. But the thought of sharing her body with strangers seemed even more horrible than the starvation, disease, and hard work she'd endured when she was in the other block in the camp.

"Why are you here?" Sigrid asked, then she looked away. "I probably have no right to ask you that."

"You mean why was I arrested?" Steffi asked, "or why am I here in this block?"

"Well, I know why you were chosen for this block. It's because you're pretty, and blonde even if your hair is shaved. And the Nazi's like blondes. But why were you arrested? What did you do?" Sigrid said.

There was a long silence. Steffi was trying to choose her words carefully. But before she could speak, Sigrid said, "I'm sorry. Please don't be offended. You're right, it's none of my business why you were arrested. The fact is most of the girls don't like to talk about how they ended up here. So, you don't have to answer."

"No really, it's all right. I'll tell you," Steffi said. "I was hiding a Jewish girl in my home, she had been my neighbor, and she was so young, just a teenager. A lovely girl. I knew her parents before they were arrested. But sometimes young people are foolish. I suppose that's part of youth." Steffi said with tears in her eyes, "This girl fell in love with a German boy. And he seemed to be in love with her. She trusted him and told him the truth, that she was living as an Aryan, but she was really Jewish. But he'd been in the Hitler Youth, and he turned her in to the Gestapo."

"What happened?" Sigrid asked.

"Of course, they came for her." Steffi closed her eyes. "Yes, they came like demons from hell, in their black automobile with their loud horns blaring. We were terrified. I wanted to hide her. But it all happened so fast that there was no time. Anyway, one of them shot her. Poor thing, Zita, her name was Zita. She's dead now." There was a long hesitation, then Steffi continued, "Well, at least they can't torture her anymore." Steffi's breath caught in her throat. Her mouth was dry. "Then they arrested me. And brought me here. And now..." Steffi sighed. She tried to sound as calm as possible, but she wanted to scream. "I'm here."

"Oh God. That's terrible," Sigrid said, patting Steffi's arm.

Steffi looked away. "Please, don't take God's name in vain. He is all I have left."

"Don't tell me you're religious. I don't know how anyone can believe there is a God with all that we are going through. I ask myself that constantly. If there really is a God, how could he let this happen? How could he let innocent people be murdered every day?"

"I don't know, Sigrid. I wish I had an answer for you, but I don't. I only know that I still believe that there is a God, and that He will save us from the Nazis."

"I don't. Our only hope of being saved from the Nazis is the Allies," Sigrid said firmly. "But then again, I wasn't raised with religion, or any belief in God. My mother died when I was ten. I was alone so I turned to the streets. I guess you might say I grew up hard."

"You don't seem hard. You are very kind."

"Yes, well, everyone says that. But I learned how to steal at six. And, even before she died, my mother was no mother. When I was eight years old, she sold my virginity to some old man who gave her enough to support her drug habit for one more day. By the time I was fourteen I was a mistress to a man who was old enough to be my grandfather."

Steffi didn't know what to say. She took Sigrid's hand in hers. "I'm sorry," she whispered.

"The Germans call me an outcast," Sigrid laughed. "But I am still young and pretty enough to be one of the girls who the Nazis chose for the brothel. Unlike some of the other girls, I have plenty of officers who come to visit me."

Steffi nodded. Then in a soft voice she said, "I don't know how I am going to do this. I don't have a lot of experience with men, and I am afraid I won't be able to."

"It's not as difficult as you think. Just close your eyes and let them do whatever they want. Don't feel anything. Don't think about what is happening. The guards and the occasional prisoners are only allowed to do it to you in the missionary position. So, all you must do is lie there. Now, on the rare occasions when I have an SS officer come to see me, things are different. They can do as they please. And trust me, they do. You don't want to attract one of them if you can help it. They give you little gifts from time to time. And for me, it's all right, because I have experience and it doesn't bother me. I like the gifts, and I ignore their perversions for the most part. But you would be horrified by some of the things they demand from you. I suggest that you never look any of the officers directly in their eyes. That can make them want you. And when you see one of them here at the brothel, stay out of their way as much as possible."

Steffi felt a chill run down her spine. She was just about to ask Hilde what they did, but then a guard poked his face into the hole in the wall and said, "Come on you two. It's time to start working."

CHAPTER ELEVEN

Steffi's first visitor was a low-ranking Nazi guard. He didn't take his clothes off, and he didn't remove hers either. And she was glad that he finished quickly. But after it was over, she went to the latrine and vomited. The second one was another guard who told her he would have preferred one of the girls without a shaved head, but Steffi was the only one who was available. "I know your hair will grow back," he said, "but for now, you look ugly." Just like her first one, he also finished quickly. He left her in the room without another word. But this time she noticed several guards were watching everything through the hole in the wall. She looked away, trying to avoid their lecherous gazes.

Finally, the night's work ended, and it was time to sleep. "Are you all right?" Sigrid turned over in her cot and asked Steffi.

"Yes," Steffi said. But she really wasn't.

"Good. Rest now. You'll need it."

A mosquito buzzed somewhere near Steffi's ear. She swatted at it. Then she said, "Hilde?"

"Yes?"

"What happens if we get pregnant?"

"Haven't you been sterilized?" Hilde asked.

"I don't know. Mengele said he was going to close my womb. Then he gave me an injection," Steffi choked on the word. "Have you?"

There was a long silence "That should take care of it."

"So, I am sterile? Is it permanent?"

"I don't know. Probably." Hilde said. "I don't care. I don't want to bring a child into this world. I wish my mother had never given birth to me."

"Don't say that. Life is a gift," Steffi said.

One of the other girls across the room overheard them talking and said, "It sounds like you were given the chemical sterilization. Sometimes it works. Sometimes not. It's best for you if it does because if you get pregnant Mengele will give you an abortion. And most of the girls who he performs abortions on suffer terrible pain and then they don't survive."

"He's a terrible man. Is he a real doctor?" Steffi asked.

There was a long pause, then Sigrid sighed, "I don't know. I find it hard to believe that he is. But from what I have heard, yes."

The other girl across the room said, "The prisoners call Mengele the 'Angel of death.' He's a bastard. A sadist and a bastard. He has a lot of power here in Auschwitz." She was quiet for a moment. Then in a soft voice she said, "He sterilized me by surgically removing my female organs... and he did it without any anesthesia. So, even if I should somehow live to see the end of the Nazis, if they ever end, I will never have a child of my own."

Steffi wanted to say something to comfort the girl, but she couldn't think of anything to say. There was a long silence, and she thought Sigrid and the other girl had fallen asleep. But then Sigrid said to the other girl, "Well, it's probably for the best anyway. Do you think you would know how to be a good mother? I know I wouldn't because I never did have much of a role model."

CHAPTER TWELVE

The girls in Block 24 were expected to service twenty men each night. There was a good-sized hole in the wall through which the guards could amuse themselves by watching. No matter how a girl felt about one of the men, she had no choice but to service him. Refusals were not permitted. And there were rules for the guests as well. Each man who had been granted permission for a visit was required to make an advanced appointment, and his visit was only permitted to last for twenty minutes. This, the officers decided, allowed for the optimum use of each girl's time. Since a visit to the brothel was a highly regarded bonus that was only bestowed on those guards and occasional prisoners who proved themselves worthy, the men worked hard to receive an invitation. And once they were awarded a much-coveted visit, they followed the rules to the letter. However, when it came to the SS officers, none of these rules applied. After all, they considered themselves superior Aryan men, and so they arrived and left whenever they felt like it. And when they were exercising their rights as superior men, they treated the girls as they pleased.

For Steffi each night when the sun went down, it was like a

descent into hell. She endured the long line of men who came to her bed by closing her eyes and thinking of Pitor. Thoughts crept into her mind that made her cry, even as the strangers mounted her. But it didn't matter; if they noticed, they never acknowledged her tears. By the time the night was over, she felt filthy, exhausted, and alone. But she rarely slept through an entire night. Most of the time she lay in her cot staring at the wall and asking God what He wanted of her.

But the days were different. Once the sun rose, everything looked a little less gloomy. Or at least Steffi tried to convince herself that this was true. At least, she thought, during the day, there were no male visitors, and as time passed, she found she did enjoy the company of most of the other girls. A casual friendship developed between Steffi and Sigrid, and having someone to talk to brought Steffi some peace.

One night as Steffi lay waiting for the next visitor, a young male prisoner walked over to Steffi's bed. He was a tall, slender fellow, dirty, and smelly. And far too thin. When he removed his uniform top, she could see his ribs jutting out of his paper-thin skin. When she looked at him, she felt sad. She could tell that before he'd been starved and beaten, he had been very handsome. He tried to get on top of her, but something stopped him, and he sat down on the edge of her bed. As he picked up his uniform shirt, she saw a pink triangle had been sewn on to it. She touched the triangle and looked into his eyes, but she didn't say a word. Then, as if he heard her thoughts, he whispered so she had to strain to hear him, "Yes, I am a homosexual. They sometimes send us here to you girls to see if you can rehabilitate us."

"I see," she said, nodding.

"The guards are watching us through the peephole so please help me. Will you? I need you to try to pretend that we are having sex. If they think I've failed, they will beat me again," he was still whispering.

She nodded, then she answered him in a whisper, "Of course, I will do as you ask."

"I'm sorry for putting you through this. I truly am. I can imagine how unpleasant it is for you. No one should have to go through what you girls go through," he whispered in her ear as he lay on top of her.

"I'm all right," she tried to reassure him. But his face was only a few inches from hers, and when he looked at her and she could see in his eyes that he was sincerely regretful. "If I was ever going to be with a woman, I would not have wanted it to be this way."

She nodded. "I understand."

"Although, I will try if you want me to, but I don't think I can."

"It's all right." She said, "Just lay here and move up and down. They can't see what's happening."

He nodded and then did as she asked.

"Do you have a boyfriend?"

"I have a very special boyfriend. He is the love of my life. But I don't know where he is or if he is alive. He was not only a homosexual, but he was a Jew. That's two terrible strikes. And you know how the Nazis are."

"Enough talking over there," one of the guards, who was glaring through the peephole, said. "Your time is almost up, faggot. And you had better be normal when this is all over or you are going to suffer."

"Think of him. And maybe you should try," Steffi whispered. "Do your best so that they don't beat you."

The man closed his eyes, and he tried. Sweat was pouring down his face, and he apologized for dripping it onto Steffi's face. But he could not achieve an erection.

"Time is up," the guard yelled. Then he came in and grabbed the young man roughly by the arm. The guard pulled him out of the room, and the next man in line was sent into the room. This one was a coarse, heavy-set guard. His hands and face were filthy but not because he was a prisoner and not allowed to wash, but because he chose not to. As he violated Steffi roughly, she covered her ears to muffle the screams of the young homosexual as the guard was beating him in the hallway right outside her room.

When the night finally ended, Steffi was exhausted, but she could not sleep. She lay in her bed weeping softly.

"Steffi, don't cry," Sigrid whispered. "It doesn't solve anything. Just try to rest. You need your strength."

"I know. But I can't help it."

THE FOLLOWING NIGHT, the first man to enter Steffi's room was a political prisoner. He was handsome and rugged and in some ways he reminded her of Pitor. She lay on her bed as he approached. "I'm sorry to have to do this to you," he said. "I haven't been with a woman in three years. And, well, I don't know how to put this, but I suppose I will just say it. I am in need of the release. I will be very gentle. And I am sorry. I am so sorry."

She swallowed hard. His tenderness made her feel almost worse than the roughness of the guards. But she just nodded.

He looked into her eyes, then in a soft voice he said, "You're very pretty."

Again, she nodded, remembering how it had been hard for her to accept being plain when she was a young girl. She wasn't ugly, not exactly; she just always thought of herself as plain. But when she was growing up, she had longed to be pretty. Steffi knew that this poor man was lying to her. He wanted to make this terrible thing he was about to do easier for her. But beauty no longer mattered to her. It was a trivial thing in comparison with health and food and survival. And besides, she was sure that since she had been imprisoned, she had grown to be ugly. Once, right after they had shaved her head, she'd caught a glimpse of herself in a mirror, and she had been shocked and horrified by her appearance. Now her hair had started to grow back, but when she looked at her body, she could see that her chest was concave, and she could feel that the bones jutted out of her face and neck. She smiled wryly, remembering how naïve she'd been as a girl, truly believing that beauty alone would bring a lifetime of happiness. How wrong she had been. Beauty meant nothing. Nothing at all. Suddenly laughter bubbled up in her throat and before she could contain it, it rang through the room. The man standing above her stared at her, not knowing what to say. She wanted to apologize, but she couldn't because her laughter had turned to wrenching sobs. "Go ahead, do what you must do," she told him. "Please, just get it over with."

He stood over her, looking down at her. Then he shook his head and said, "I can't. Not like this." His manhood was limp as he turned away from her. "It's all right. I am sorry I made you cry."

"It's not your fault. You didn't make me cry." She managed to say. "It's not your fault. You are a prisoner here too. And that means that you are as much a victim as I am."

He didn't answer her. But when she turned her head away from him, her breath caught in her throat. There was Reinhard. He was smiling at her as he peered through the peephole. Under her breath, she quietly cursed him. "You demon," she whispered, "may you rot in hell."

Then Steffi, seeing the prisoner was embarrassed, reached for his hand. "It's all right. Really. I think you still have a few minutes left. Do what you must do."

"No, I can't, not like this," the man said. "Even though I am starved for a woman. I won't do this. I refuse to stoop to their level." He turned and walked out of the room.

CHAPTER THIRTEEN

Reinhard Woolf went back to his office. He sat waiting for Steffi to arrive. He had sent one of the lower-ranking guards to retrieve her from the brothel and bring her to him. And now as he waited, he was thinking about the political prisoner whom he had seen walk out on Steffi just a few minutes ago. Her bed was probably already occupied by another guard, but he didn't care. He needed to see her. Reinhard glanced outside through the window in his office. Across the yard, he saw several prisoners who had just returned to the camp from working on a hard construction detail. They looked battered, and many of them were having trouble walking. *Some of those prisoners will not survive the rest of the week,* he thought. *But since they are all enemies of our Reich, mostly Jews, why should I care? They deserve whatever happens to them.*

As Reinhard stared out the window waiting, to his delight, he happened to see the political prisoner who had so proudly refused to force himself on Steffi. Even after suffering a terrible beating, he openly spat at Reinhard. So, Reinhard stormed out towards the Kapo in charge of the work detail, and told him to work him exceptionally hard. "Make sure that you give him the most difficult jobs." *He will die working at a job that is so hard his body will give out.* Satisfied with this thought, Reinhard smiled to himself. "I'll bet you're sorry now, aren't you? You stupid fellow." *Since he was arrogant enough to refuse the gift of a woman and he proudly walked out on her, I will see to it that he regrets his decision. How dare he think he has the right to refuse a gift from the Reich? That idiot defied me. So now I'll punish him severely. I'll cut his rations and make sure that he'll work so hard that he'll be dead within a couple of days.*

There was a knock on the door. "Yes?" he answered.

"I've brought the prisoner you requested, Herr Kommandant."

"Good, bring her in."

Steffi almost fell when the guard pushed her through the door. But as soon as she reclaimed her balance, she stood staring at Reinhard defiantly. The guard, who brought Steffi to Reinhard's office, followed her in.

"Leave us," Reinhard said to the guard as he waved him away with his hand.

The guard nodded. "Heil Hitler," he saluted.

"Heil Hitler," Reinhard replied.

The guard turned and immediately left the room.

Once they were alone, Reinhard said, "I was planning to let you rot in the brothel. After what you did to me, you deserve it. But then last night I was bored so I decided to come and watch you through the peephole. You were with that idiot, that political prisoner. I'm sure you remember him even though you've been used by twenty men a night, every night since you were transferred to the brothel." He smirked. "Field whore, that you are. But when I saw what happened in that little room, I could see by the way you looked at him you had found a way to pretend that you are still a good girl. And you used that to manipulate him into feeling guilty, so you would not have to do your job. That man was treating you like you were some sort of angel. Not like the whore that you are. Well, you should know that because of you, he is being severely punished. And my guess is he won't live through the week."

She looked at him stunned.

He shook his head. "Steffi, Steffi," he said in a condescending tone of voice. "I thought I would enjoy watching you, but alas, I found that I didn't care much for observing. In fact, I found that I really didn't want to share you with all those other men. You see, I would much prefer to keep you for myself," he smiled and winked.

She cringed inside. What she'd endured was horrible beyond belief. But the thought of having to give herself to Reinhard Woolf made her want to die.

He waited for her to speak, but she didn't. She couldn't. She was too horrified.

"Steffi," he said her name with such contempt that it made her shudder with fear. "I've decided to bring you here to visit with me, because it will bring me great pleasure to let you know why I chose to put you in the brothel. Most of the female prisoners would appreciate the increase in food and the opportunity to keep their hair. But I know you. And I know that allowing strange men to use your body would be the most painful thing I could do to you. You were never one of those girls who might give in to a boy because she was weak. Not you, you never went on dates. I know, I watched you. And I knew you always thought you were above that sort of thing, didn't you? Everyone in town thought of you as a good girl. Such a perfect little angel." He laughed. "Every week I saw you walking with your mother to church and I secretly cursed you. Because you were always doing something for charity, everyone thought you were so good. But I knew better. I knew you were just the type of person to rat someone out. I knew because you did that to me, causing me so much trouble."

There was a long silence as he glared at her. "I am sorry I caused you so much trouble. But, Reinhard, you treated that poor boy so badly."

He let out a laugh. "I'm going to do worse to you."

She felt her skin growing hotter and thought once more that she might be breaking out in a rash.

"Now, I will let you think about just what I might have in mind.

Quite often your thoughts can be even more terrifying than reality. And that's what I want for you, Steffi. I want you to live in constant fear of what is coming next."

His words reminded her that if she begged or cried, he would not have mercy on her. He would find joy in her pain, and so she must be strong; she must hide her fears.

"So, once again, I chose the brothel, because I never found you attractive enough to bother with. I mean, of course I could do as I wished with you. I just wasn't inclined to force myself on you. But I had to avenge your stupid actions concerning a lousy worthless cripple. That was when, I figured that being used sexually by men would be the most torturous thing for a girl like you. Was it Steffi? Was it as bad as I hoped it would be for you?"

How am I to answer this? If I say yes, he will give me more of the same. But if I say no, he will do something even more terrible. I just don't know what to say. So she stared at the ground and stayed silent.

"You are a pig. You can't even give me the common curtesy of an answer to my question. But don't you worry. I don't really need your answer. I think you were getting used to the brothel, and so it was no longer terrible enough. No, not for you, my dear Steffi. When I saw you in that room with that man, that dirty good-for-nothing enemy of our Reich, you were so gentle, and you handled yourself with such grace. So, that was when I decided that, well, I could do better. I could find more effective ways to make sure you would really suffer." He smiled. "And...by the way, that cripple who I pushed out of my way so many years ago. What was his name again? Seigbert or something like that? Well, anyway, he's dead now. I made sure of that."

She felt her insides trembling. *How can any human being enjoy being so cruel? I am terrified of him. His heartlessness knows no bounds. I tremble to think of what he might have in store for me now. The brothel was a living hell, and yet he couldn't leave me alone. It just wasn't enough for him. And now he takes such pleasure in telling me that the poor fellow who he pushed down the stairs is dead, and he is responsible. Oh, dear Jesus, I need you now. I am not strong enough to endure this man's horrible vengeance. Please help me... please.*

"Don't look so frightened. I don't plan to kill you. At least not quite yet." He smiled. "On second thought, fear looks good on you, Steffi. You were never a pretty girl. But I find the terror in your eyes to be very stimulating."

As she looked into his menacing eyes, she thought, *why don't you just kill me? I wish you would. I am tired of living. The Nazis have taken everything away from me. My home. Everyone I care for. Everything I ever had.*

He was still speaking, but she couldn't hear him.

Her mind was racing. *Why do we cling to life when there is no reason left to go on living?* She closed her eyes tightly for a moment to stop herself from shedding any tears because she knew he would enjoy seeing her cry. Then a thought came into her mind. *Reinhard can hurt me. And the Nazis can take everything I love away from me, but they can't take my love of the Lord away. They can never take that.* She squeezed her eyes shut even tighter. And it was then that she saw a face in her mind. It was Pitor's face. His eyes brought her comfort. And a warm glow of light seemed to come over her. *How kind Pitor had been. What a wonderful man he was. Perhaps by some miracle, if I do survive this, I might see him again.*

Reinhard slammed his fist on the table. "Don't fall asleep when I am talking to you!" he shouted in her face. He broke her daydream as her eyes flew open. His face was dark red with anger as he walked over and slapped her so hard across the face that her chair fell backward. "You are a clumsy idiot. Now get up, get on your feet. You don't deserve to sit in my presence. You will stand until I am finished talking to you." He cleared his throat, took a cigarette out of a pack on his desk and lit it. Reinhard walked over to Steffi and stood very close to her. Then he blew a large puff of smoke into her face. Her eyes burned, and she coughed.

"Now, I have decided on the perfect job for you. I am going to make our time together lots of fun for both of us." A vicious smile turned the corners of his lips upward as his eyes twinkled. Her body shivered, and she hoped he hadn't seen her tremble. "Steffi, my dear old friend Steffi. I plan to employ you as my family's maid, and nanny. A demeaning position for sure. Of course, I don't intend to pay you. Since you are a prisoner of the Reich, your labor is free to me. You chose the weak, Steffi. I chose the strong. And it turns out that I am the victor, and you are the loser. It will bring me great delight to watch you clean our toilets and scrub our floors, and you better pray if I see one speck of dirt or dust anywhere. Meanwhile, by having you in my home I can use you whenever I want. You can satisfy all my needs. If I have a bad day, I will beat you. If I want you sexually, I will use you in any manner I see fit. And, not only this, but having you in my home will allow me to keep a watch on you every minute of every day. I will own your life, Steffi. When I want to see you humiliated, naked or on your knees, I won't have to gaze through some peephole at you. You will be right there at my beck and call, and you will obey me no matter what I tell you to do. Because you will have to." He smiled and took a puff of his cigarette.

She glanced at him, and the look in his eyes was so repulsive that she had to turn away.

"I will have you delivered to my home this afternoon, after you've finished working. Until I send for you, you will be at the rubber factory. I want to see to it that your lungs suffer for as long as possible while you inhale the fumes from the rubber. So, that's all." He put out his cigarette, then looked up at her. "Rest easy my dear girl, you are about to learn a very valuable lesson about playing hero. By the time I am through with you, you will wish that you had never defended that worthless eater, that good for nothing cripple when we were in school."

Is there any way I can reason with him? Is there anything I can say or do to make him less angry with me? Her mind was racing. *I must find a way to soften him, or he is going to make my existence unbearable.* "Reinhard," she said softly. "I know that in your heart you are a good person. I don't know why you have chosen to do this job, but I don't believe that you are truly evil. I refuse to believe it."

He let out a laugh. "You don't huh? Well, then I'll just have to convince you otherwise. Before you are delivered to my home this afternoon, you will have your hair shaved again. Then you will be expected to clean the entire house before you are returned to the original block where you did not have a bed of your own. And it will be very late tonight when you return. Unfortunately, you won't have much time to sleep because you are expected to report for roll call before you are sent back to my home. Poor thing, you will certainly be tired today after eleven hours in the rubber factory followed by an entire day's work in my home. And then very little sleep on top of it? You had better make sure you don't pass out from exhaustion tomorrow when you arrive at my house bright and early. You will be expected to clean it again from top to bottom. And if you faint, you will suffer a severe beating."

CHAPTER FOURTEEN

That afternoon, Steffi returned from the factory, hungry and exhausted from the long day at work and then the four mile walk back to the camp from the rubber factory. The noxious odor of chemicals still stung her nose and throat. She wished she had some time to rest. However, she was handed a small bowl of watery soup. It was the only meal provided each day. But before she could eat it, a guard came over. He had been waiting for her. "No time for you to eat tonight," he said. "Herr Kommandant is waiting for your arrival at his home."

The guard grabbed her arm and pulled her forward. "There is no time to waste eating. Get up and let's go," he said.

Steffi followed him, and he led her out of the gate and over to the large home that stood just outside the barbed wire. She had once noticed the house through the fence — a graceful two-story structure. And she'd often wondered who lived there. Now she no longer had to wonder. She knew.

When they arrived at the house, they stood in front of a large wooden door with a heavy gold door knocker. The guard clicked the knocker, and a few minutes later, a woman opened the door. "Come in," she said. She was close to Steffi's age, but she looked younger. Her skin was radiant, not gray like Steffi's, and her blonde hair was shiney and braided tightly. The woman wore a casual, yet expensive dress. "Herr Woolf is expecting you," she said.

Then, as if he were directed by a director, on cue in a play, Reinhard Woolf entered the room. He had removed his jacket and now he wore a clean white sleeveless undershirt tucked in to his uniform pants. "You can go now," he said to the guard. Then he turned to Steffi and, gesturing towards the woman with the blonde braids, said, "This is my wife, Uta." His smile was not really a smile at all. It was a challenge of sorts. A terrifying display of power.

Uta studied Steffi for a moment and then, once she was satisfied with what she saw, she said, "This girl you are bringing into our home is not a Jew, right?"

"No, I promised you that I would not bring a Jew to care for our house. I know you are repelled by them." Reinhard said, then remembering that he was in charge of not only Steffi but also his wife, he added. "How dare you question my choices? Besides, do you take me for a fool? If she was a Jew, do you think I would let her in our home?"

"Good, I know you are too smart for that. And I am glad she's not one of them," Uta said. "She'll do just fine." Then Uta turned to Steffi and said, "Our son, Liam, is in his room. Go and get him and give him a bath. Then after you've finished, clean the bathroom. Once you've finished that, clean the rest of the house."

Steffi nodded, keeping her gaze on the ground.

"Our son's room is at the top of the stairs, on the right."

"Yes, Fräulein," Steffi said.

Steffi climbed the stairs slowly. Her entire body was aching, and her stomach was growling. She had no idea how she was going to get through the evening. But when she walked into the little boy's room, she glanced over at the child, and she was stunned. *Have I gone mad? Could I be imagining this?* She thought as she stared at the little boy with his blond curls, who looked up at her and smiled. Steffi returned his smile, but she closed her eyes for a moment to recall, as accurately as she could, the photo that Pitor had given her of his son. *The likeness of this boy to Pitor's son Jakup was uncanny. When I met him, Pitor had been searching for his son, who had been stolen by a Nazi. Was it possible that Liam was actually Jakup?*

"Hello," she whispered softly to the little boy. She didn't want him to be afraid of her. After all, she was a stranger, and she was about to give him a bath.

"Hello," he said bravely, and his smile was so broad and so confident that she was certain she saw a strong resemblance to Pitor. "What are you playing with?" she asked him.

"My toy gun. I'm killing all the enemies of the Führer," he said in his childlike voice. Hearing those words coming out of his mouth sent a chill down her spine.

"Well, how about we put that toy gun away for now, shall we?"

"I'd like to play some more. Do you want to play with me? I have another gun. It's an old one. But you can use this one, and I'll use the old one if you want. We can be soldiers."

"Maybe tomorrow. Your mother sent me upstairs to give you a bath."

"Ick. I hate taking baths."

"I know. But we can pretend that you are in the navy, and that your bathtub is the ocean. That might be fun. What do you say?"

He giggled. "I like that idea. And I like you." He said, and her heart swelled. For a moment she imagined herself and Pitor together raising this little boy with all the love that he deserved. And with a respect for humanity that would make him into a fine man, like his father.

"Well, I like you too," Steffi smiled. "Where do you keep your clean pajamas?"

He pointed to his dresser.

"Which drawer?"

Liam stood up and opened the drawer. He took out a pair of pajamas. Steffi smiled at him. "Perfect," she said. "Can you show me where the bathtub is?"

"Of course, silly. Come on. Follow me," Liam said.

Steffi followed Liam to the bathroom. And as she bathed and dressed him for bed, she thought of Pitor and how sure she was that this was his son. *I did not want to come here. But now that I've met Liam, I know why the Lord sent me, and I will do everything in my power to protect this child.*

CHAPTER FIFTEEN

Gretchen and Horst spoke in whispers as they walked to work one morning. "Konrad is an officer. Killing him is a serious offence. How do you plan to do something like that without getting caught?" Gretchen asked.

"I don't know. But I don't know how else to hide our secret."

"Do we really have to kill Heidi too? I really don't like the idea of that." Gretchen whined.

"I think it's best. We don't want to leave any lose ends. Besides, I thought you didn't like her as much as you used to."

"I don't, she has become awful and unbearable to be around since she met Konrad, but I don't want to kill her. I mean, she and I have been friends for a long time. We were roommates too. So, the thought of murdering her is rather unnerving." Gretchen admitted.

"They both know too much about us. Unless you can come up with something better, we have to do this."

"But Horst, I really don't think Konrad or Heidi would turn you in, because if they did, then they would have to disclose the fact that Liam is really a Jew. And as you know, Konrad is obsessed with adopting that child, and only that child. But he certainly couldn't adopt the boy if everyone knew Liam was really a Jew. The Gestapo would take Liam and dispose of the child immediately. Konrad knows this. He would never take that risk."

"But *can* we be sure? Can we take such a risk with our lives? You know how the SS officers are. They can be so unpredictable. One minute they are on someone's side and the next minute they turn on them. Even this strange story about Liam looking like Konrad's brother is odd. I must admit, I am not convinced that story is entirely true, nor that it's the real reason why Konrad wants this particular little boy. I think there is something very strange going on here. I remember Konrad from school, and he was nothing like the man who married Heidi. He was not humble and never kind. He came from a wealthy family and was very arrogant. He could be a bully. And, I know they say people change, but the man we know now, is not like that at all. The Konrad we know is really very kind and very fair."

"That's true. But he is older now and he has served in the army. They say that combat can change a person."

"I served and it didn't change me," Horst said.

"Were you in combat?"

"Of course," Horst said uncomfortably as he remembered how he'd hidden in a foxhole like a coward while the rest of his platoon was fighting on the Russian front.

"Didn't it make you feel humbled to see how fragile life is?" she asked.

"If you're asking me if I witnessed the death of my fellow soldiers, the answer is yes. But I did not allow it to weaken me. I knew that if I did, I would face the same fate. So, I forced myself to follow Nietzsche, the way our Führer follows him. And as you know, Nietzsche said that if I did not die in the process, surviving all my fears and horrors would make me stronger. And this is because I am a true Aryan man, and we must never forget that we are the superior race."

"All right then, so what is it you are trying to say?" She was losing patience with him. Soon she would arrive at work, and this conversation would have to continue later that evening.

"What I am trying to say is that I think Konrad Hoffmann is an imposter."

"What? How could he be an imposter? He's been promoted and no one but you seems to think that he is a fraud. Oh Horst, I thought you had an intelligent idea. But this sounds like nonsense to me."

"I am not so sure you're right. I think people look at him and see what they expect to see, not what he really is."

"I don't know. You might be right. I hope you are. But I am not sure how this affects us. Can you please explain?"

"I'm not sure how it will affect us. It depends if my theory is correct, and then if it is, who he turns out to be. If we can prove he's just some German soldier, even a deserter perhaps, who is unimportant and not fit to be in the position he is in, it will be a lot easier for us to make him have a little accident. Something to get him out of our way. We couldn't turn him in to the Gestapo because he knows too much, and there is a chance he might tell them about me stealing Liam. However, if he had an accident and died..." Horst paused for a moment, smiling at the thought of killing Konrad. "Well then, we could act as if we had just learned that he was an imposter. That way we couldn't get in trouble for not turning him in sooner."

"But how can we possibly find out?"

"Well," Horst was silent for a few moments. And a light rain began to fall.

Gretchen grunted. "This rain is going to ruin my hair. Of course it would rain. I slept with my hair in pin curls last night."

Horst was unaffected by the rain. He was deep in thought. Finally, he said, "I will go through the files at my office and try to find some men who served in the same platoon as Konrad when he was in the army. Then we will have a party and invite Konrad's fellow soldiers, as well as Konrad. They will recognize that he is a fraud, and they will expose him."

"And if he is not, then we will have had a party for no reason at all. Besides, Horst, why would these men who are strangers to us, want to come to our party?"

"Because they are friends of Konrad's, and although the invitations will come from us, we must hope that they will want to see him again. We will write a letter in the invitation, explaining that we are Konrad's good friends. We will say that we are having a special surprise party to celebrate his new marriage to our other friend, Heidi. Hopefully this will work and there will be several men who will want to reconnect with their old friend. And to sweeten the deal, we will be sure to tell them that Konrad has achieved a prominent position in the party. Everyone is always looking to better themselves, and what better opportunity to do so than to reconnect with an old army buddy who has some influence. After all, a recommendation from a good friend can help a fellow rise quickly, and get a better position."

"It is a rather good idea. Especially if it turns out that you are correct and he is a fraud. I am hoping it turns out that he is a deserter," she admitted brushing her hair from her forehead with her fingers.

"I know that I am correct. I remember Konrad, and the man we know is not the same person."

She nodded. "But how will you find the names and addresses of the soldiers in his platoon? And how will you know which ones we should invite? Do you have access to that information."

"I don't have access to it. But when everyone goes to the lunchroom, I can sneak into the office and look it up. I will do that today. And then we will invite all of them. All the men that are still alive, anyway..." Horst said.

Gretchen nodded. "Be careful sneaking into the office. If you get caught you will be in trouble."

"I won't get caught, and I won't get in trouble. Normally I hate it, but right now I am glad to be invisible."

"So, if we can get our hands on this list and we can get some of these fellows to agree to come, where will we hold this party? Our apartment isn't large enough. It's not even a one bedroom."

"I realize that. And because of it we are going to have to spend some money to have it at a beer garden."

"Oh, Horst. If we do this, it will mean that we'll have to spend a lot of the money we have been saving. Do you really think it will be worth it? What if it backfires and it turns out that Konrad is who he says he is? What if all his friends embrace him and are happy to see him? Then we've just spent so much of our entire savings for nothing. And so far, I don't see the party awarding you with a house, so we need to save our money, or we will never be able to move out of our tiny apartment."

"You know I want to move to a better apartment. But we have to do this. It's our only chance."

The rain was slowing down, but Gretchen's hair was soaked. She stopped for a moment and pulled her hair into a ponytail and squeezed out the water. "I wish we were doing better. I wish we had an automobile and a decent apartment," she sighed.

"Gretchen, please just listen to me. You and me are on the same side. And, if, for some reason I am wrong about Hoffmann—which I doubt that I am—but if I am, and Heidi's husband really is Konrad Hoffmann, then we will be his very best friends. He and Heidi will love us because we are the friends who organized a surprise celebration to honor their new marriage. And Konrad and Heidi will be so grateful, they will never tell anyone about what I did with Liam. However, if I am right and this man is a fraud—and I believe I am—his lies will be discovered. Then if I do kill him, I might even be promoted for killing a traitor and that might be enough for us to receive a house as a reward from the Party."

"Hmmm..." She nodded. "Who do you think he is, if he is not Konrad Hoffmann? A deserter? There are plenty of those running around."

"We can only hope he is. But I think he's probably some low-ranking soldier who was in the same troop as Konrad. I think he probably admired and befriended the real Konrad. Everyone always wanted to be Konrad's friend when we were in school. He was very popular. He was confident and a little bit of a braggart. So, here is my theory. I assume that Konrad must have told this imposter about his upcoming promotion. He probably told him that he was on his way to the Eagle's Nest. Then this low-ranking soldier probably thought it was his lucky day when he saw Konrad fall in battle. And that's when this imposter decided to desert his platoon and assume Konrad's identity."

"You are very convincing. I hope your theory is right," she thought for a moment. "And it would be far better to have Konrad's undoing be of his own making, rather than you and I trying to get away with murdering him and Heidi. I must admit, although I don't care for her very much anymore, I still found the idea of actually killing her rather unsettling. This way, we just sit back and let things happen, and there are no messy loose ends for us to worry about. But we have to hope you're right about Konrad."

"I know I am."

She thought for moment. "The other day I ran into an old girlfriend of mine. She has recently been hired to work as a secretary in the same building where Konrad works. She and I went for a coffee, and I casually asked her if she had met him. I may have told you about her. Her name is Birdie Schmitz."

"Didn't you say she was a rather loose woman?" Horst blushed.

She laughed a little. "It figures that you remember that. Well, anyway, she said that she recalled having spent a rather intimate evening with a man by the name of Konrad Hoffmann several years ago. I told her to look for him because he was currently working at the same office as she was. And I suggested she look him up."

"Did she agree?"

"She was actually quite enthusiastic about the idea. Of course, after I did it, I felt sorry for Heidi, because I know Birdie, and if she does take the time to look him up, she'll have him in her bed that same afternoon," Gretchen couldn't tell Horst the real reason she'd done this. It had nothing to do with doubting Konrad's identity. Gretchen had gone out of her way to mention Konrad to Birdie because Gretchen was jealous of Heidi having a husband who was handsome and successful, and she wanted Konrad to cheat on Heidi.

"Do you know where to get in touch with her?" Horst asked.

"Yes, of course I do. But I don't want to telephone her yet. She said she would call me as soon as she had a chance to talk to him."

"Call her," Horst said insistently. "Call her as soon as you can. We might not have to give a party. Birdie just might be able to tell us what we need to know."

CHAPTER SIXTEEN

Several days passed and Steffi came each morning to Reinhard's home to clean, and care for Liam.

Reinhard worked long hours, and when he arrived back home, he seemed to hardly notice Steffi at all. Even so, she did her best to stay out of his way. She was relieved to be left alone, but in the back of her mind, there was always the fear that he would call for her and the torture he promised would begin. But to Steffi's surprise, Reinhard was different when he was at home. He was quiet and stayed alone in his study for hours at a time. Uta and Reinhard did not speak to each other very often, but when they did, he was respectful but not affectionate towards Uta. And when he saw Liam, he was tolerant but not loving towards the child. None of this seemed to matter to his wife, Uta. She was busy with her social life, and that was just fine for Steffi, because, in the short time that Steffi had come to know Liam, she had also come to adore him. He was affectionate, smart, and funny. And for Steffi, every day with the little boy was a blessing. She saw so much of Pitor in him she was more convinced—although she could not be certain—that Liam was really Jakup.

Steffi, having grown up on a farm, had no trouble keeping the house in perfect working order. Each day, Reinhard's uniform and Uta's dresses were cleaned and pressed. Steffi hung them carefully in their respective closets. The floors were washed, and the furniture was dusted each afternoon when Liam took his nap. And when Reinhard returned from work, his dinner was on the table, and Liam had already eaten and was bathed and ready for bed. The first time Uta told Steffi to prepare the evening meal for the family, she warned Steffi not to dare steal a single morsel of food. However, Uta was not home very often, and with no one watching her, Steffi was able to eat small amounts of food that would not be noticed.

By the end of her first week of working for Reinhard Woolf's family, Steffi realized that she was happy. And she knew it was because of Liam. He had given her a reason to live. But she also knew she must never let Reinhard know she was experiencing any joy from the child, because she was sure that he would do whatever he could to snuff it out.

But then, one afternoon when Uta was at home sitting by the pool in the backyard with Liam, the phone rang. Steffi was in the kitchen preparing dinner, and she wasn't sure whether to answer the call. She quickly ran outside and asked, "The phone is ringing. Shall I answer it?"

"Of course, you idiot." Uta said, annoyed. But she got up and followed Steffi inside to see who was calling.

"This is the Woolf's residence," Steffi said as she picked up the telephone receiver.

"This call is for Uta Woolf," a telephone operator answered in broken German. Steffi thought she detected a Polish accent.

"Frau Woolf, it's a call for you," Steffi turned to tell Uta, who stood in the doorway looking lovely and sun-kissed in a red bathing suit.

Uta walked over and picked up the telephone receiver. For a moment, Steffi went back to her work of chopping onions for dinner.

But then she remembered Liam was outside alone by the pool, and he couldn't swim. Her heart began to race as she ran outside. When she saw Liam floating in the water on his stomach, she gasped and ran outside. Still wearing her uniform, she jumped into the water. Having grown up near a lake, she'd learned to swim at an early age, so Steffi was a strong swimmer. She was at Liam's side in seconds. She dragged him to the edge of the pool and pulled him out. Then she laid him on his back and began to breathe into his mouth. Several moments passed. It felt like a lifetime. But then a gush of water came pouring out of the child's mouth and Liam began to cough. Steffi sat back on her haunches and tried to catch her breath. When she looked up, she saw Uta was standing a few feet away from them, her hand on her heart. For a moment, Steffi was afraid that she would be blamed and punished for Liam being left by the pool alone and almost drowning. But then Uta said, "Thank you. I don't know what I was thinking... I should never have left him out here alone." Tears were running down her cheeks as she knelt on the ground, beside the child. Then she took him in her arms. "Liam, Liam, are you all right?" Her pretty red bathing suit was wet from picking the child up, but Uta didn't seem to care. And suddenly Steffi realized that even though Uta was a selfish woman, who usually ignored Liam, she wanted to be a good mother to this little boy.

"He'll be all right now," Steffi said.

Liam was still coughing.

"Thank God you were here," Uta said.

Steffi looked down. "I'm glad I was able to help," Steffi said, and she meant it. She hated Reinhard and didn't really care for his wife either, but she was quite sure that Liam was Jakup, and Jakup was Pitor's son. And Steffi still did, and always would, love Pitor.

Finally, Liam stopped coughing and caught his breath. He sat on the ground quietly, breathing heavily. The ordeal had exhausted him.

"Let's bring him inside. I think we've had enough pool time for today," Uta said.

"Can you walk? Or shall I carry you?" Steffi asked Liam.

Liam didn't answer, but he reached up. His short, chubby arms beckoned Steffi, showing that he wanted her to pick him up. She smiled at him. Then she took him in her arms and carried him into the house. He kissed her softly on the cheek before she put him down, and her heart melted.

CHAPTER SEVENTEEN

That night when Reinhard returned from work, Steffi served the family their dinner. "I think Steffi deserves some extra food tonight, Reinhard. We had a terrible incident this afternoon and well, without her help we might have lost Liam."

"Lost Liam?" he asked, but he didn't look very concerned. "What does that mean?"

"Liam fell in the pool and almost drowned. You know I can't swim. So, Steffi jumped in and fished him out."

That wasn't the whole story, Steffi thought. And at that moment, she realized Uta was a little afraid of Reinhard. She didn't tell him she'd left the child alone outside. But of course, Steffi would not say a word.

"I was thinking," Uta went on. "Perhaps it might be a good idea for Liam to learn to swim. I mean, with him unable to swim, having a pool in the yard is rather dangerous. I was thinking Steffi could teach him."

Reinhard nodded and shrugged. "Yes, sure. If that's what you want, then go ahead and arrange it. But just because Steffi is giving the boy swimming lessons, doesn't mean she is permitted to slack off on her housework. Make sure that she completes all her tasks each day. I won't have her swimming and enjoying the pool. That's not why I brought her here. If her other work is not done, she will be sent away and you won't have a maid to help you. So, make sure she does her work." He gave Steffi that special wicked smile that made the fine hair on the back of her neck stand up.

"Of course, I will make sure that she does all her other work first. The swimming lessons will just be something additional that she can offer us."

He nodded, "Very well then. Do as you please."

CHAPTER EIGHTEEN

Uta had a secret. She would never have told Reinhard, but Uta was terrified of water.

As Uta lay in bed that evening after the swimming pool incident with Liam, she thought of her childhood. A week following Uta's thirteenth birthday, her mother began acting strangely. She had made a new friend who seemed to consume her world, leaving Uta to wonder who this friend was. Sometimes when her mother thought she was in her room playing with a doll, Uta was busy watching her mother rush out to meet the delivery driver, or to get a telegram before Uta's father returned home from work. So, one day curiosity got the best of Uta. She skipped school, and she secretly followed her mother to see where exactly she went. Uta, careful not to be spotted, followed her mother into town. She hid behind a building and peeked her head out, when she saw her mother exchanging a passionate kiss with a man that was not her father. She cautiously trailed her mother and this man to a café, watching as her mother laughed, more lighthearted than she ever was at home. Then finally, Uta observed her mother and the stranger walk into a hotel. She felt sick to her stomach and threw up in an alley off the main street. Uta had to face the fact that her mother was having an affair. So when her mother returned home that afternoon, Uta wanted to strike her, but she couldn't. She was struck dumb by what she had seen that day. She couldn't speak to either her mother or her father about the situation, so instead she harbored internal anger that grew and then sometimes surfaced in strange ways. She found she would secretly do small things that she knew her mother would not approve of.

One day a few months later, Uta's mother had left Uta in charge of her younger sister for the afternoon. Uta knew where her mother was going, and this made her bitter. *She's ruining our family*, Uta thought. But she couldn't discuss her feelings with anyone. About an hour later, there was a knock at the door. As Uta looked out the window, she saw Marta, one of her friends who lived down the street.

"Hi Uta! It's been so hot outside this weekend. Let's go to the public pool." Marta said excitedly.

"I can't. I am stuck home watching my little sister," Uta said, trying to avoid going because neither Uta nor her sister could swim, and her mother would never have allowed it.

"Oh, come on! It will be fun, and you can bring your sister. We will watch her," Marta smiled, trying hard to convince her friend.

"I would love to go, but I don't have a swimsuit."

"Don't you worry. I have one you can borrow. I'll bring one for your sister too!" Marta said.

And although Uta was uncomfortable, out of anger toward her mother, Uta agreed.

It was a bright, cloudless day, and school was out for summer. Uta was so excited and enthusiastic because she was sure that lots of the local boys would be at the pool. She packed lunch for the three of them, and then they walked half a mile to the pool. When they arrived, Uta looked around. It was crowded with young people. She had never worn a bathing suit before, and she felt self-conscious. Some of the other girls her age, including Marta, had begun to develop. They had tiny breasts and hips, and to Uta they looked grown up. While she was as flat as a piece of wood, and had no shape at all. She tried to avoid the eyes of the boys as she and Marta laid their towels down on the pool chairs. Her sister had already begun to eat the bread and jam that she'd packed for their lunch. Uta was about to scold her when Alex, one of the most handsome boys from her school, glanced over at her. Their eyes connected, and then he smiled. Her heart skipped a beat, and she returned his smile. He stood up and sauntered over to her chair with such confidence that it made her blush. "Uta, you look great," he said.

She smiled and looked away. Her face felt hot, and she knew that if she looked in a mirror, it would be very red.

Someone on the other side of the pool called Marta over to her. "I'll be right back. Ingrid is over there, and I want to go and say hello." Marta said to Uta.

Uta nodded.

"I hope you don't mind if I sit here," Alex said when Marta got up to go to Ingrid.

"No, of course not," Uta answered nervously.

He smiled. "Boy am I glad school is finally out. I could hardly wait for this school year to be over."

"Yes, me too," she said. But it wasn't true. She actually liked school.

There was a long silence.

"I'm thirsty, so I am going to get a drink of water from the fountain," Uta's little sister said.

"All right. But come right back," Uta answered her firmly.

The conversation between Uta and Alex was light. They talked about their teachers, and he made jokes and imitated Herr Mueller, the mathematics teacher's lisp so well that Uta found herself laughing out loud. She looked into Alex's bright blue eyes, and she was entranced. And so, for the next ten minutes she was lost in him. But then one of the lifeguards blew a whistle and everyone evacuated the pool. The sharp trill of the whistle brought Uta back to reality, and she suddenly realized that her sister had not returned after her trip to the water fountain.

The sound of the whistle-stopped Alex from talking. He sat watching the lifeguards. Uta stood up and was frantically looking for her little sister. She already knew that something terrible had happened; she could feel it in her bones. Nothing good ever happened to her unless it was followed by something terrible. Her heart felt like it might explode, and then she saw it. A teenage boy lifeguard was dragging her sister's body out of the pool. Uta let out a piercing scream. She ran over to her sister. The lifeguard did everything he could to revive the little girl. But it was too late. Uta's sister had drowned.

Uta's parents were distraught. They blamed her for being negligent. And from that day on, Uta's mother and father had become cold and distant towards her. And Uta never forgave herself.

Hiding her fear of water had been challenging when she was a young girl in the *Detuche Maidels* because fear and weakness were not well regarded by the Hitler Youth groups, and the group often went swimming. But she begged off, claiming that she was on her monthly cycle, and no one seemed to notice or care. Then, when she was just seventeen, she met Reinhard. At first she didn't really like him, but he took her out for nice dinners, and so she continued to date him. A month later, he proposed. And she'd married him. If she were honest with herself, it was more to get away from her parents' accusing eyes than out of any affection or love for him. And as the years passed, the relationship between her and Reinhard had never grown into anything deeper.

Because of her fear of water, when she and Reinhard first moved into this house in Poland, she hated it. The last thing she wanted was a pool in the yard. But as time passed, she began to relax. Not enough to go in the water, or to allow her adopted son to go in, but enough to sit in the sun on the deck. And at first Liam had shown no interest in going into the pool. So, she wasn't worried about him drowning. That was until she had gotten lax and left him for just a single moment to answer that phone call. *I almost let him drown*, Uta chastised herself in bed that evening. It had brought back such terrible memories of her sister, she hardly slept.

The following morning, Uta begged Reinhard to ask for a promotion so they could move. And he got angry with her for asking. "I am the Kommandant of this camp. And I am the man of this house. I will make the decisions." His voice was a low growl that told her not to bring it up again. That was when she realized they would not be moving out of this house anytime soon.

Uta spent all day in a daze. Partially from not sleeping the night before, and partially from her fear consuming her every thought. *I am going to have to live with this pool. The only way I am going to feel safe again is if Liam can learn to swim. And as much as I am dreading it, I should learn too.*

After Uta received permission from Reinhard to use Steffi to teach her and Liam to swim, she gave Steffi one of her old bathing suits. Steffi was very slender, and this suit was too big for her, but she had taken a needle and thread and sewed it by hand to fit her body.

The next day, Liam's swimming lessons began. He had no fear of the water and took to it instantly. He jumped and played in the sunshine, and watching him, Steffi felt even more certain that this was Jakup. She was a good teacher, and he learned quickly. By the end of two weeks of lessons every day, Liam was already doing the backstroke, and the breaststroke. He glided through the water like a dolphin.

"I suppose it's my turn now," Uta said to herself, more than to Steffi.

"Whenever you are ready Frau Woolf," Steffi said gently.

Uta's knees almost buckled as she climbed down the stairs into the pool. Her entire body was trembling. "Don't be afraid. I won't let anything happen to you," Steffi said.

Uta was terrified, and each step along the way took coaxing from Steffi, followed by praise once they were achieved. At first, Uta treated Steffi like a worthless servant, and she hardly spoke to her. However, now, as sweat formed on Uta's brow as she lowered herself into the warm water, seeing how kind and patient Steffi was, Uta felt a sense of peace with her. Steffi's calm reassurance made everything easier for Uta. Before she knew it, Uta was on the way to conquering her deepest fears.

One afternoon when Uta finally felt ready, with Steffi watching and promising that she would not allow anything bad to happen, Uta swam the length of the pool. When she finished, she was beaming. She stood up in the shallow end and said, "I can't believe I was able to do that."

"Of course you were," Steffi said, giving Uta the extra boost of confidence she needed. "You are a good swimmer. You are doing so well."

Uta had warmed up to Steffi. She saw the girl as valuable. And found that she liked her.

"Come, let's go inside so that we can have some lunch. Why don't you make sandwiches for all of us," Uta said. Then she remembered Reinhard had told her firmly that she must never allow Steffi to eat from their dishes. "But, I'm sorry," she found herself apologizing. "You must make sure you don't use our dishes for your sandwich or our cups for your water. I'm sure you understand. Reinhard insists on this. And even though you are not a Jew, and I would never permit a Jew to touch our things, because you are sleeping in that camp, you have had a lot of direct contact with the Jews. They are dirty, they carry disease. You do know that don't you?"

"There is a lot of disease in the camps. I am not sure it's because the Jews carry disease. I think it's the conditions everyone is forced to live under that breeds illnesses," Steffi said, looking away, but not before Uta saw a look of disgust on Steffi's face.

"And..." Uta winked. She wanted to change the subject. "I have a surprise for you."

"Oh?"

"Since it's such a special day for the both of us, I've decided that you may have an apple today."

"Thank you, Fräulein Woolf" Steffi said humbly.

Since Uta and Liam had learned to swim, the two of them went in the pool often. Uta found it a refreshing way to spend the hot summer days. Liam loved swimming and was always asking to go into the pool. To her surprise, Uta began to trust Steffi. So, even when Uta was out with the other wives of the SS officers, she allowed Steffi to take Liam swimming. And when Reinhard wasn't at home, she found ways to give Steffi extra food. However, as much as she liked her, and even though Steffi wasn't a Jew, Uta still could not tolerate Steffi drinking from her family's cups or eating with their utensils. But Steffi didn't care. For her, the extra food was a godsend. She ate a little of it, but most of it she carefully hid and took back to the camp to share with Hilde. Although she and Hilde no longer shared a room, they still ate all their meals together.

CHAPTER NINETEEN

The past few months had been much more tolerable for Steffi. And that was because of Liam. She adored the little boy, and he openly returned her affection.

One night, when it was well past midnight, Steffi was lying on her wooden cot, fast asleep from complete exhaustion, when she was awakened by the sound of one of the guards calling out her number. At first, she thought she was still asleep and dreaming of roll call. But when the guard's voice became louder and more insistent, her eyes flew open, and a pang of fear gripped her. Not waiting for her to get up, the guard found her. He hit her across the legs with a rifle butt. Pain shot through her legs and up into her back. Quickly, she jumped out of bed.

"Come with me," the guard said, "Herr Kommandant has requested you to be brought to his house."

Reinhard, she thought. Fear jolted her awake. *It's the middle of the night. I am sure he is up to something terrible.* But she knew she dare not ask any questions. So, she followed the guard obediently.

When they arrived at the house Uta and Reinhard were in the living room waiting for her.

"Heil Hitler," the guard saluted proudly. "Here is the prisoner you asked me to bring to you."

"Heil Hitler," Reinhard said, nodding. "You may go. The prisoner will remain here."

The guard nodded and left.

STEFFI GLANCED OVER AT UTA. She had never seen Uta so disheveled. Uta's hair was a mess. Her face was unwashed and tear stained, and her eyes were red from crying.

The room was completely silent apart from Uta's soft cries, and suddenly Reinhard spoke in a very deep, strong voice that scared Steffi to her core. "Have you been sick in the past couple weeks? And you better answer honestly, or this will end poorly for you."

"No... no..." Steffi stammered to get out the words. "I promise. I swear. Why? What has happened?"

Uta rushed over to where she stood. "It's Liam," she cried. "He's very sick. He's running a high fever. The doctor left instructions for us to bathe him every hour. I have been doing my best to follow the instructions, but Reinhard doesn't want me to continue. He said we needed to send for you. He doesn't want he or I to be exposed to whatever it is that Liam has come down with."

Steffi nodded. "May I go to his room?" she asked Reinhard.

"Yes, go now."

Steffi walked quickly to Liam's room. The child looked so small as he lay whimpering softly in his bed. Uta was behind Steffi but kept a good distance from the boy.

Steffi turned to Uta, who stood in the doorway. "Did the doctor say what he thought Liam might have?"

Liam reached his arms up to Steffi and she lifted him into her arms. The little boy's skin was clammy and very hot. She pressed her lips to his forehead, "He has a fever," she said softly.

"The doctor thinks it's viral meningitis. If it is, it isn't contagious. But Reinhard said that since we can't be sure, he doesn't want me to handle Liam at all. He has always been very afraid of catching diseases. So, since he and I sleep in the same bed, he is afraid I will get sick, and he will catch it. In fact, he says he really doesn't want me to come into Liam's room at all. But before you got here, I had to take care of Liam, I couldn't just leave him all alone when he was so sick. But, now that you're here, I must not come in here anymore."

Steffi nodded, "It's all right. Don't worry, I'll take care of him."

"My head hurts," Liam said, whimpering. Then he vomited all over the front of Steffi's uniform.

"Shhh, it's all right," Steffi said, pushing his blonde curls off his sweaty forehead. "You're going to be all right."

Uta backed away. "Get rid of that uniform. I'll have one of the guards bring you a clean one tomorrow morning. Until then I am going to give you one of my old dresses. We must be careful. We don't want these germs spread all over this house."

"Yes, Fräulein," Steffi said.

"In the morning I'll have a bed set up in Liam's room where you will stay. Until then, I will give you a blanket and you can sleep on the floor in here with him. And since I'm sure Reinhard will not want you to touch our food, we'll have another prisoner come and prepare our meals until this ordeal is over. I'll make sure that food is sent to this room each day for Liam. And I'll see to it there is food for you, too."

"Thank you," Steffi said. She didn't know what was wrong with Liam. If he did have meningitis, she didn't care if it was contagious or not. She was glad to be able to offer her help to this little boy who made her feel alive, and who she was sure was Pitor's son. Steffi was sure she would never see Pitor again, but she felt blessed to share her love for him through his precious son. A little boy whose affection had brought her happiness and sunshine in the darkest place on earth. A child whom she had come to love with all her heart. And she knew that no matter what was wrong with Liam, she would never turn her back on him. *Even if he is contagious. I will never leave him to suffer alone.*

Uta told Steffi that the doctor had instructed them to bathe Liam every hour with a sponge and cool water, which Steffi did with care. For the first several nights, he was unable to sleep. And although Steffi was tired, she did not sleep either. She stayed awake and lay beside him, singing to him softly and smoothing his hair—wet with heavy perspiration—away from his face. Reinhard did not send Steffi back to the camp. Because he didn't want to expose himself to Liam's illness, he allowed Steffi to stay with Liam all day and night. She was only permitted to leave the room to use the toilet. Otherwise, she was expected to care for Liam around the clock. Reinhard didn't care if Steffi caught the disease. He was repulsed by the entire situation and chose to turn his back on it completely. What he didn't realize was that Steffi would not have had it any other way. She cared for Liam as if he were her own child, comforting and cuddling him. For three days, he refused to eat. He gagged as liquid poured out of his small mouth from his empty stomach. Steffi knew she must coax him to drink water. And so, she continued to try until he finally drank a little. And then he drank a little more. Once he kept the water down, she spoon-fed him the soup that the family's temporary maid brought each day. Finally, on the morning of the fourth day, when she put her hand on his forehead, she could feel that Liam's fever broke.

He opened his eyes and looked at her, "I'm hungry," Liam whispered in a soft broken voice. She put her arms around him and squeezed him gently, her heart aching with relief.

"I'll let the maid know that you'd like some food," Steffi said. "But first, let me get you out of these wet clothes. And let me change your sheets. Sit on my cot for a minute and I will take care of you."

He did as she asked, but he was shivering. Quickly she gathered fresh pajamas for him and changed his clothes. Then she wrapped him in a blanket as she changed his sheets. When she lifted him to put him back into his bed she felt his skin, it was slightly cool, and he was no longer sweating.

Steffi sighed with relief. "You're going to be all right," she said as she kissed his forehead.

The maid arrived with a bowl of hot potato soup, which she handed to Steffi. Steffi fed Liam, who ate greedily. She was so happy to see him able to eat again that she began to cry and laugh at the same time.

"Why are you crying?" Liam asked, as Steffi blew on a spoonful of hot soup before giving it to him so he wouldn't burn his tongue.

"I'm so happy that you're better now Liam. I've been so worried about you."

He leaned over and kissed her cheek, "I love you, Steffi. I wish you were my mommy." He said, and her heart melted.

CHAPTER TWENTY

The doctor came later that afternoon and examined Liam. "I think it's best that you wait for another week before we allow Liam to leave this room. He is better but he's still recovering, and he could relapse."

Steffi nodded. But she knew in her heart that Liam was going to be all right. And at first, although Liam no longer had a fever and was able to eat, he was still extremely tired. He slept through the night and then for hours at a time during the day. But as each day passed, he became stronger and slept less. And then he was no longer tired—he was restless and bored.

"When can we go swimming again?" Liam asked Steffi.

"Not until the doctor says it's all right," she answered. "But I'll ask your mother if she can get me some children's books so I can read to you. Would you like that?"

"Yes, I would like that very much."

Now that Liam was doing better, Uta came to visit him daily. However, when she came, she remained in the doorway and never stayed very long. Steffi noticed that Uta never touched or held the little boy. But she'd heard that the Nazis frowned upon cuddling their children. They believed it made a child weak. Steffi did not agree. She wanted Liam to feel loved every minute of every day. And she knew by the way he responded to her affection that he did feel loved by her.

When Uta came to Liam the following afternoon, Steffi asked her if she could bring some children's books so that she could read to Liam.

"Yes, I'll have the maid drop them off later," Uta said.

Steffi was excited to read to Liam. She was sure he would enjoy it. That was, until the books arrived. She had been expecting Uta to send a book of fairy tales, but that was not the case. The maid dropped off two books. The first was titled *Der Giftpilz, The Poisonous Mushroom*, and the second was a picture book titled *You Can't Trust a Fox in the Heath, and a Jew on his Oath*. That afternoon, as Liam slept, Steffi thumbed through both books. She was disappointed to find that they were nothing more than propaganda written to perpetuate hatred and fear of the Jewish people in children. *I will never read these books to Liam. I am going to have to rack my brain and try to recall as many folktales as I can, so I can tell him the stories from memory. I will also tell him stories from the Bible and tales I remember by Hans Christian Anderson. I don't think that the stories by Hans Christian Anderson have been banned by the Nazis, so if he tells his parents, it will probably be all right. But I know his parents would not approve of me telling him biblical stories. Even so, I simply refuse to read these terrible propaganda books that Uta brought to this sweet, innocent child. He doesn't need to have his heart and mind poisoned with hatred. And although I doubt he will ever learn that he is Jewish, and it is probably better that he never knows, if by some miracle he does find out, I don't want him filled with hatred towards himself and his own people.*

And so, she hid the books that Uta sent and began to tell Liam every story she could remember.

Two weeks later, Dr. Mengele, the camp doctor, came to visit and to check on Liam. Steffi didn't trust Mengele, but she had no power to refuse to allow him to examine the child. Mengele insisted she leave the room while he checked Liam over. Steffi waited outside the door, wringing her hands and remembering how Mengele had enjoyed her pain. *Please, Lord, don't let this horrible man hurt Liam,* she thought as she waited, praying that she would not hear the child cry. A few minutes later, Mengele walked out of the room and smiled. Steffi felt her skin crawl. But Mengele didn't notice. He turned to Uta, who was standing a few feet away, and declared Liam to be healthy and healed. After Mengele left, Liam was permitted to leave his room, and the next day he was allowed to resume his swimming lessons. However, since Liam's illness had given Uta a scare, she talked to Reinhard about moving Steffi into the basement of their home.

"I would rather she stay here with us. If she is going to prepare our food and care for the boy, it's better if she is not exposed to all the diseases in the camp. If she catches something from one of those dirty Jews or gypsies, she could bring an illness here to our home, and we could catch it," Uta said.

Reinhard contemplated this. He had always been afraid of contracting some terrible disease when he was working at the camp. And even though his job was considered a good one with lots of benefits, he longed to be promoted to another position far away from the filth and illnesses that surrounded the prisoners at Auschwitz. He'd seen far too many guards come down with bouts of malaria or typhoid, and the very thought of it made him shiver.

Steffi was nothing but a prisoner and therefore no one consulted her about the Woolf's decision to move her into the basement. She was sure that now that Liam was better, she was going to be sent back to the camp. But she was pleasantly surprised when Uta told her she was going to be moved to the basement in the house. And although the basement was dirty and filled with spiderwebs and mice, she was glad to be away from the camp and close to Liam in case he needed her.

CHAPTER TWENTY-ONE

The basement was cool at night in comparison to the rest of the house. And although she was exhausted, Steffi had spent her first night cleaning the area. It was dark and damp, but she was able to steal a candle from the kitchen, which gave her enough light to work by. Reinhard said it was fine for her to sleep on the floor, but she found some dirty pillows, which she lined up to create a mattress. Neither Uta nor Reinhard knew of the pillows, so she assumed they had probably been the property of the previous owners of the house. Whenever she heard the door to the upstairs open, she quickly hid the pillows in the dark corner where she'd found them. Then, one night, she was awakened by the quiet sound of footsteps on the stairs. Quickly, she jumped up and hid the pillows. She prayed nothing was wrong with Liam; she hoped it was only Uta coming to demand something from her. However, it was something far more sinister.

As soon as she saw his form shadowed in the darkness, Steffi knew Reinhard had come to exact his revenge. He did not speak until after he walked over to her and slapped her across the face. Then in a low growl he said, "That was because you have been on my mind."

She stood trembling; she knew better than to answer him. "Take off your dress," he said coldly.

Steffi wanted to beg him to please let her be. But she knew that begging would only encourage him. And she knew if she tried to fight him off, he would kill her, although she wondered what he would tell Uta had happened when she was not in the kitchen preparing their breakfast the following morning. Her stomach felt queasy, and she tried to keep from vomiting, but the bile rose, and she threw up. "You're a swine, a pig," Reinhard laughed a wicked laugh. Then he threw her onto the hard concrete. Roughly, he pulled at her breasts and then inserted his fist into her most delicate and private parts. Steffi began to cry silently, forcing herself not to make a sound. But when he stood over her and pulled down his trousers, his manhood was limp. Even in the darkness, she could see that he did not have an erection. Frantically, he pulled at himself trying to prepare for intercourse. And for a moment or two his penis became erect. However, it grew limp again almost immediately. Angry and frustrated, he struck her. The crack resounded in her eardrums, and the pain was overpowering. As blood ran down the back of her throat, she knew he'd broken her nose. He punched her in the stomach. Then he kicked her in the stomach and legs several times before he called her a 'Field Whore.' Finally, he turned and made his way back upstairs.

The following morning, her eyes were purple with bruises, and her nose was crusted with blood. Uta looked at her suspiciously, but she didn't ask any questions. However, that afternoon when she and Liam were in the pool, he asked, "What happened to you?"

Careful not to scare him, she said, "Oh silly me. I fell down."

"Does it hurt?" the little boy touched her face gently.

"Yes, a little. But I will be all right," she smiled.

Then he said, "Let me kiss it and make it better the way you kiss me and make it better when I get hurt."

Her heart swelled as she leaned down, and Liam placed a gentle kiss on her face.

After Reinhard broke her nose, Steffi went to bed terrified each night. She never knew if he might return and try to force himself on her again. She thought about it constantly, and her fear gave her constant anxiety. She developed a red, itchy rash on her chest that she had to force herself not to scratch. But a few weeks passed, and when he did not return, Steffi began to feel calmer. Then, one night after she'd just fallen asleep, she heard Reinhard's boots on the stairs. Jumping up, she hid the pillows. This time he smelled of alcohol. However, try as he might, he was unable to consummate his lust. Reinhard beat her with his belt buckle, but because he was very drunk, the blows were weak. She was relieved, but terrified of his return. He returned several more times, and the results were the same. The beatings left her battered and bruised. Had it not been for her love for the little boy who slept upstairs, Steffi would have taken her own life.

Once Reinhard left in the morning, Steffi didn't mind her job. There was a lot of work to do in the house, and Uta was demanding. She wanted the house to be spotless, but Steffi didn't mind the work. If only Reinhard would leave her alone, she felt she could bear anything. Uta expected breakfast to be prepared and served before Reinhard left for work each morning, and then dinner must be ready to serve when he arrived back at home from work each evening. Uta could be demeaning, but Steffi tried not to hate or resent Uta. She tried to remember that Uta was only behaving the way she had been raised to behave. She was not intentionally cruel; she was just very good at closing her eyes to all the cruelty that surrounded her.

However, because Liam was a joy, Steffi was grateful that Uta had given her the opportunity to be with him. Every day, Steffi felt more certain that Liam was Pitor's son, because he was growing up to look more and more like Pitor. And even though her love for Pitor was only a memory, and she knew he had never felt the same way about her. The tenderness of the memory was one of the few things she could hold on to, and so she refused to let it go. Steffi poured all the love she had buried in her heart for Pitor into his little boy. And in turn, Liam grew up to be a warm and affectionate child. When he awoke each morning, he ran to Steffi and hugged her as she took him into her arms. When she put him to bed at night, he told her he loved her. And even amidst all the misery surrounding her, this was enough to keep her alive.

Then one night when Reinhard was supposed to be out of town on business, he appeared in the basement carrying a lit candle. She had slept too well and had not hidden her pillows. "What's this?" He put down the bottle of schnapps he'd been carrying in his other hand. Then he grabbed the pillow from under her. "Where did you get these?"

She didn't answer.

He kicked her in the stomach. "I said where did you get these? Did my wife give them to you?"

"No, I found them, here in the basement."

"I didn't give you permission to have pillows," he said angrily. Then he took a pocketknife out of his pants pocket, slit the fabric of the pillow and shook the feathers out all over the floor. "You will sleep on the concrete. That is what you deserve." He put the knife back into his pants pocket. Then he pushed her uniform skirt up over her stomach. *Oh, dear God, please not again.* In the candlelight, Steffi could see his eyes were puffy and red, and when he pressed his wet lips hard against hers, she smelled the alcohol on his breath. She wished she could reach the knife in his pocket. *I would kill him if I could. But then what would I do with his body? What would happen to Liam? What would he think when he heard I had killed his father? He's too young to know or understand any of this.*

Reinhard's face was so close to hers that she felt beads of his perspiration falling onto her face. "Oh, little Steffi," his tone was sarcastic, "you don't fool me for a minute. I know you want me. You know you do too. You've wanted me since you first saw me here in my position of power. The power I have excites you, doesn't it, Steffi? Shall I continue to call you Steffi? Or shall I call you by your number? That's what you've been reduced to. Just a number," he let out a laugh.

She turned her face to the side so he wouldn't be able to see the fear in her eyes. But he grabbed her face and turned it back towards him. "Now, now... don't you dare try to hide from me. Forget about your religion. Your love for your God hasn't saved you yet, now, has it? You see, Steffi, your God doesn't exist, I am your God now. I am the only God who can save you."

This angered her so much that she felt a sudden burst of courage rising in her blood. "You are not God. And you will never be God. You are just a cruel and miserable man. There is only one God..."

He slapped her across the face. "I didn't say I *was* God. What I said was that I am *your* God. Do you know why that's true? It's because it is in my power to decide if you live or die."

"Go ahead and kill me if that's what you want."

"I want you to say that I am your God."

"Never," she growled, "I'd rather die."

"You make me sick," he said. Then somehow he was able to have an erection, and he entered her. She whimpered. Her muscles were clenched so tightly against him that severe pain shot through her. She winced at the pain, but she didn't make a sound. Again, she turned her head away from him. "Look at me. Look directly at me. Turn your face to me so I can see your eyes," he growled.

She did not look at him. "I said look at me," he said, and again he grabbed her chin and roughly turned her head towards him, this time even more forcefully than before. Steffi bit her lip hard, and she tasted the metallic taste of blood. Hot tears were forming in her eyes, but she held them back, refusing to let him see her cry. He held her face tightly, and she stared at him as defiantly as she could manage. And then his manhood went soft. He let out a loud curse and slapped her so hard across the face that her head jerked to the side and her neck spasmed. "Why is it that I can't do this with you or with my wife? I can only do it to that Jew prisoner." He was speaking to himself, not to her. But then he turned to look at her and spat in Steffi's face as he still hovered over her. She wished he would leave, just go away forever. *If only someone would kill him.* She thought. But she wouldn't dare beg him to go, because if she did, she knew he would only stay longer. He reached down to check his limp manhood. Then he finally got off her and stood up. Steffi sat up and immediately pulled her skirt down to cover herself. "I'll tell you why everything works with that Jew woman in the camp. It's because she is a witch. She is a devil. I know what I am going to have to do. I am going to burn her at the stake. I'll do it tomorrow. What do you think of that?"

Steffi did not speak. But he didn't care; he was speaking more to himself than to her as he went on, "I am going to light that whore on fire for bewitching me. And as for you," Reinhard picked up the candle, "What if I chained you to this post?" He pointed out a pillar that held up the house's foundation. "And when you couldn't get away, I lit a blanket on fire and covered you with it? Do you think your skin would melt off before you died?"

She shuddered. But she knew she must not let him see her fear, or he would do it. And although she was terrified for herself, she was also afraid that Liam would die in the fire. Taking a deep breath, she said, "Reinhard, don't be foolish. If you set me on fire, you would burn this house down. Then you would be in a lot of trouble with your superiors. They would not be happy that you had done that."

He contemplated what she said for moment, then he nodded as if she was making sense to him, "That's true," he said casually, "but I could take you outside and burn you there."

She felt dizzy and sick to her stomach. However, she didn't let on at all. Steffi just looked at Reinhard and smiled as calmly as she could manage. "If you do that, you will need to train another prisoner to care for Liam. The child trusts me. What if you can't find someone else who Liam is comfortable with? Then he might just become a real bother to you and Uta."

Reinhard paused for a long moment. "And so, the great Steffi has convinced me to let her live another day. Bravo to you, Steffi," he said, slurring his words. "However, I am going to make you regret this. I am going to make you wish I'd killed you. Do you know the real reason why I am letting you live? It's because if you're dead, I won't be able to torture you anymore. And I do so enjoy it."

Then Reinhard stood up, took the candle and walked back up the stairs. She heard the door slam, and then she heard the lock turn. Once she was sure she was alone, Steffi got out of her bed and vomited into the slop bucket she kept in her room. After she emptied her stomach, she sat down on the concrete and wept. Her body shook, but she felt some release in crying. She wept for a long time until her mind grew clear, and she began to think. *I am stuck in a terrible situation. I know that even though this is horrible, I still have it better than most prisoners. Reinhard is at the camp all day. Uta is not so bad. She is a drunk, but I don't care. At least she gives me extra food. And she doesn't beat me. Even so, I am at the mercy of a horrible man. The next time Frau Woolf leaves me alone here, I could take a kitchen knife and slice through the veins on my arm. Suicide is a sin, but I believe God will forgive me. The guard who watches this house is always distracted. He pays no attention to me because, although Reinhard doesn't know it, the guard is having an affair with the SS officer's wife who lives next door.* She sighed aloud. *I would like to die. The only thing that stops me from ending my pathetic life is Liam. If I am gone, that poor little boy will be all alone in this house with my dead body until someone returns home. During that time, anything could happen to him.* She shuddered. *I can't let him get hurt. I could be going mad, or it could just be wishful thinking, but I truly believe Liam is Jakup, Pitor's son. And since I love Pitor, and I love Liam, I will do my best to go on living for them. I will live as long as I can bear to.*

CHAPTER TWENTY-TWO

Since Liam's illness, Uta had become even more relaxed around Steffi. She sometimes talked to Steffi about things she could not tell anyone else. She would even tell Steffi bits and pieces of her childhood memories. One afternoon when Uta returned from a luncheon with Frau Jager—one of the wives of a visiting officer who ranked higher than Reinhard—Uta seemed angry and frustrated. She plopped down on the sofa and called Steffi to come into the room. Then she began to tell Steffi her true feelings about this woman. "Since I know that you would never dare tell anyone what I am about to tell you, I can trust you. Of course, if you did ever get it into your head to open your mouth, I would have you executed in a second," Uta said. "You do know this, don't you?"

"Yes, Fräulein," Steffi said, looking down towards the ground. She didn't want to hear whatever Uta was about to tell her, but she dared not voice her feelings. She just sat quietly and listened.

"Frau Jager is obnoxious. She was constantly bragging and showing off. I can't stand her," Uta said as she poured herself a full glass of wine. "She likes to flaunt the fact that she married well. And because her husband is more successful than the other husbands here at the camp, and he chose her, that makes her better than the rest of us."

Steffi said nothing.

Uta downed her glass of wine and then poured herself another.

"I am glad to have you here to talk to because I can tell you these things and it doesn't matter. I mean, you will never be around this group of women, so you can't say anything that will make me look bad."

"Yes, Fräulein," Steffi said. *If Uta starts to regret telling me these things, it could be dangerous for me. I wish she wouldn't feel so comfortable.*

Uta took a large sip from her glass, then she said, "Why don't we go outside, and I'll get some sun while you take Liam into the pool?"

It was a rhetorical question. Steffi nodded. "I'll go and get us both ready," she said.

"Yes, do that. But before we go outside you can make some sandwiches, and we'll eat by the pool. I am starving. I couldn't eat a thing at the luncheon. I was so infuriated with that woman."

Steffi nodded.

Uta hadn't hugged or held Liam since his recovery. She had not gone into the pool with him either. And she made no secret of the fact that she wanted to be sure that he was completely healthy and not contagious before she had any physical contact with him. Steffi didn't mind. She held the little boy as if she were his mother, and he cuddled into her, basking in her love and attention.

Uta was drinking another glass of wine, and she was slowly getting drunk. Steffi was glad that at least she was not going to go into the pool, because she didn't want to be responsible for rescuing her if she started drowning.

Uta and Liam ate the sandwiches that Steffi prepared at an outdoor table by the side of the pool. Meanwhile, Uta gave Steffi half of a sandwich to eat while sitting on the ground at Liam's feet.

"He is a very handsome little boy, don't you think?" Uta asked. "I'm glad we chose him from all the children at the Lebensborn home. I mean if we must have a child, at least this one is a beautiful specimen of Aryan perfection," she was slurring her words.

"Yes, I do think he is a beautiful little boy," Steffi smiled, thinking of Pitor.

"You know, even though you are a Jew lover, I find that I like you. And you must admit, I am rather generous with you," Uta said, and she winked.

"Yes, very generous," Steffi tried to sound agreeable.

"You're not really a bad person. Now I am glad that at least you're not a Jew or a Gypsy, because if you were, I would never have you in my house at all. But as things stand, you are a German, but you're just a confused woman."

There was a long silence. Then Uta said wistfully, "You know, I never wanted him."

Steffi looked up at her, afraid to ask what she meant by that. *Does she mean she never wanted to marry Reinhard?*

"Liam, I mean. I never wanted Liam. I never wanted to adopt a child. If I was going to put all the effort it takes into raising a baby, I wanted the child to be my own. But try as we might, I couldn't get pregnant." She laughed bitterly. "Something is wrong with Reinhard. He would never agree or admit it. He's far too proud. But you know what?" She whispered. "I am going to tell you another secret. His manhood doesn't work. He can't keep an erection. That's right, Reinhard, isn't able to have intercourse." Then she laughed bitterly, and Steffi looked at her nervously. She wished Uta would stop telling her these things. But Uta didn't notice the nervous expression on Steffi's face. She just rambled on in a drunken stupor, "Reinhard, acts like he is such a big important fellow, but his male parts just don't work. I certainly didn't deserve such a fate, now did I?"

Steffi knew Uta was drunk. And she was terrified that if Uta remembered what she had just told Steffi, she might be so embarrassed that she would send Steffi away. *I don't care about Reinhard or Uta, or even myself, but it would devastate Liam.*

"So, he had to find a way to satisfy the whims of his superior officers. They were constantly demanding that we have children. You know all about the awards that German women are receiving for having lots of children. And since we couldn't get pregnant, Reinhard blamed it on me. He even got that louse, Dr. Mengele, to say that it was my fault. Mengele wrote up a paper saying that something was wrong with me." She let out a bitter laugh. "But it was Reinhard all along. However, I dared not tell anyone. Can you imagine what Reinhard would have done to me if I told anyone that he was impotent? Anyway, it was important to Reinhard's career that we have a child. So, we had to go to Munich and get one from the Lebensborn."

It hurt Steffi's heart to hear Uta talk this way in front of Liam, and she wondered how much the little boy understood. But Uta had had too much to drink, and she was not thinking before she spoke. "I never wanted to marry Reinhard either. There was another boy who I was in love with. He was very handsome, but he was poor. And he came from a bad part of town. When my father found out I was sleeping with this other fellow, he beat me and threatened to kill me if I ever saw him again. I was heartsick, but there was nothing I could do. A few months later I met Reinhard. My parents were impressed with him because he was from a decent family with a little bit of money. And not only that but he had an uncle who was helping him to rise to a good position in the Nazi party. So, my father insisted I marry him. As you know, girls don't have much say in anything. My father said I had to marry him, so I did. But being married to Reinhard wasn't so bad, that is of course until we ended up here in Auschwitz. What a terrible place this is. I hate it here." She admitted. Then she began to laugh a drunken laugh. "I've never told anyone else that I feel this way. But the stench of this place never leaves me. I feel slightly nauseated all the time. All those filthy Jews in there carrying disease. When I think of it, it makes me sick."

Steffi was glad that the sun was in Uta's eyes, so Uta could not see her clearly. She knew she couldn't conceal her disgust for the woman, and she was afraid Uta would see it in her face. Steffi's heart was racing as she thought about Liam. Now that she knew Uta didn't really love him—and she doubted Reinhard did either—if they ever found out that Liam was really a Jewish child, they wouldn't keep him. In fact, she shuddered to think of what they might to do him.

"Liam is getting tired. Shall I put him down for his nap?" Steffi asked, hoping Uta would agree so she could leave before Uta told her anything else that was too personal.

"I'm not tired. We still haven't gone swimming," Liam protested.

"Yes, but you are looking very tired," Steffi said, kissing his forehead. "I don't want you to overdo it. You are still getting over being ill."

"Yes, that's a good idea. Why don't you take him in and put him down for a nap. Then go and start dinner."

"Yes, Fräulein," Steffi said. She lifted Liam into her arms. He hadn't been swimming, but it was very hot outside, and just playing in the heat had made him tired. As he laid his head on her shoulder, she whispered into his ear, "I love you."

Liam put his thumb in his mouth and was fast asleep before they even got to his bedroom.

CHAPTER TWENTY-THREE

Horst spent several days looking things up until he was able to locate men who had served in the army with Konrad. Most of them were still in the military and therefore unavailable. However, after extensive work, he located four men who had fought side by side with Konrad Hoffmann and had been disabled in the war. These men had been left unable to fight, and therefore they were forced to leave the army and stay at home. Three of the men had been married before they left home to serve. And each of them had children. The fourth was a young man who had lost both his legs in battle, and he had never been married. When Horst telephoned him to invite him to the party he was giving to celebrate Konrad's recent marriage, the wounded soldier proudly told Horst that Konrad had been a hero. Then he professed how happy he was that Konrad had found a wife, and then he admitted that in his condition, he would probably never find a wife. But at least, he said self-importantly, he'd given everything he could to serve his Führer. All four of the men who Horst spoke to had said they had fond memories of Konrad Hoffmann, and they all agreed to attend the upcoming festivity.

Gretchen and Horst went to the biergarten around the corner

from their apartment, and Horst made a deal for a good price with the owner that he felt was fair. The party was arranged for the following week.

Although the get together was to be a celebration of Konrad's marriage to Heidi, and it was supposed to be a surprise, Gretchen decided that if things were to work the way that she and Horst hoped, they would need Heidi's cooperation. So, the following day, Gretchen told Heidi that she and Horst wanted to give a party to celebrate Heidi and Konrad's marriage.

"That's so very kind of you," Heidi said sincerely.

Gretchen smiled. "Horst and I need your help, because we want to make the party a surprise for Konrad. We have arranged the party for Friday night at Gunther's beer garden. Do you know where that is?"

"Yes, it's not very far from here. What time is the party scheduled for?"

"Eight o'clock. Now, since this is going to be a surprise, Horst and I need you to bring Konrad to the biergarten, but don't tell him why. Just tell him you want to go out for dinner and that you'd like to go to Gunther's. Everyone will be waiting for the two of you. I am sure he will be delighted to see all his old army friends."

"Yes, I am sure he will."

"So, you'll be there? And you will bring Konrad?"

"Of course I will. I know he will really enjoy it. And I wouldn't miss it. Thank you for being such a good friend to me, Gretchen."

CHAPTER TWENTY-FOUR

Day and night, Pitor racked his brain for a way to get his son back. He had to be strategic, not only for his own safety, but because if he made any mistakes and was caught, he would be arrested or shot, and that would leave Jakup at the mercy of these merciless people. And if somehow it was discovered that he, Pitor, was actually Jewish, and Jakup was his biological son, that would be disastrous. He shuddered to think of what might become of his little boy. Pitor lay awake at night beside Heidi, listening to her even steady breathing. She was happy, and marrying Konrad had made her dreams come true. She told Pitor so constantly. And in a strange way, he felt sorry for her, because he knew that eventually he was going to be forced to break her heart. She was one of them. An Aryan with the dark heart of a Nazi. And to Pitor, working for the Nazi party was unforgivable. But she was also a woman. His mother had instilled a respect for women in his heart and mind when he was just a boy. So, he felt a stab of guilt at the way he was treating Heidi. However, his priority was his son, and the promise that he'd made to Mila, the love of his life and Jakup's mother.

Pitor continued to work each day, living as Konrad Hoffmann.

But he found it difficult to laugh and joke with the other bodyguards. His façade was becoming harder to maintain; now that he had all the information he needed to find his son, all he could do was agonize about Jakup. As Pitor sat on a bench having a cup of coffee one afternoon, he observed as a mother walked past him pushing a stroller with a little boy sleeping inside. *Perhaps I am not doing Jakup any favors by taking him.* He thought. *I hate these Nazis, but the truth is that my son is currently safe where he is. They have no idea that he is a Jew. Horst, Gretchen, and Heidi are the only ones who know the truth. And if it ever came out, they would be in trouble too. So, right now my son is safe. If I go to Jakup and kidnap him, then I will have to hide in the forests with him. Hopefully, I can find my way back to the partisan's camp. But living in the forest is not an easy life. Maybe I should leave well enough alone. I could go and see him, keep a watch on him and make sure he is safe, and his needs are being met, until the war is over. If it is ever going to be over.* Pitor took a sip of his coffee and sighed. *Hitler is one relentless, miserable, power-hungry monster. But I have overheard some of my higher ups talking to each other about the war in secret. And although the Germans hate to admit it, Germany is losing the war. So, waiting and watching my son might be the smartest thing to do. But he is so young, and who knows how his upbringing in the home of an SS officer will affect the rest of his life? Do I take him and raise him with Heidi as my wife? That is an option. But then again, he would be raised to be a Nazi. And what if there is a turn of events and, God forbid, the Nazis win this war? Then it would be better for Jakup to never learn of his Jewish blood. My son was born a Jew; his mother and I were both Jews. And I have never been very religious, but I want my son to know the depth and beauty of his heritage. After all we have been through, I want him to live as one of God's chosen people. Not as a blind follower of a madman like Hitler.*

A loud whistle brought Pitor back to the present, and he looked around. "Hoffmann!" One of the other officers called out to him. "Come join us."

Pitor walked over to the table and sat with the rest of Hitler's staff. While they were discussing women and local restaurants, Pitor was mulling over all the possibilities surrounding Jakup. When the others tried to pull him into their conversations, he just smiled but did not speak. They attributed his lack of interest to his being tired. "He's a newlywed, his wife is keeping him busy all night. You must be tired, yes, Konrad?" one of them asked him.

"I am," Pitor said, glad for the excuse.

The rest of the men at the table laughed warmly at this and then spoke among themselves.

A week or so later Pitor lay in bed awake; after telling Heidi he was too tired to have sex. He'd kissed her gently and told her he'd been working very hard. However, he would make it up to her on his day off. She was satisfied with his excuse. And now, Heidi was snoring softly. As quietly as he could, Pitor got out of bed and went into the living room, where he poured himself a glass of schnapps. He sank into the large chair in front of the picture window and stared out at the stars. Closing his eyes, he could see Mila's face as clearly as if she were before him, and his heart ached to hold her close. *I miss you, my love. I miss you every day of my life. I don't know what to do. Tell me, what should I do, Mila? I must be so careful not to put our little boy in danger.* He felt a cool breeze, a soft gust of wind brush across his cheek. Yet a breeze was impossible because the window was closed. *Was that you, Mila? Are you here with me? Or am I just dreaming? Dear God, how I want to believe you are here.* Hot tears began to sting the back of his eyes. *We were such a happy family; we had everything. We had each other and our beautiful child. And now you are gone, and I am alone here trying to figure out what to do. Help me, Mila. Please help me. I'm lost.* He sat silently, as if waiting for an answer. But he knew it was only wishful thinking. He poured another glass of schnapps and drank it quickly. The schnapps both burned his throat and warmed his belly. Pitor closed his eyes. Then he saw Mila in his mind's eye. She was smiling at him, and suddenly he knew what he needed to do. He needed to see Jakup. He needed to go where Jakup was living and see how his son was being raised. I will not plan to take him. Not yet. First, I will just go and observe. I won't confront his new family. I'll hide outside the house where he is living, and I'll wait for him to come outside. Pitor sighed out loud and took a swig of schnapps, emptying his glass. *Tomorrow morning, as soon as I get to work I'll put in a special request to take a few days off next week. I'll tell my superior officer that my mother is sick, and she might die. I'll say I must go home to see her. He likes me, so even though he's not happy that I married a little brown sister, he will probably grant me the time off. Then I will tell Heidi that I must go away on business, and I cannot take her with me. She will not question me. Once I am relieved from work, I will travel to Poland—to the address that Heidi gave me—and I will watch and wait until I see Jakup come out of the house. Once I see him, I'll know what to do.*

CHAPTER TWENTY-FIVE

The following morning, Pitor went into work and requested the time off.

"I understand that your mother is ill, and you would like to leave as soon as possible," the Sturmbannführer in charge said, "however, you can't take any time off right now, we are expecting important guests to visit us next week, and you must be here. There is to be an important meeting between these men and our Führer. And as always, there is a possibility of danger to our Führer, so he needs men here who he can trust. He has made it mandatory that his specially chosen bodyguards be present."

Pitor felt his heart sink. "My mother is quite ill," he said lamely, knowing that this would not make any difference. The Führer's needs always came first.

"Family is important. But our Führer is more important. He is our leader, our savior. He *is* Deutschland."

"Yes, of course," Pitor said. "Can I go the following week?"

"If your mother is still alive, of course I will arrange for you to have the time off," the Oberstrumführer said.

"I hope she will be able to wait for me," Pitor said.

The Oberstrumführer nodded. "If she does pass on, at least you can take comfort in the knowledge that you've done your duty to your Führer, and your country. And you will be able to attend the funeral."

"Yes, of course," Pitor said. *These people are not human. They have no feelings at all.*

As he walked away, he thought, *another week. I can hardly stand the wait, but I must be patient. The truth is, I don't even know if Konrad's mother is still alive. So, I must be very careful not to do anything that might raise suspicion. The last thing I need is for any of these Nazis to check on Konrad's mother's health.*

The rest of the day passed slowly, as it always did. A new secretary by the name of Birdie had recently been hired. When she had been introduced to Pitor, she smiled broadly, and he could see in her eyes that she was attracted to him. All the men at the office noticed that Birdie's shirts were a little tight, her skirts slightly too short, and she walked with an easy swivel to her hips that aroused them. But try as they might to ask her out, Birdie showed no interest in any of the others. The more Pitor ignored her, the more she seemed to appear everywhere he went. Sometimes he would look up from the paperwork on his desk to find her gazing at him and smiling from across the room. And she often tried to strike up conversations with him about anything, but most of all she seemed to be very curious about his private life. She even suggested that they have a drink after work one evening. "Why don't you come to my apartment this evening. We could have a drink, and dinner perhaps?" she said.

He was cordial as he informed her he was newly married and was very faithful.

"How unusual," she laughed a little.

Pitor thought that would be the end of it, but Birdie was not one to be discouraged easily. And so, she wore even more provocative clothing and made subtle sexual suggestions to him whenever she was able to find him alone. Pitor needed to discourage her more. She was always asking questions about Konrad's family, his youth, his private life. Questions he did not know the answers to. So, he did his best to avoid her. Then, one Friday, she brought cookies she'd baked into work. Some of the men flattered her, saying what a wonderful hausfrau she would make, and she flirted with them. But when Pitor did not go into the lunchroom and try her cookies, she brought a plate of them to Pitor's desk. He thanked her, but still kept his distance. And the more he tried to push her away, the harder she tried to entice him, flirting openly and shamelessly with him. He was fairly certain that she was only asking him questions about his life as a way of showing interest. He didn't think she had any idea that he was an imposter. However, her constant pursuit of him unnerved him and left him jittery. He was concerned that her obsession with him might cause her to search through the files on Konrad in the office. And if she looked too deeply, she could come out knowing more about Konrad than Pitor did.

After his superior officer told Pitor he could not take off work for a week, he was feeling anxious. Birdie was even more attentive than usual. When she saw him sitting at his desk eating alone during lunchtime, she pulled a chair up and ate her lunch beside him. He tried to be polite, but he was glad when lunchtime finally ended. And at the end of the day, relieved that he would not be confronted by Birdie with her broad, inviting smile anymore—at least until tomorrow. On his way home, exhausted from making so much effort to avoid the new secretary, he decided that the next time Birdie tried to talk to him, he was going to tell her she was making him uncomfortable because he was afraid his wife would find out and be suspicious of his friendship with another woman at work.

CHAPTER TWENTY-SIX

Gretchen had promised Horst she would call Birdie and see what Birdie had found out about Konrad. So that evening she picked up the telephone receiver and asked the operator to connect her to the phone number Birdie had given her. It took a few minutes, and then the voice of an older woman came on the phone. "Allo."

"I'd like to speak with Birdie Schmitz, please," Gretchen said.

"I'll see if she's in her room. Hold the phone, please. I'll be right back."

Gretchen waited. From the sounds of women's voices and laughter in the background, Gretchen assumed Birdie was staying in one of the hotels for single women. *It would be nice if Birdie could identify Konrad as an imposter. Then Horst and I could cancel this party, and we would not have to spend so much of our money on a party for Heidi and her husband. She certainly doesn't deserve it. She's never done anything like this for me.*

"This is Birdie Schmitz," a voice on the phone interrupted her thoughts.

"Birdie, this is Gretchen. How are you doing at your new job?"

"I like it. Lots of handsome important men," she giggled.

"So, have you had a chance to see Konrad Hoffmann, and do you have any information for me?"

"Actually yes, I have seen him several times. But I am rather embarrassed to admit this, but I don't remember him. I was so drunk that night that I spent time with him at his hotel, that I just couldn't really say what he looked like. However, the man I met is very handsome. And I wouldn't mind getting to know him better. I've tried to spark his interest, but he is always so busy and so distracted with his work. And it seems he is actually in love with his wife. Now that is rather unusual, yes?" she laughed, then asked, "By the way, are you and Konrad friends?"

"Yes, and no. I mean, we know each other."

"Well, the next time you see him, could you put in a word for me?" Birdie asked.

"I would if he hadn't just gotten married. You're right about his love for his wife. He seems to be mad about her," Gretchen said, trying to hide her disdain.

"Most men don't take marriage so seriously," Birdie said.

"I know. He is quite the gem. His wife is a friend of mine."

"Lucky girl," Birdie sighed. "He is a handsome devil. And faithful too. That is a rare combination. That is for sure."

"Yes, she is lucky," Gretchen said. *So far, Heidi has been lucky, but if Horst is right, her luck might be about to run out.*

"I'd love to have a husband who is so handsome, devoted and successful," Birdie said.

"Yes, well..." Gretchen sighed, thinking of how her own husband was devoted, but not successful and certainly not handsome. "I must get going. Let's keep in touch, shall we?"

"I'd like that. Perhaps we can go out and have a beer sometime."

"Sure. Just give me a call."

"I will."

Gretchen hung up the telephone. She was frustrated and ready to cry. Not that she hated Heidi. She didn't. There was no reason to hate her. But she couldn't stand seeing Heidi doing so well. And she really wished that Horst was right, and Konrad was a fraud. This would change everything. Heidi wouldn't be so smug. This would put Heidi back in her place.

CHAPTER TWENTY-SEVEN

On the night of the party, it rained. The sky turned gray and then opened up with a heavy downpour. At first, Heidi was concerned about her hair getting wet on the walk to the biergarten. She'd spent the entire previous night unable to sleep because her hair was set in pin curls, and the clips pulled on her scalp. She'd gotten permission to leave work early to get ready. And now, as she looked in the mirror, her hair was absolutely perfect. She wore a classic German green and white dirndl skirt with a crisp white blouse. Heidi watched the rain subside as she waited for Konrad to arrive home from work, and she breathed a sigh of relief that she was not going to get wet. When Konrad walked through the door and into the apartment, she ran to greet him and hugged him tightly.

"You look nice," he said, smiling. "But why are you so dressed up?"

"Because I have a request."

"Oh?" he managed to force himself to smile. "What's your request?"

"Will you take me to dinner?"

"Of course," he said. This behavior was unusual for Heidi, but

Pitor wasn't alarmed. She was usually happy to prepare a meal each evening and then stay at home with him so she could have him all to herself. But he wasn't concerned about her wanting to go out. "Where would you like to go?" he asked.

"Gunther's biergarten," she smiled broadly.

"Why Gunther's?" he asked curiously, but still unsuspecting that there might be any special reason.

"I like their beer."

"All right. Sure. Let's go there. Give me a few minutes to get cleaned up."

"Of course," she said, grinning.

Pitor went into the bathroom and leaned his forehead against the wall. The tile felt cool against his face. *I have to get through this week. I must do everything I can to keep up this façade, even though it's driving me crazy.* After splashing a good deal of cold water on his face, Pitor felt a little more in control. He walked back to the living room, where Heidi waited.

"All right. Gunther's it is. Let's go," he said, smiling and trying hard to hide his inner anxiety.

Gunther's Biergarten was walking distance from their apartment. And since the rain had stopped, it was a lovely night for a short walk. As they made their way to Gunther's, Heidi hooked her arm through her husband's. She was proud to be married to such an important and handsome Aryan man. And as they walked along, Heidi was greeted by several people who passed on the street. When she saw them, she smiled smugly. She was no longer the ugly little brown sister. She was the wife of an important man. And she wanted the world to know it. But secretly she had never, in her wildest dreams, hoped for such good fortune.

Konrad looked so handsome and tall as he held the door for Heidi, then followed her into the Biergarten. She beamed with pride as she looked at him. But before they could even get inside and look around for a table, a loud cry echoed from a group of people sitting at a long table, "Surprise!"

Pitor turned to look at Heidi. She was smiling broadly. "Surprise, sweetheart," she said, leaning in and kissing him. "Gretchen and Horst are giving us a little get together to celebrate our marriage. Horst invited some of your army buddies. At least the ones he was able to contact." The walk had calmed him, but now he was really unnerved. He glanced at the door and considered running away. But before he could move, Horst and Gretchen were at their side.

Gretchen smiled at Pitor. "A little surprise party to celebrate your marriage," she said, then Gretchen reached out and gave Heidi a long hug.

"Heil Hitler," Horst said, smiling at Pitor.

"Heil Hitler," Pitor answered.

"I contacted as many of your army buddies as I could find," Horst said slyly.

Pitor glanced over at the table. His heart was sinking. *How can I get out of here? What can I do? They are all staring at me. They must realize that I am not Konrad.*

"Don't you recognize these fellows? I mean you should," Horst said slyly, "After all, you served in the military with them. They served with you, and they were all so excited to see you again."

Pitor caught the distinct, menacing look of a predator in Horst's eyes. Cold beads of sweat began forming on Pitor's forehead. *He knows the truth. He knows that I am not Konrad. I wonder if he knows I am a Jew, and that Liam is not some strange child, but my son that he stole from the ghetto. I am not sure what he knows exactly, but I have a feeling that he plans to expose me to the Nazi party. I could kill him here and now with my bare hands. But of course, I dare not touch him with everyone here watching. All these men that he invited to come here to this party know Konrad. They are going to tell everyone the truth. I don't know what to do.* Pitor's heart was racing. *If I run out of here and try to get away, I will automatically look guilty of something. I must stay and hope that I can convince these men that I am Konrad Hoffmann. We look a lot alike, Konrad and I. But will they believe I am him? Can I make them believe it? I have no idea how I am going to do that.*

Only four men and their wives, including Gretchen and Horst were in attendance. Other than Horst, the men all had suffered some form of disability from the war. One was missing an arm. Another had only one eye, the other covered by a black eye patch. And the last one was unable to walk.

Pitor was worried about being recognized, but none of them seemed to know he was not Konrad. And he decided that they probably hadn't really known Konrad very well. As each of the couples congratulated him and Heidi, Pitor watched them to see if any of them were trying to trick him by pretending they believed he was Konrad Hoffmann. However, they all seemed to be sincere in their congratulations. And strangely enough, not one of the men seemed to realize that he was an imposter. Pitor was still anxious. He couldn't trust his good fortune. At any moment, one of them might say or do something that revealed that they knew the truth. Pitor wondered if they had really served with Konrad, or if they just showed up with hopes to mingle with higher ranked Nazi officers. But as the night wore on, Konrad's friends drank to Konrad and Heidi's marriage, and if they suspected anything, not one of them gave any indication. And finally, Pitor began to relax.

It was getting late, and the biergarten was about to close when a handsome young man in a black SS officer's uniform sauntered in. It had begun to rain again, and he shook the water off his coat just inside the door. Then he turned and glanced around the room. When he saw the group of Konrad and his friends, he smiled and walked over to them. Horst stood up, "You must be Erich Keller. I'm Horst. I'm the man who invited you."

"Heil Hitler," Erich said, standing proud at attention.

"Heil Hitler," Horst replied, smiling.

Then the others all chimed in, "Heil Hitler."

"Hans!" Erich said to the man with the black eye patch, "How are you? It's been a long time."

"Yes, it certainly has," the man answered.

Erich smiled, then turned and looked around at the others at the table, and said, "So, where is Konrad? Where is the guest of honor?"

Pitor was sitting with his back to the man called Erich. But when he heard Erich's words, Pitor felt his pulse begin to race.

"He's sitting right here," one of the soldiers answered. "Don't you recognize him?"

Erich didn't answer, but he walked over to the other side of the table to see Konrad's face. He stared at Pitor for a long moment. Then he shook his head and declared in a firm voice, "This man is not Konrad Hoffmann. I served with Konrad for over five months. We were good friends, and I'd know him anywhere. But I know who you are, and I know you are not Konrad," he said, pointing to Pitor's face.

"You're drunk," Heidi said to Erich. She tried to sound causal, but her voice was quivering with fear that what the man was saying might be true. Still, she tried to stand up for her husband and hold fast to her dreams.

"I might have had a drink or two, but I am telling you something. I know for sure that this man is not Konrad Hoffmann."

When Heidi glanced over at Horst, he looked like a man who had just trapped his worst enemy. And Gretchen was smiling. "I knew it," she said. "Horst and I both knew it. This man is nothing but an imposter."

"He's not only an imposter. He's a Jew," Erich said.

CHAPTER TWENTY-EIGHT

The entire room went silent when Erich yelled out the word 'Jew.' The other men at the table let out a gasp of surprise. Erich was staring at Pitor as he went on, "You see, I worked as a guard for a while in the Warsaw Ghetto. I recognize this man because he was a real troublemaker there. Strong as an ox too. We received our orders to liquidate the ghetto, but this man, along with other Jews who were just like him, resisted and they caused the deaths of plenty of good German soldiers. When the uprising broke out and the Jews got out of hand, this man was one of the men we thought was probably behind it. SS-Brigadeführer Stroop, was in charge. He sent several of us into the burned-out buildings to search for the trouble making Jews so we could put an end to the uprising. But the Jews were dirty fighters, and so to put a quick end to it all, we finally set the entire ghetto on fire. It was a filthy place, full of disease, and it was probably best that it burnt to the round. Anyway, the fire drove some of them out into the street where we shot them, and others were either already dead, or they disappeared. This man was one of the ones we couldn't find. Stroop said he thought that some of these Jews might have been burned in one of the fires or the bombings. But now I see that was not the case. This one escaped, and he had the nerve to impersonate a German officer." Erich shook his head in disbelief. "My guess is that he must have killed the real Konrad Hoffmann in order to assume his identity."

Heidi's face was bright red. Her fists were clenched. Her body was trembling. "None of this is true. It's all impossible. You don't know that my husband is not who he says he is. These are horrible, devastating accusations," she said.

Pitor glanced over at Heidi, and then at the faces of all the other people who were sitting at their table. Only a few minutes ago, they had been laughing, telling stories, and drinking. But now, it was as if their eyes were opened, and they saw him for the first time. They were glaring at him, their mouths open as if they were in shock, and he could feel their razor stare cutting through him, slicing through him. *Is it too late to run?*

"You did this. You did this on purpose to ruin my life!" Heidi glared at Gretchen. "You and your lousy husband. You were so jealous of me that you couldn't stand it. So, you had to find a way to ruin everything for me, didn't you? And you disguised your wicked plan by pretending you wanted to give a party for Konrad and me, to celebrate our marriage. You are evil, Gretchen. You are a terrible friend, and a miserable person. I hope you rot in hell for this."

"I...I..."

"Shut your mouth. You know in your heart that you are a terrible person, Gretchen. And since you've made it your business to destroy my husband, I will pay you in kind. I will destroy your life too. I am about to ruin your husband, because I know the truth. And you know that I do. Now, everyone here seated at this table will know the truth about Horst too." Her voice was shaking with anger as she turned to look at the others. "Gretchen and I used to be best friends. Or at least I thought we were. And she told me in the strictest confidence that Horst stole a child from the Warsaw Ghetto—a Jewish child. He couldn't fill his quota of Polish children, so he did something unthinkable. He brought a Jew into Heim Hochland to be Germanized. He lied to everyone and said the little boy was Polish. But Gretchen knew the truth. She should have turned him in and sent the child to whatever place that we send Jew children. But she didn't. She let that boy be adopted by a good Aryan family. Didn't you, Gretchen?"

"You knew too, Heidi. I told you all about it, so you knew. And because you didn't turn Horst in, you have just implicated yourself as well as Horst and me," Gretchen said. "Why didn't you turn him in? I didn't turn him in, because Horst is my husband. But you should have had allegiance to the Reich, and you should have turned him in."

"I didn't for your sake, because I thought you were my friend," Heidi stared directly into Gretchen's cold eyes.

"I am not your friend. I hate you," Gretchen said, her face crimson with anger. And for a moment she looked insane. No one moved. And before anyone realized what had happened, Gretchen grabbed a sharp knife off the table and stabbed it into Heidi's chest. Heidi looked shocked as everyone in the biergarten gathered around. Then Heidi clutched her chest and fell to the floor. Chaos ensued. Gretchen was screaming in shock at what she had done. The knife fell from her hand, and tears ran down her cheeks as she knelt at Heidi's side. "I'm sorry. I'm sorry. I didn't mean it. Don't die. You can't die."

Someone must have called the police, because two officers appeared and grabbed Gretchen's arms. Horst let out a cry of dismay. "No, please don't take her. She didn't mean it; it was an accident. Let her go. Let her go. She didn't mean it."

But the police were dragging Gretchen away, her hands and her dress covered in her friend's blood.

In the midst of all the confusion, everyone had forgotten Pitor for the moment. As quickly and as silently as he could, Pitor slipped out the back door of the biergarten and into the dark night. He began to run as fast as he could. Before anyone noticed he was gone.

CHAPTER TWENTY-NINE

Horst's mind was whirling as the police dragged Gretchen away from the dead body of her best friend. Since the day they met, Gretchen had been Horst's rock, his constant source of strength. Without her, he couldn't go on.

Horst walked all the way to the police station, where he knew they'd taken his wife. He walked as quickly as he could, his mind racing. *Heidi is dead. And I know Gretchen didn't mean it, but she is gone, and there is nothing anyone can do about it. If I'm honest,* Horst thought to himself, *I don't care at all about what happened to Heidi; I don't even blame Gretchen. But now, most importantly, I must find a way to get her out of this mess.* His heart was pounding. *If Gretchen is found guilty, she will be punished severely. She could even be executed or put into a work camp.* The idea of Gretchen dying, or going into a prison camp made Horst feel weak. And then it made him angry. *I never cared about rising in the party. And I never really cared about Hoffmann. I didn't trust him, and I knew he was an imposter. But if Gretchen had only kept her mouth shut about that little boy, we wouldn't be in this mess. Why do women need to talk so much? I was forced to hide my crime by exposing him. I had no other choice, or I would never have bothered to pursue this. It wasn't worth the effort. Everything that happened tonight was that lousy Jew's fault. If he had not posed as Konrad Hoffmann and married my wife's best friend, we would not be in this trouble today. I am not surprised to find out that he is a Jew, and that the child I took was probably his son. It makes sense now why he wanted that particular child so badly. Well, as usual, our Führer was right again. He always said that the Jews were at the root of all the trouble in the world. That Jew is as Aryan looking as Liam. Both of them have the blue eyes and blond hair of pure Aryan Germans. From that, I can assume that the Jew is probably a disciple of the devil. He has somehow masked his Jewishness and now he looks like an Aryan. I should tell the police everything I know,* he thought. Horst was out of breath. He had recently begun smoking again, and he found it difficult to walk such a long distance. He leaned against the side of building and closed his eyes, waiting for his heart to stop pounding. As his heart rate slowed, his breathing grew less labored, and his mind became clearer. Then he started to form a plan. *If I tell the police what I know, then I will have no power. The police will send the Gestapo to get him, and that will be the end of it. I don't care about that man at all. But I can, and I will use him to free my wife. So, if I tell the police that I think I can find and catch Hoffmann's imposter, and that I will bring him in to face justice, I might be able to use the fugitive to bargain with the police to release Gretchen in exchange. I know Gretchen gave Heidi the name and address of the couple who adopted Liam. But I don't have it. And now with Heidi gone, and the only person who would know is Gretchen. So somehow I must find a way to make the police allow me to have a private moment with her. Because I am sure that the Jew is headed to find the child.*

CHAPTER THIRTY

Pitor was in good shape. He had always been a strong man, and since food had been plentiful since he began working for the Führer, he had gained back all the weight he lost when he was imprisoned in the ghetto. He looked handsome and every bit an SS officer in his black uniform, and several women turned to look at him as he stood in the station, waiting for the train to Berlin. Pitor was sure that Horst and Gretchen had told the Gestapo all about him and his son. Gretchen had probably given them the address of the family in Poland who had adopted Liam. They would assume that Pitor was on his way there, which he was. But they would probably think he would be on a train headed for Krakow, and from there he would transfer to a train to Auschwitz-Birkenau. So instead, he'd taken an alternate route. *It might take a little longer, but taking a train from Munich to Berlin, and then from Berlin to Krakow seems like a smart idea. The Gestapo would be less likely to look for me on a train from Berlin.* It was a long train ride from Munich to Berlin, even though the cities were not that far apart. Military trains always took priority over civilian trains, so the ride took hours. Every minute would be nerve racking because at any moment the Gestapo might stop the train, board it, and arrest him. He was sure that they were already searching for him. There was no trust in the Nazi party, not even amongst the most highly regarded party members. Everyone was always under constant scrutiny. They were always searching each other's backgrounds for Jewish or Gypsy blood. So, after what had transpired at the biergarten, he knew no one was standing up for him. All the men who he worked with, men who professed to be his friends, would have turned on him now that his pure German identity was in question.

Despite Pitor's constant anxiety, the train ride went smoothly. Each time the train made a stop, he shuddered. Sometimes SS officers boarded the train. When they saw his uniform, they nodded and occasionally saluted with "Heil Hitler." He had grown so accustomed to hearing it, and he returned the salute casually. But otherwise, no one spoke to him or approached him. A young woman with a child in her arms smiled at him flirtatiously. He returned her smile, then turned away, putting his attention on the darkness outside the window. A little later he thought he could feel her eyes on him, and he couldn't help but glance over at her. She was staring at him. It unnerved him. *Does she recognize me from somewhere?* This time he did not smile or encourage her attention in any way. Instead, he closed his eyes and pretended to be asleep. When the train arrived in Berlin the following morning, Pitor got off quickly. He did not have any luggage, so there was no reason to hesitate for even a moment. "The first train to Krakow this morning will be departing in less than an hour." The man at the ticket booth said to Pitor.

"Thank you," Pitor said, putting a few Reichsmarks on the counter to purchase his ticket.

It was almost dawn, and soon the train station would be crowded with people going to work, but right now it was still early, and so the station was almost empty. Pitor grabbed himself a cup of coffee, found a bench and sat down. *Waiting until the time is right is always the most difficult part of any mission.* He remembered hearing this from one of the partisans. Pitor thought about those men, those brave freedom fighters. And he missed them. *Once I find Jakup and I have my son with me, I will need to find a place to go. I will either take Jakup to Steffi's farm or retreat to the forest with him and try to find the partisans again. It's difficult to bring a child to such a dangerous place. But it really doesn't make any difference where Jakup and I go, because all of Europe is a hotbed of danger right now. Especially for Jews. And after all that's happened, I can't risk leaving him where he is. Damn Heidi. She opened her mouth, and now they know Jakup is not a Polish child. They know he is Jewish. I am hoping the Lebensborn is so ashamed of their mistake that they don't know how to tell his adopted family what happened. But I am sure they will think of a way. And once the family finds out, I can't trust them to protect Jakup anymore. Even if they have come to love him, Nazis don't love the way other people love. They put their country and that lousy Führer above everything else. So, I think they would surrender Jakup to the Gestapo. Then, I shudder to think what would happen.* He shook his head. His mouth was as dry as sand. *I must get to him before they get there.*

Pitor fidgeted nervously as he waited on the bench for the train to arrive. His hands were clammy with sweat. *Every second is crucial. At any time, they might seize my little boy, and well... what they might do with a Jewish child is unthinkable.* Two young, healthy, and vibrant SS officers wearing clean pressed uniforms walked briskly past him. They both turned, nodded and smiled at Pitor. "Heil Hitler," they said in unison.

"Heil Hitler," Pitor answered. He too smiled, but his lips were quivering, and a bead of sweat ran down his forehead and into his eyes. He wiped it away with the back of his hand, glad they hadn't noticed.

As the two Nazis crossed over to the other side of the station, a train whistle blew. Pitor stood up immediately, and the train came rumbling into the station.

"All aboard, this train is bound for Krakow."

Pitor's legs were weak as he climbed the stairs to board the train. He quickly glanced around to see if anyone was following him, relieved when he saw no one.

Once on board the train, Pitor walked to the back of the train car and then quietly slipped into a seat by the window where he stared out at the station, waiting for the train to leave. A German soldier wearing the gray green uniform of the Wehrmacht boarded the train. A young, pretty woman laughing gayly hung on to the soldier's arm. Pitor turned his head at the sound of the laughter. The soldier nodded to Pitor and respectfully uttered, "Heil Hitler, sir."

"Heil Hitler," Pitor answered. He was hoping they would not sit by him. He didn't want to be forced into a conversation with a soldier. So, he was relieved as the young couple left the train car and entered another one.

The train whistle blew again. "Last call for Krakow."

A few minutes passed, and then the train sprang to life. Pitor took a deep breath. He was finally on his way. It would be afternoon before he would arrive in Krakow. He took several long, deep breaths trying hard to relax. Please, *God, let me get there in time,* he thought, closing his eyes and trying to let the rhythmic motion of the train help him relax. Finally, after half an hour, his breathing slowed down to normal for a moment, and his heart stopped pounding in his chest. He closed his eyes as the gentle, even rhythm of the rails lulled him to sleep. But then the train stopped abruptly, and Pitor's eyes flew open as a group of Nazi officers climbed on board. They were not smiling or talking to each other. They had the look of predators, and Pitor was sure they were looking for someone or something. *Is it me they are searching for?* He sat up, watching and waiting. He held his hand on the gun beneath his jacket. His entire body was on high alert.

CHAPTER THIRTY-ONE

"Steffi." Uta said as she sat at the kitchen table eating breakfast after Reinhard left for work. Liam was still asleep, so she was speaking quietly. "I have a luncheon today with that awful woman, the one I can't stand. You know who I am talking about?"

Steffi did not answer. She knew better than to say anything. Keeping her eyes cast down, she waited to see if Uta had any orders for her.

"I am going to be coming home late. From what I understand, it is some sort of award ceremony for the local women in the party who have the most children. Absurd. Don't you agree?" Uta scoffed. She didn't seem to notice that Steffi wasn't answering. "So, you may have half of a sandwich for lunch. And once you've fed Liam, you may take him swimming, if he wants to go."

"Yes, Fräulein," Steffi said.

"I am good to you." Uta smiled. "You know if you were in that camp, you would never have it so good."

"Yes, Fräulein. Thank you."

Uta smiled, satisfied with herself. "I'm going to go and get dressed for the luncheon."

CHAPTER THIRTY-TWO

The Nazi officers were making their way through the train car asking to see everyone's papers. Pitor had his papers in his hand. But when they saw his uniform, they did not ask him for them.

They quickly stopped in front of him. "Heil Hitler."

"Heil Hitler," Pitor repeated.

One of the officers nodded and smiled.

Pitor returned the smile. But he kept his hand on his gun, just in case it was a trick. The Nazis loved playing cruel tricks. Pitor knew this, and so he didn't trust them. He kept his eyes on them until they left the train car. *I don't know who they are looking for, but for some reason they don't seem to be looking for me yet. I can't believe that a search hasn't begun. I hope I outsmarted them by taking the train from Berlin. Either way, I am grateful for the good fortune. Every second counts...*

However, from that moment on, Pitor could not relax. He was on high alert, just in case the Nazis returned. This could all be a trick to trap him. And he must not let his guard down for a second. No one spoke to him for the rest of the trip.

Pitor stepped off the train in Krakow in the early afternoon. Pitor immediately walked into town to see if he could find someone to give him directions. He needed to get to the town of Oswiecim, where a camp called Auschwitz-Birkenau was located.

Realizing he had eaten nothing since the night before, Pitor stopped into a bakery. He hated to waste the time, but he was feeling weak, and his head was aching.

A heavy-set young girl with chubby cheeks greeted him with a broad smile. Her strawberry blonde hair was neatly braided around her face. And he recognized right away that she wore the uniform of the League of German Girls, a dark skirt, a short-sleeved white blouse with a black scarf tied around her neck. "Heil Hitler, officer," she said, smiling proudly.

"Heil Hitler," Pitor repeated. "I'd like one of those pretzels, please."

"Of course," the girl said, she was about to charge Pitor when an older woman came walking out of a room in the back of the bakery. "Vera, where are your manners? This man is an officer," then the older woman smiled at Pitor and said, "Oberstrumführer?"

He nodded.

"Please excuse my daughter. There is no charge for you today."

Pitor smiled. "Thank you," he said. Then he took the pretzel and asked, "Do you know how I can get to a place called Oswiecim? I'm looking for a camp called Auschwitz-Birkenau?"

"Ewww," the younger girl said. "Have you ever been there before?"

"Hush," the older woman said. "You'll have to excuse my daughter. She sometimes speaks out of turn and says things she shouldn't. Young people." The woman said, hitting the side of her daughter's head with the back of her hand.

"Don't hit me mother," the daughter scoffed. "I'm just telling the officer the truth. Auschwitz-Birkenau is an awful place. The entire town smells terrible because of it. And depending on when you go, sometimes there is a big fire at the camp, and ashes come shooting out of a chimney and get all over your clothes."

"Enough, Vera! The officer did not come here to hear your thoughts on anything. Go in the back room before I punish you."

Vera looked at her mother blankly. "What did I say wrong? I just told him..."

"Go, NOW!"

Disappointed and rejected, Vera hung her head as she walked slowly to the back of the bakery. Once her daughter was gone, the mother turned to Pitor. "You can either take a bus or a train. It's about forty miles from here," she said. "If you are in a hurry, you will probably have more luck with a bus, unfortunately we can't use it anymore, but being an SS Officer, you can. You may have to wait for the next train, and it could be a while."

"Which way is the bus station?"

The woman pointed in the general direction. "When you leave here, walk south until you come to the bank, then turn left. You'll see it. It's right down the street from there."

Pitor nodded. "Thank you for the information and for the pretzel."

The woman nodded, "Heil Hitler," she said.

"Heil Hitler," Pitor answered, then he walked out the door.

CHAPTER THIRTY-THREE

Gretchen sat in her jail cell, looking alone and forlorn. Her face was smudged with dirt. There was dried blood on her hands and smeared all over the front of her new flowered dress. When Horst arrived at the police station, he could see her from across the room, and it hurt his heart to see her looking like this. He had never seen her—in all the time he'd known her—when she was not well groomed. And today she did not look like *his* Gretchen. She looked like a woman in trouble, and she was. Her face was red from crying. And when she made eye contact with Horst, he could see her getting emotional again. "I didn't mean to kill her," she yelled out hysterically to Horst when she saw him standing at the front of a counter, waiting to be permitted to talk to her.

"I know," he called back. "But don't yell here in the police station. Everyone is looking at you. Wait until I can come over there to talk to you."

A police officer walked up to the desk. "Can I help you?" he asked Horst.

"Yes, please help me. That woman is my wife. There's been a terrible misunderstanding.'

"I see."

"Please let her go. I am begging you to please let her out. She is not a criminal."

The officer nodded. "I understand, but I can't just let her out. She is going to have to face a trial. She murdered a young German woman."

"Please, officer. Please." Horst said, "Can I at least come into the station and have a moment to speak to her?"

Just then, an old friend of Horst's, a boy he served in the army with for two years, walked over. "Horst? My old friend. Is that you? Could it be? It's been so long."

"Albert!" Horst returned the greeting, happy to recognize someone. "How good to see you. I didn't know you had returned home to Munich. I thought you were living in Hamburg."

"Yes, I was. But then I got a job offer here at the police station. And since my mother and sister are here, I decided it would be nice to come home. How have you been?"

"All right, I suppose. At least I was all right, until earlier this evening."

"What happened?" Albert asked.

Horst told Albert what happened at the biergarten, but he conveniently left out the part about his crime of stealing a Jewish child from the ghetto to fill his quota. "Please, can I just speak to my wife? I am begging you," he said, waving his hand towards Gretchen. "She's so upset, and I can't blame her. My Gretchen is not a murderer. She didn't mean it. She was in shock when she found out that her best friend had married a Jew. Things happened so fast."

"I can certainly understand how shocking that must have been," Albert said, nodding. "Married to a Jew. How horrifying. And since you were friends, you must have socialized with the Jew."

"Yes, we did. And so, my wife was temporarily out of her mind when she found out. I don't have to tell you, you know how those Jews are. They are treacherous."

Albert nodded, "Yes, you're right. That certainly is true. Well, I can't see any harm in you speaking with her. Go ahead, but don't be too long. I don't want to get in trouble."

"Yes, of course. I completely understand, and I will be very quick," Horst said as Albert opened a large door and allowed Horst to enter.

"OH, HORST," Gretchen gripped the bars of her cell as her knuckles turned white. "What a mess I am in. I am still in shock. Heidi is dead. She's dead, Horst! This all went too far. I am covered in her blood. I don't know what came over me, Horst!" She sucked in a ragged breath, then continued, "After all the terrible things that happened tonight, I feel so horrible and strange. In my whole life, I never thought I would be arrested and put behind bars. I can't go to jail, Horst. I just can't. Please, you must do something. Contact everyone you know. See if they can't find a way to get me out of here. Cash in on every favor you have ever done for anyone. You must get me out of here. I simply can't serve time."

"I will do that. But I have another idea. Do you remember the name and address of the couple who adopted that little boy who I took from the ghetto? I think his name was Liam."

"Of course, I remember. How could I forget? That child is the entire problem. And that's because he is a Jew. We know that Jews cause problems. I still can't believe you did what you did. That's why we're in this whole mess." Gretchen was hysterical.

"That's in the past, Gretchen. There is nothing we can do about the past. And keep your voice down." Horst growled at her, then he took a deep breath and, in a nicer tone, he continued, "We must do something right now to save you. I must find a way to get you out of here. Now I've been thinking... if that man who was posing as Hoffmann is really Liam's father, and I know that you gave all the information about the couple who adopted Liam to Heidi, and she gave it to the Jew. So, if I am right, my guess is that he is on his way to get his son right now."

"But what about the fact that Heidi told everyone at the party tonight that you took Liam from the Jewish ghetto to fill your quota? I'm surprised you haven't been arrested for that."

"The police already questioned me at the scene. I told them that Heidi was mad with vengeance towards you, because you told her that she had to turn her husband in. She refused to believe it, and you told her that you were going to turn him in. That was when she made up that story about me taking Liam from the Jewish ghetto. The police found it quite feasible. And besides, since Konrad—or whoever he is—was gone, they were eager to believe me."

"Vengeance? But why?"

"Because, Gretchen, you found out her husband was a Jew. And you thought that she was helping him to hide from the Reich. You were appalled and because you love your country and our Führer, you told Heidi that you were going to have to turn him in."

"Did they believe you about Liam?"

"Yes, but they wanted more proof. They gave me an hour to deliver it."

"Oh Horst, what are you going to do."

"Don't worry, I already took care of everything. I know this Polish fellow very well. He is living here in Munich now. I went to his house and made a deal with him. Then I took him back to the tavern with me. He's a rather nice man, even if he is a Pole. Anyway, instead of paying the tavern owner for the party, I gave the money to this fellow so he would lie to the police and say Liam was his son. He said I bought Liam from him when he lived in Warsaw, and that was how he got the money to move to Munich."

"Did they know which child it was that was involved? Did they even ask?"

"No one asked and no one mentioned Liam's name."

"Then you just might be right. They probably aren't searching for Liam, because they don't know his name. And they don't believe Heidi, they believe what you said." Gretchen was beginning to calm down a little.

"Exactly. And so, we won't tell them Liam's name. And we will never tell them the truth about him. Meanwhile, I will find that Jew, who was impersonating Oberstrumführer Konrad Hoffmann and bring him to justice. The Gestapo will be so pleased with me; they will probably release you right away. And, who knows, I might even get a promotion."

"Oh Horst, this is brilliant. But could this plan possibly work?"

"It's working already, my dear. The police said that they were only allowing me to leave the tavern to bring back the Polish man who sold Liam to me, because I have a decent reputation with the party. The police officer who arrested you said that was why he trusted me to return with this Polish man and the evidence they needed to set me free."

"I feel encouraged right now," she said, sighing. "I really hope that this will be enough to get me released. I mean after all, everyone saw me stab Heidi, and now she's dead."

"I really believe that this will work. We can blame it all on the Jew. If I bring this Jew to justice—this wretched fraud who dared impersonate a high-ranking official—the police will be so grateful they'll release you. After all, just think of it, this horrible Jewish rat dared to put himself in a position where he could have brought harm to our precious Führer. The Party will want to make an example of him. I am sure of it."

"I'll give you the address and the name of the couple. He is a Kommandant at one of the camps."

Horst nodded.

"Are you ready? Do you need to write this information down, or will you remember it?"

"Tell me the name and address. I will remember."

CHAPTER THIRTY-FOUR

Uta got herself dressed and when she was ready to leave for the awards luncheon, she looked stunning. She wore a white silk dress that set off her glowing skin, which was slightly tanned from the time she'd been spending outside in the pool with Liam and Steffi. "I'm leaving to go to the luncheon now," she said. "And I won't be back until an hour or so before Reinhard returns from work. So, it will just be you and Rainer, the guard, here today. I know I can trust you, Steffi. I know you are not a Jew, and so you won't try to run away or do anything foolish. You know how good you have it here." Uta smiled. "Anyway, I must go. Take care of Liam. And make sure that dinner is ready when Reinhard gets home."

"Yes, Fräulein," she said obediently.

"By the way, Steffi."

"Yes, Fräulein?"

Uta looked into Steffi's eyes. "I must warn you, that just because I treat you kindly, doesn't mean I won't turn you in if you try anything foolish while I am gone. Do you understand me?"

"Of course, Fräulein."

"Good," Uta said, then she smiled and poured herself a quick glass of schnapps. It was still very early in the morning, and as far as Steffi knew, Uta had just awakened.

She's drinking already, Steffi thought. Then, instead of leaving the house, Uta sat down at the table holding her head in her hands.

"Shall I bring you some coffee or something to eat? I noticed that you didn't really eat your breakfast earlier," Steffi offered.

"No, I am not hungry. Make sure you clean Liam's room today. He is always making such a mess of it. Then do the laundry, and once you have finished washing the clothes you can take him out for a swim. That should keep him busy for a while."

"Yes, Fräulein."

Uta drank the entire contents of her glass in a few sips. Then she stood up and walked out of the house, locking the door behind her.

Steffi cleaned the kitchen, and a little while later Liam came running out of his room calling for her. "I had a bad dream," he said, wiping tears from his eyes.

"Oh?" she answered, picking him up and holding him in her arms. "You are getting too heavy for me to pick you up like this."

He giggled. Then his face grew serious, "Do you want me to tell you my dream?"

"If you would like," she said, sitting down with Liam still in her lap.

"I dreamed that someone tried to take me away from my parents. My dad always says that I should be very careful and never go with strangers. He says they can do very bad things to children. And in my dream, this person who took me was a stranger. It was a big man. I remember he had very big hands, and I was afraid of him. He picked me up and carried me away from my home and my family. I don't know where we were going. But I think he wanted to hurt me." As Liam told Steffi his dream, his small body began trembling.

"Shhh, it's all right Liam. It was only a dream. We all have bad dreams sometimes. Don't be afraid. I am here with you, and I will keep you safe."

"Do you promise, Steffi?"

"I promise."
"Are you sure?"
"Do you trust me?"
He nodded.
"Then don't worry anymore. All right?"
Liam nodded.
"Now, perhaps you would like some breakfast?"
"I would," he said. "Will you fry some potatoes for me?"
"I would do anything for you," she said, kissing his chubby cheek.

CHAPTER THIRTY-FIVE

In the afternoon, Pitor boarded a crowded bus full of Nazi officers heading toward the town of Oswiecim. The smell of perspiration, sausage, and garlic permeated the air, and the noise of chatter filled the small space. Pitor stood tall and blond, with a strong build, and when the other riders who took this trip together daily, didn't recognize him, they grew quiet. Uneasy because everyone was watching him, Pitor glanced around. He would have liked to slip into a window seat where he could disappear from their direct view, but there were no seats available.

The bus rambled through traffic, stopping at what seemed like every other street. *At this rate, I won't get to Auschwitz for hours.* He thought nervously. *But I dare not get off the bus, because I don't know where I am going and it might take longer if I try to walk.* A young woman, provocatively dressed and wearing an overabundance of cheap perfume, boarded the bus. She smiled at Pitor. He nodded to her. "Hello," she said, smiling. "I'm Daria."

"Hello," Pitor said, not introducing himself.

"Where are you going?" she asked.

"I have an appointment," he tried to brush her off by saying as little as possible.

"Oh? At the camp outside of town?"

He looked at her now. "Yes," he answered.

"I have dated one or two of the guards from when I used to work as a secretary there. It's an awful place. I am happy I work for the party closer to town now," she said, "But from your uniform I can see that you are not a guard. You're an officer."

Pitor hated to be rude, but the strong smell of her perfume was making him sick to his stomach. And he had far too much on his mind to spend time talking to this woman. "I'm sorry," he said apologetically, "but I really don't feel much like talking."

She huffed and looked away. He was relieved when she got off at the next stop. However, he wondered if she would remember him if he had to kill someone and the police came around asking questions. *Well, there is nothing I can do now.* As the bus rolled out of town and into a more rural area, some of the passengers got off, and seats became available. Pitor slid into a seat by the window, where he was comfortable until a very heavy-set woman sat down in the seat beside him. He glanced around, wondering why she'd chosen to sit there when there were other seats available. She looked at him and smiled. Her hair was frizzing out of a messy bun and smelled of sauerkraut. As she spilled over into his seat, her body seemed to radiate heat. Annoyingly, she hummed to herself.

"I'm glad you German's came to Poland," she said.

He nodded.

"Things are much better here now. I even have a job cleaning in the camp."

After an hour, the woman sitting beside Pitor stood up and got off the bus. He shook his leg, which was numb, because she had been practically sitting on top of him. He felt spent and exhausted. He wished he could rest, but he knew he must not waste a single moment. Nothing mattered but Jakup. Pitor had to find his son as quickly as possible. So regardless of how he felt, he knew he must keep going. He could not relax, not for a second. He must get to his son before they did.

CHAPTER THIRTY-SIX

It was a beautiful sunny day, and Liam was getting restless waiting. "Hurry up Steffi, get your work done so we can go swimming."

"I am going as fast as I can," she answered him, smiling.

"Can I go out by the pool and wait for you. I promise I won't go in until you come out."

"No," she chided him gently, "you know better."

"But I can swim now."

"Yes, you can, but you are very important to me. So, I want to make sure you're safe."

He smiled. "All right, but hurry."

"I am. I promise."

She lifted a heavy pile of clothes and sat down on the kitchen floor with a wash bucket to scrub them. "Can I help?" Liam asked.

"Of course, you can," Steffi said. "Why don't you hand me the next piece when I ask you for it?"

"That sounds good," Liam said happily.

She leaned over and kissed the top of his head. "I love you, Liam," she whispered.

"I love you too, Steffi."

Steffi's favorite days were the days when Uta had an important luncheon or social visit that took her away from the house for a while. With Reinhard away at work, Steffi had time alone with Liam. She would spend hours reading to him, taking him swimming, or just sitting beside him on the floor where they played with his toys. Even scrubbing laundry was not so bad if she made a game out of it for Liam.

Since Steffi had come to live with the Woolfs, Uta no longer used the young girls who lived nearby as babysitters. She told Steffi that the reason she left Liam with her, rather than the babysitters, was because she had come to trust Steffi. And because Steffi didn't want to lose the privilege of spending time with Liam, she never tried to escape.

There were a lot of clothes, as well as sheets, that needed washing. And afterwards, the kitchen floor was flooded. So, Steffi had to mop it quickly. But Steffi didn't mind; she was capable of heavy work. She'd grown up on a farm and had worked hard all her life. Today, because she was eager to play in the pool with Liam, she moved through her household tasks quickly. By lunchtime, all her housework was finished. She prepared a quick lunch for Liam and herself. Since she was alone in the house, she took a thin slice of the white bread that was reserved for the Aryans, instead of the black bread made of sawdust that Uta kept on hand for her, and sliced a thin piece off a hunk of cheese that she thought would not be missed, and made herself a sandwich. If Steffi had been caught eating white bread and cheese, she would have been punished, and she knew this. Uta made it clear that she kept the brown bread that was made with sawdust for Steffi, but if she could get it, Steffi preferred the soft, sweet white bread. And since she cut her own slice very thin, she assumed Uta would not notice it was missing.

"I'll tell you a story..." Steffi said, when she and Liam were both finished eating. "Because you can't go right into the pool after lunch. It's important that you take a little time to let your food settle before we go swimming."

Liam was eager to get into the water. However, he loved the fairytales Steffi told him. So, he lay his head in her lap, and she began to tell him the story of the Ugly Duckling.

As he always did, Liam drifted off to sleep while she told him the familiar tale. And Steffi sat with him on her lap, stroking his head lovingly for over an hour.

When he awoke, still a little sleepy, he asked, "Can we go in the pool now?"

Steffi had to laugh. "You just woke up, little man. Take a minute to get your bearings. Then we'll put on your suit, and we'll go swimming."

"I've got my bearings, whatever that means," he smiled excitedly. "Let's go."

"Very well," she said. "Come, follow me into your room and we'll get your suit on. Then you must wait right here until I get ready. And don't you dare go out by the pool alone."

"But Steffi... Why did I have to learn to swim if I can't go alone?"

"Because it's good for you to know how to swim in case you fall into water someday. But we don't need to take any dangerous chances. So, promise me that you will only go in the pool when I am with you. Do you understand?"

"Yes, Steffi," he said.

CHAPTER THIRTY-SEVEN

The girl in the bakery was right, Pitor thought as he got off the bus. *This place smells very strange.* It was a sickly sweet odor that made his stomach turn. As he made his way down the main street of town, he saw a large fire burning bright in the distance. Angry orange flames leaped up into the sky. Just then, he passed an old woman with a burlap sack and a scarf on her head. "Excuse me, mam," he said politely. "Can you direct me to Auschwitz-Birkenau?"

The woman looked at him in disgust. Then, to hide the emotions on her face, she looked away for a moment. "It's over there." She pointed to the flames.

"Thank you," he answered.

For a second, she turned back and stared at him. Pitor thought she looked like there was something more she wanted to say. He studied her and waited while he looked into her gray eyes. But she shook her head and hurried away.

What strange reactions I am getting from people when I mention this place. I've heard terrible rumors about these camps being mass murder camps, but I have been reluctant to believe them. Now, I am wondering if the rumors might really be true. But is it possible that the Nazis could really be committing mass murder on such a large scale?

Just then, like a burst of snow, the sky filled with flakes. *That's so odd. It's summer. And it's far too hot for snow.*

But as the snowflakes fell onto Pitor's shoulders, he realized they were not snowflakes, they were ashes.

CHAPTER THIRTY-EIGHT

Arriving at the gates of Auschwitz, he read the sign that said, 'Work Makes You Free.'

This is a work camp, he thought, as the guard at the gate looked him over. Pitor looked very official, and very Aryan, with his blond hair and blue eyes, wearing his black SS officer's uniform. And so, the guard stood up straight and tall in the presence of a superior. "Heil Hitler."

"Heil Hitler," Pitor answered.

Then, in a very polite and respectful tone, the guard asked, "May I help you, Oberstrumführer? I know you do not work here, because I don't recognize you. So, perhaps I can assist you with something?"

"Yes, thank you. I am looking for the home of Reinhard Woolf. We have an appointment. He is a Kommandant here at the camp, and from what I understand, he lives here on the grounds. Do you know him?"

"Of course, I've been here over a year. I know everyone who works here, and I would be happy to direct you. In fact, let me get one of the guards to escort you. That way you won't get lost."

I wasn't expecting this, Pitor thought. *I would rather not have an* escort. Because I might have to kill the guard to get rid of him. "That won't be necessary," Pitor said. "I wouldn't want someone leaving their work to escort me. I can get there on my own."

"Are you sure?"

"Of course. Just point me in the right direction."

The guard smiled at Pitor. "It's the house that is right outside the barbed wire gates, just behind the main building. You can't miss it. It's a brown brick two story home. The one with the pool and tennis court in the backyard."

"Thank you," Pitor said as he hurried away. *I am glad he just let me go; an escort might have been a problem.*

As Pitor made his way to the other side of the camp, he was stunned by the look of skeletally thin people, their skin gray, their heads bald, and their large vacant eyes cast down as they walked quickly away from him. *They are afraid of me because of my uniform. But what has happened to them? Is this a camp for the sick and dying? Or are these people starving to death?* He shuddered. Then, he saw a large pile of naked, skeletal, dead bodies lying up against the side of a building. Even though they were dead, their eyes were wide open, and they stared out at him. Their mouths were frozen in grimaces of terror. He was so shocked and horrified that for a moment his feet froze, and he was unable to move. *Look away from those dead people. Don't look at that pile of bodies. These poor people are dead, and there is nothing I can do to help them. Standing here and staring does nothing for them. I must keep going through this terrible place. I am almost there. I am almost at the Kommandant's house, where my son is. I must not look or see anything else. I must focus my mind on getting to Jakup.*

The guard was correct; the house was easy to find. When he arrived, he double checked the address with the address Heidi had given him. Then he knocked on the door and waited. He wasn't sure what he was going to say when they answered. All he could think of doing was offering the money he'd saved in exchange for his son. If the Kommandant refused, he would be forced to kill him. It was as simple as that. Pitor reached under his uniform jacket to touch his gun. Its presence reassured him. He knocked again, harder this time. There was no answer. He knocked again, harder. Still, no one came. *They must not be home.* He was about to leave when he heard laughter coming from the backyard. It was the laughter of a woman and child.

CHAPTER THIRTY-NINE

Quietly, Pitor sneaked around the side of the house and peered through the gate. That was when he saw Jakup, who was in the pool playing a game with a petite blonde woman. His heart leaped. *My son. Dear God, my son. He's here. He's alive. And he is safe. Thank you, Hashem, thank you.* The woman in the pool turned around as she lifted Jakup into her arms. Jakup giggled. Pitor was frozen in shock when he saw the woman's face. *Steffi? Is that really Steffi? Am I imagining this? What is she doing here? Is it possible that she is married to Reinhard Woolf? Is she Jakup's adopted mother? Even if she married the Kommandant and had turned and become one of them, I trust her.*

Pitor whispered her name just loud enough for her to hear. He saw her close her eyes, as if she thought she was dreaming. Then he called her name a little louder, "Steffi. It's me, Pitor. Turn around. I'm over here in the bushes."

Her eyes grew wide when she turned and saw him, and for a moment she was stunned. Her mouth flew open. Then tears began to fall down her cheeks as she picked Jakup up into her arms and took him out of the pool.

"Why are we getting out? I've waited to go swimming all day. Please Steffi. Just a little longer. I want to keep swimming," Jakup said.

Steffi couldn't answer Jakup. She was too shocked, and her eyes were fixed on Pitor. She sat Jakup down on a towel with a few of his toys. "I promise I will be right back," she said to him as she walked towards the bushes.

"Is that..." Pitor said, unable to actually get the words to leave his mouth.

"Yes, I think he is." Steffi stammered.

"Are you his adopted mother?"

"No, I am not." Steffi looked down at Liam. "I was arrested for hiding Jews. I am a prisoner at this camp. But I've been fortunate to work at this house for the Kommandant and his wife. My job is to keep the house and to care for Jakup," she said. "I've cared for him as if he were my own child because I knew in my heart that he was yours."

"Come with me. We'll take Jakup, and we will get out of here," Pitor said. "We need to hurry. Jakup is in danger. I'll tell you more when we are safe. But right now, get the both of you out of those swimming clothes and get dressed as quickly as you can. You do want to go, don't you?"

"Of course I do. We will be very quick," she said, taking Jakup's hand and leading him into the house.

"Steffi, who is this man? I don't want to get dressed yet. Come on, please, you promised we could go swimming, and we just got outside. We hardly had any time at all in the pool," Jakup whined.

She didn't explain who Pitor was; she figured they would explain together once they were free. "I know. I promise, I'll make it up to you," Steffi said. Then she took Liam into the house and dressed him in a pair of short pants and a shirt. She packed a small bag of his clothes.

Then she took his hand and led him to Uta's bedroom with her. She quickly put on one of Uta's house dresses and a pair of walking shoes. Then she packed two more of Uta's casual dresses, and a pair of Reinhard's slacks and one of his shirts. Within minutes, she and Liam returned to the backyard where Pitor was waiting.

"We have to go right now. At any moment someone might come and start asking questions. The quicker we get out of here, the better." Pitor said to them.

Steffi glanced around, searching for the guard. But she was sure he was visiting the woman next door. "It looks like the guard is not here. He's busy with his girlfriend. The Kommandant is at work, and his wife won't be home until dinner time. So, we have a minute. Let me pack up the food from the kitchen," Steffi turned to Pitor.

"All right, take as much food as you can get, quickly."

"Liam, listen to me." Steffi said, kneeling down so she could look into the little boy's eyes. "You stay here with this nice man and wait for me. I'll be right back. All right?"

"No, I want to go with you. I don't know this man. I don't want to stay with him. He's a stranger and my father says I should not talk to strangers."

"Very well, then come with me. But we must hurry."

Pitor's heart ached when he heard his son call him a stranger. *He was so young when he was taken away from his family. He doesn't remember me. He probably doesn't remember his mother, either.*

Steffi and Jakup returned in minutes. "Let's go," Pitor said, as he began to lead them away.

Jakup began shaking his head. "Where are you taking us? I don't want to go with you. I won't go."

"Please Liam. You must trust me. You know I love you, don't you?" Steffi said, "And I would never do anything to hurt you. You know this."

He nodded.

"You must trust me now, please Liam. It's very important that you don't argue with me this time. I need you to behave. It's very, very important," Steffi begged.

"All right, Steffi," he said, squeezing her hand, but giving Pitor a skeptical look.

As they were walking quickly towards the exit, but not quickly enough to draw attention, Reinhard came up from behind. "Hello Steffi," he said. "Where exactly are you going?"

They were alone. There was no one else around.

She heard his voice. And she turned, her eyes wide with fear. "You should be at work," she said, more to herself than to him.

Pitor felt for his gun. But then he thought perhaps he should not shoot. The sound would alert the others. He might have to kill this man with his bare hands.

"Yes, I should be at work. You're absolutely right. However, a few minutes ago, the guard at the gate came into my office and said that an SS officer who he didn't recognize had just arrived here, and was on his way to my house for a meeting with me. Can you imagine, a meeting with me?" He laughed a wicked laugh. "Of course, I found that rather suspicious, because I knew I didn't have any meetings scheduled with anyone at the house today. So, I decided to come home and see exactly what kind of tomfoolery was taking place. And..." He let out another sarcastic laugh. "Wouldn't you know it, Steffi, I was right. You devious little minx. You were up to something. Now, I see that there is another person involved. And since I don't know who this fellow is, my guess is, he is not an officer at all. He is some sort of Polish workman who you have convinced to help you escape from here. And I have been so kind to you. I really expected better treatment from you. You even took my child." Then he shook his head condescendingly. "Dear, dear, Steffi," he sighed, "you and I both know that it's impossible for you to escape from here. And not only to escape, but to kidnap Liam. Well, of course, I am not going to let you get away with this. You are in very serious trouble, my dear. You will pay for this. And this friend of yours, this idiot who is posing as an officer, has just earned himself a place right here beside you, as a prisoner in this lovely camp." Then his lips curled into a crooked smile, and his eyes were fixed on her with a cruel stare.

"Please." she begged. "Please just let us go."

Pitor glanced at Steffi. He knew she was hoping for mercy, and that was something beyond this Nazi's capabilities. Pitor could see the coldness in the man's eyes. He wanted to say something, but he knew that there was nothing he could say or do that would soften this man. So, Pitor did not speak. He stood quietly, watching and waiting.

"Daddy, I want to go home," Jakup said to Reinhard. "I'm scared. I don't know who this man is, and you said not to ever go with strangers."

"Shut up," Reinhard said to Jakup, dismissing him in a voice that was harsh. Jakup looked at Reinhard pleading, but Reinhard did not comfort the child. His eyes threatened Jakup, telling him to be quiet. Jakup's small body shook with fear, then he began to cry.

Steffi bent down and folded the little boy into her arms. She cradled him gently. "It's all right, Liam. It's all right," she whispered, even though her voice was filled with fear.

"Don't cuddle him you idiot. That's not the way to treat a child. How can you expect him to grow up to be strong if you treat him like that. You are not doing him a favor, Steffi, you're making him weak, like a Jew."

"Daddy?" Liam begged, looking directly at Reinhard.

"I said shut up," Reinhard growled at Liam.

Jakup was distraught and confused. He broke free of Steffi's embrace and ran to Reinhard, grabbing on to his leg. At first, Reinhard tried to ignore him. His gaze was fixed on Steffi. But Jakup squeezed tighter, and then, to shake him off, Reinhard kicked his foot. Jakup was thrown to the ground, but still he tried to attract his father's attention. His little hands reached up into the air towards Reinhard, and his tiny voice trembled as he said, "Daddy, you're scaring me."

Reinhard was clearly annoyed now. He kicked the little boy in the chest. Jakup doubled over, struggling to breathe. Steffi's eyes grew wide as she picked the child up and held him. Finally, he drew a breath, but he did not try to get away this time. He did not look at Reinhard. He buried his head in Steffi's chest and was weeping.

Pitor felt rage running through his blood. It was unbearable to watch this man treat Jakup this way. Steffi was holding Jakup tightly, but she was crying softly.

Reinhard shook his head as he watched Steffi. "You are a stupid woman," he said. "You had it good here. But you've ruined it for yourself." Reinhard reached over and grabbed Steffi's arm, pulling her so hard that she dropped Jakup. Jakup fell to the ground and began screaming in terror. As quick as a shooting star, and before Reinhard even realized what was about to happen, Pitor grabbed Reinhard by the throat and began to choke him. Reinhard was struggling, but Pitor was much stronger, and he held Reinhard down. Reinhard kicked and squirmed. Then blood shot through the whites of his eyes as they bulged in his head.

"You are a weak, worthless excuse for a man," Pitor growled. "You beat up on a woman and a child to make yourself feel powerful. And who knows what other terrible things you have done to people in that camp. I can only imagine. You simply don't deserve to live." With that, Pitor twisted Reinhard's head and instantly broke his neck. Jakup's eyes were as full as the moon. He was terrified and crying uncontrollably now. Even Steffi could not comfort him. Pitor quickly looked around him. Pitor checked the pulse on Reinhard's neck to make sure he was dead. Satisfied that he was, Pitor stripped Reinhard of his clothes. Then he lifted Reinhard's corpse and carried him into the camp where there was a large pile of dead bodies, and buried him under piles and piles of other dead bodies—the bodies of emaciated dead Jews. Then, he took all the money out of Reinhard's pockets and stuffed it into his own uniform pocket. He rolled Reinhard's clothes up into a ball and put them under his arm. And made sure that he took Reinhard's gun and bullets.

No one will ever find him here. He will burn in the crematorium just like all his victims, and he deserves it, Pitor thought, as he hurried back to where Steffi and Liam waited.

"Let's go," Pitor said to Steffi. "Try to quiet Jakup. If he keeps screaming, he will attract the attention of the guards."

But try as she might, she couldn't quiet him. Jakup was screaming in terror. And just as Pitor had predicted, one of the guards walked over to ask if he could help. "Isn't that Kommandant Woolf's little boy?" the guard asked.

Pitor smiled calmly and said, "Yes, it is. I'm Oberstrumführer Hoffmann. I've been sent here to take this child and his nurse to a special hospital. The little boy is very ill. That's why he is crying. And you must be careful not to get too close, because he is contagious," Pitor said, knowing that would put the guard off, because he'd learned that the Nazis were terrified of catching diseases.

"All right. Well, go on then. Safe travels," the guard said, backing off.

"Thank you. Heil Hitler."

"Heil Hitler."

By the time Pitor, Jakup, and Steffi left the camp, Jakup had fallen asleep from crying. They found an area of trees where Pitor changed into the shirt and pants Steffi had taken from Reinhard's closet. Now she and Pitor looked like a young Polish couple with a son as they made their way out of town and headed into the large dense forest that waited for them with open arms.

PART TWO

CHAPTER FORTY

They walked in silence, going deeper and deeper into the forest as Jakup slept while Steffi carried him. Pitor carried the bags of food and clothing Steffi had taken from the house.

The sun was still hot as it began to set, and Steffi's face was red with exertion. Her hair had dried from the pool, but was now stuck to her head with perspiration.

When Pitor glanced over at her, he realized he had been inconsiderate. He was so lost in thought up until now, worried about where he was going to take them, trying to remember where he'd camped with the partisans. So lost in his own thoughts, he had not realized how hard this journey must be for her. "I'm sorry, Steffi. I don't know what I have been thinking. I should be carrying Jakup."

She shrugged, "It's all right. You have the bags. That's enough."

"Please, let me help you," Pitor offered. "I'm sure your arms are aching by now."

"Are you sure you don't mind?" she asked.

"Of course, not. He's my son." Pitor looked into her eyes as he took the sleeping child into his arms.

"Are you hungry?" she asked.

"Yes, very."

"Me too. Shall we eat something? I brought a whole bag of food. I took whatever they had in the kitchen."

"Yes, let's eat something. Then we'll sleep here for the night. We can continue on our journey in the early morning."

Steffi took the other dress out of her bag and laid it down on the ground. Pitor gently put Jakup down on top of the dress, then he took the jacket from his uniform out of the bag and laid it down. "Please sit here," he said to Steffi, indicating the jacket. She sat down and began to unpack the food. Gently, she nudged Jakup to wake him up. But when he awoke it was dark, and somewhere close an owl hooted. Jakup was disoriented at first, but when he looked over and saw Pitor, he let out a scream.

"Shhh, you can't scream like that," Steffi said gently. Then she turned to Pitor. "He's terrified," Steffi said. "He doesn't understand what is happening. The Nazis took him from you and your wife when he was very young. He doesn't remember you," she said to Pitor as she held Jakup in her arms.

"I want to go home," Jakup said.

"I know. But you are safe, because you are here with me, and I promise no matter what happens, I will take good care of you," Steffi said. Then she touched Jakup's cheek. "Liam," she said, "I have something very important to tell you."

"What?" he asked.

"Your real name is Jakup. And this man..." She put her hand on Pitor's shoulder, "is your real father."

"No, he's not. He's a stranger. And I want to go home," Jakup said, gripping Steffi tightly.

"He is your real father," she repeated, "and he loves you. He has always loved you. I love you too. You know I do."

"Yes, I know. And I want you to come home with me. I don't know that man. He is a stranger."

"I'm not," Pitor said gently. "Steffi is telling you the truth. I am your father, and I love you very much. I would do anything for you, Jakup."

"My name is Liam. You are not my father."

Pitor was devastated. Then Steffi reached over and took Pitor's hand. "I know that Jakup is hurting you right now, Pitor. But he is just frightened and confused. And he is only a little boy. Give him a chance to get to know you. Let him get used to you. You'll see, it will be all right."

"Why don't you eat something," Steffi said, handing Jakup a piece of bread and a hunk of cheese. He began to nibble on the cheese as he sat close to her.

There was a long silence, then a wolf howled, and Jakup jumped.

"I will protect you," Pitor said. "I promise I won't let any harm come to you. How about this? How about you look at this as an adventure."

"Yes," Steffi tried to sound lighthearted, "like one of the fairy tales I've told you."

This seemed to settle Jakup down. He nodded, then he finished eating. Once he was done, he lay down on the ground, and fell asleep.

"Do you know where we can go? We can't go back to my farm. I wish we could." Steffi said, "But they've confiscated it and from what I've heard from other people in my neighborhood who were imprisoned in Auschwitz with me, a German family is living there now."

"I know the Nazis do that. They steal homes and children, and people's businesses. They call it Germanization. It's terrible. They take whatever they want as if they are entitled to it, people's lives and their families, they don't care."

"Yes, they certainly do," she said, shaking her head, "I never thought I was capable of hate. I always thought I could forgive, but you can't imagine how wonderful I felt when I saw you standing there in the Kommandant's backyard. I thought I was dreaming," she said, "except for finding Jakup and being with him, that place was hell for me."

"I was surprised to see you too. I can't tell you how happy I am that Jakup had you to take care of him. Not that I am happy that you were arrested."

"Yes, well, being arrested was terrible."

"What happened? Did the Gestapo find Zita?"

"Yes, they did." She looked at him sadly. "It was horrible, but it was even more complicated than that. You see after you left, Zita's brother was killed by one of them. And, as you know my mother was ill. She passed peacefully in her sleep. It was very lonely for me and for Zita. So, we decided to try something, to take a chance. We knew it was risky, but she was growing very ill living in the space under the floor in darkness all day, so we decided that she should come upstairs and live with me. It had been several years since anyone in the neighborhood had seen her, and over that time she'd grown up. Besides, even before the Nazis came, she had not gone into town very often. So, we were relying on the hope that no one would remember her, or if they did, they wouldn't recognize her. We changed her hair color and if anyone asked, which they hardly even noticed her, I said she was a relative of mine. For a long time, everything went very well. And it would have continued to be all right, I believe, but then she fell in love with a boy, a German boy." Steffi sighed. "We went to church each week. I thought that would keep suspicion away. But that's how she met him. Poor Zita, she had no one left in the world but me, so she fell very hard. He told her he loved her too. And she believed him, giving him her heart and soul. Zita longed for a family, a husband, children, and so she trusted him. I begged her not to tell him the truth about her past. I told her that we must never let anyone know that she was Jewish. But she didn't listen. Without asking me, she told him the truth, that she was a Jewish girl and that I was hiding her. Well, he was a German boy who had been in the Hitler youth. And everything they taught him took precedence over his feelings for her, so he turned us into the Gestapo. When the Gestapo came to the house to arrest us, the boy, who Zita was in love with, was with them. She was so heartbroken. She cried and called out to him as they pulled her away from the house and tried to push her into the back seat of their automobile. One of them punched her in the face, her nose was bleeding. I watched the blood drip onto the ground as she cried out to her lover, "I love you, please Gustav, don't let them do this to me." But he turned away from her, he wouldn't even look at her. They were pulling me towards the car too. I did not resist. I was too sickened by Zita's pain. But then she tried to break free of their grasp. I think she was trying to get to him. But she couldn't get away. Then one of the Gestapo shot Zita. She was so small and slender that she fell to the ground so softly, without even a thud. It was so unbelievable to me that for a second, I was frozen, unable to move, mesmerized by how red the blood was that was running like a river across my land. I should probably have tried to run. But I couldn't. I was so crushed. And, then the Gestapo agent yelled something at me. I can't tell you what he said. I didn't hear him because my mind was running in circles, racing around like a rat in a cage. One of the agents grabbed me and threw me in the back of the black car. That was how they arrested me. I was so shaken that I wasn't even afraid for myself. In fact, I can't remember the ride that brought me to Auschwitz. All I can remember was arriving there and seeing that terrible sign 'Work Makes You Free.' Even then, even before I saw how terrible the camp actually was, somehow I knew it was a lie. I knew that the only way to get free from this place was to die," she shook her head. "But then..." she cleared her throat. "Then you came, like a light from heaven."

He smiled. "I'm no light from heaven. I'm just a man trying to save my son, and to save a friend...you."

She began to cry.

It was too dark to see each other's faces, but Pitor heard her soft weeping. "I'm sorry," he said, "I'm sorry you had to endure all that."

"I know you are. You are a good man, Pitor. You always were. I am sorry for all of us, but mostly I am sorry for poor Zita."

"You are a good person too, Steffi. You are always putting others before yourself."

She didn't answer. There was a long silence. Then in a whisper she said, "I would rather die in this forest than live in Auschwitz. I am so grateful to you for rescuing us."

"I have no intentions of any of us dying. We will not starve. I can hunt and I can fish, remember? I know how to find water. Besides, somewhere in these forests I have a group of friends. Partisans who I stayed with for a while. I have a vague idea of where they might be. So, we are going to try to find them. If we can find them it will be easier for us to live in the forest."

She reached out and touched his knee. "Thank you for everything, Pitor. God bless you."

Then she lay down beside Jakup, put her arm around the little boy, and fell asleep.

Pitor was exhausted, but he couldn't sleep. As he listened to the gentle rhythm of his son's breathing, he gazed up at the millions of stars in the sky and whispered, "Mila. Look, I've found him. He is here with me right now. It seems like it took a million miracles, but God must have been with me, because I found him. Our son is alive, and he is safe. And I promise you, I will do anything, anything, even give my life if I must, to protect him."

CHAPTER FORTY-ONE

That night when Horst went back to the apartment that he shared with his wife, Gretchen, he couldn't rest. Not while she sat in jail, and there was so much uncertainty. *For now, at least, I am out of danger. No one suspected me of lying. They believed me that the little boy had belonged to a Polish couple. And I hope they will never question me about the child again.* Horst plopped onto the couch in the apartment and looked around. Nothing seemed to matter to him right now, because Gretchen was gone. *I hadn't realized how much I had come to depend on her. She is my best friend. Not only does she prepare all our meals and keep the house clean, but she listens to me. She was the only person I could trust completely.* Horst felt so alone. He closed his eyes, and flashbacks of the last time he felt this alone flooded his mind. In his mind, he was hiding, cowering in a foxhole somewhere on the Eastern Front, listening to the death cries of his fellow soldiers. And at some point, between the echoes of war and missing Gretchen, he fell asleep.

The following morning, Horst got up early and, instead of going to work, he went into town and straight to the police station. When he arrived, he did not see Gretchen in the cell where she'd been the previous night. But he did see his old friend, who worked at the station. "Where is my wife?" Horst asked. He was shaking, but trying to remain calm.

"In a cell downstairs," Horst's old friend said.

Horst nodded. It hurt him to think of Gretchen spending the night behind bars. Then he asked, "Did you happen to get statements from all the soldiers who were at the tavern last night? There was a soldier who said he had encountered the man who was impersonating Konrad when he was working as a guard in the Warsaw Ghetto. Do you know where he is staying in Munich?"

"Why would you want to know that?"

"I want to bring this lousy impersonator to justice." Horst said, "He's not only a fraud, but he is a trouble making Jew and he is the reason my wife is behind bars."

"I wish I could help you. I really do." The policeman said, "but the truth is, I don't know where that soldier is staying. I don't know if he is still in town. When he came in last night to give us a statement, he said he was leaving Munich. Said he had to return to his platoon."

"What else did he say?"

"Well, nothing new. Just all the stuff that he said last night. The stuff you already know."

"Please, just tell me again. I am very distraught about my wife, and I can't remember exactly what he said."

"Sure," the policeman smiled at Horst. "The soldier said that he recognized the fellow who was pretending to be Oberstrumführer Hoffmann. He said he knew him when he was working as a guard at the Warsaw Ghetto. That he thought the man's real name was Pitor Barr. And he was sure that Barr was definitely a Jew."

"That doesn't surprise me at all. He acts like a Jew, tricky, and manipulative. Only thing is he sure doesn't look like one with that blond hair, those blue eyes, and that strong jaw."

"Well, he sure is one. The only reason the soldier remembered him was because, he said, Barr was a real troublemaker. He also mentioned that he was pretty sure that Barr was involved in that terrible Uprising that caused us to lose so many good German soldiers. I am sure you heard about that."

Horst nodded, "Of course, everyone heard about it. And from what I heard, that uprising was brutal. The Jews really got out of hand. They have some nerve, don't they?"

"They sure do. I knew a fella who died there. A good German solider."

Horst nodded. Then he hesitated for a moment before he asked, "Any chance I can see my wife?"

"I'm not supposed to let anyone downstairs where the cells are. I'm afraid your wife is not allowed visitors."

"Can't you break a rule just this once, for an old friend?" Horst begged.

"Sorry, Horst. You know better. It's not up to me. I'm just following orders."

Horst nodded. Then he turned to leave. "Heil Hitler. And thanks for the information."

"Heil Hitler. I hope you find that Jew, Barr."

"Yes, I hope so too."

CHAPTER FORTY-TWO

Pitor finally drifted off to sleep, but it was not a deep sleep. During the time he'd spent living among the partisans, Pitor learned how to sleep lightly. So, although he slept, he heard every sound. And from the cry of the wolves to the hoot of the owls, he could assess just how far away each of the animals was.

The following morning, Pitor was awake before dawn, before Steffi or Jakup. He sat with his back against a tree, watching them as they cuddled together against the cool morning breeze. Soon, he knew the sun would rise and with it the relentless heat of day. As he looked at his son, he thought of Mila and how happy they had been before the Nazis came to power in Poland. They were not rich, but they had enough to eat, and a place to live. But most of all, they were a family then, and although they lived a simple life, Pitor had felt like he was the richest man in the world. *Now, without Mila, I am missing a part of myself. I will always feel alone in my heart, even though I have my son and Steffi, my friend. I will never be able to fill that emptiness. But I must remember to be grateful. God gave Jakup back to me. And that is such a blessing. And I am also thankful to have Steffi. She is a good friend to both Jakup and me. God was good to send her to care for Jakup when he was living with that Nazi family.*

Jakup stirred, and the leaves rustled softly beneath him. Pitor turned to see the little boy's eyes slowly open. The shock on Jakup's face hurt Pitor's heart. "Where am I?" Jakup asked. "I want to go home."

Steffi woke up immediately. A nervous look passed between her and Pitor. "It's all right," she whispered as she gently rubbed Jakup's small back. "You are here with me and with your papa. We are going to take good care of you."

"I don't want to be here. I want to go home. Bad things happen in the forest. All the fairy tales say that the forest is where danger lies. I want to go home," Jakup said, then he began to cry. Pitor reached for him, but Jakup recoiled away from him.

"Jakup," Pitor said softly, "I am your father. Try to remember me. Please, I know you were very young when I last saw you, but try to remember."

"I don't know you. You are a stranger, and I am afraid of you," Jakup said firmly. "And I don't know who Jakup is, but my name is Liam."

Steffi nodded. "It's all right. In time, you will remember everything." She took Jakup in her arms and held him for a few minutes. Then she said, "I'm hungry. You must be too. Why don't we eat some of this food, and then we can start walking again."

"Where are we going? Are we going home?" Jakup asked.

"We are going on an adventure. We are going deeper into the woods to meet up with some of your father's friends," she smiled at Jakup as she handed him a piece of bread.

Jakup looked at her with his eyes wide with fear. "I hate the forest. There are wolves, and witches, and monsters in the forest."

"You will be safe. I promise you. Have I ever lied to you, Jakup?" Steffi asked him as she turned his chin up, so he was looking directly at her.

"No," he admitted, "you've never lied to me."

"And I won't lie to you now," she said, handing him a hunk of bread.

Jakup took a bite of the bread. "Eww, this bread is too hard. It's too old," Jakup said. "Mother would throw it in the trash. Do you have any fresh bread?"

"No, I'm sorry. It's not as soft as you're used to, but it is still good. Please, eat it," Steffi said, "You need to eat." She wanted to tell him about how many people were starving in the camp and about how they would give anything to have this hunk of day-old bread. But he was just a child, and she knew he would never be able to grasp the horror of the starvation going on in the camp. *And why should he have to? Why should anyone have to?* She thought.

Jakup bit off a piece of the bread. Then, as he tried to chew, he said, "I don't want to go further into the forest to meet this man's friends." He pointed to Pitor. "I want to go home and go swimming in our pool."

Pitor was angry for a moment. But he had to remind himself that Jakup was only a little boy who was confused. He had been living among the Nazis, and he had been led to believe that the Kommandant was his father. Rage shot through Pitor. *My son behaves just like one of them. He has been living a charmed life, while the rest of the world has been suffering because of Hitler. The Nazis took him from his family, but he doesn't realize that. They made him one of them. They gave him the best food and sent him to play outside in the sunshine while other children his age were rotting away, hiding in attics or basements, or worse, being murdered.* Pitor looked at Jakup. He was ashamed of his child's lack of caring. Then he had to remind himself once again that Jakup was still just a little boy. He only knew what he'd been taught. *It's not his fault. None of this is his fault. Jakup knew no other life. He was too small to remember me or his mother. And how would a child of that age ever know that anyone else was suffering? All he knew was what they told him. And they told him that he was an Aryan, and he was living his life the way it was supposed to be.*

"Please sir," Jakup said to Pitor, and the politeness of his reference to Pitor as sir as well the begging made Pitor feel sad, as if he had lost something he might never recover. *Will he ever come to know me? Or will I always be someone he sees as a stranger?*

There were tears in Jakup's eyes as he looked at Pitor. "Please, sir, please, I am begging you not to hurt me. Please just take me home." He cleared his throat, and the tears ran down his cheeks. Pitor watched him and realized he was just a little boy. Shaking, Jakup went on, "I saw what you did to my father. But if you will just take me home, I promise I won't ever tell anyone what I saw."

Pitor was speechless. It was as if he had been hit by a bolt of lightning. He put his hand to his temple. *He understood what happened between the Kommandant and me. I didn't know if he realized I killed that man. I was hoping he wouldn't understand what happened because he is so young, but he knows.*

There was a moment of silence. Then Steffi patted the ground next to her. "Come here Jakup. Sit beside me, yes? I want to talk to you for a moment. All right?"

Jakup nodded reluctantly. Then he got up and walked over to sit next to Steffi. She put her arm around him, and he cuddled into her side. "Now," she said, smiling, "do you remember the story of Robin hood? I told you that story. You must remember how they lived together in the forest? Yes?"

At the mention of the story, Jakup brightened up. "I remember that story. I love that story, Steffi. Can you tell me again?"

"Well of course I can. But first you must understand what I am trying to tell you. All right?"

He nodded.

She continued, "The three of us are going to have a big adventure. We are going to live in the forest just like Robin Hood. And once we find Pitor's friends, we will be with a whole group of merry men."

"Really?"

"Absolutely. This is going to be fun. Pitor will take you fishing and hunting. And I will roast fish and meat outside. Then, once we find the merry men, we will all live together in the forest."

The idea of this seemed to appease Jakup. "I might like that. But I don't want to do it forever. Just for a little while. I want to go in the pool. So, I want to go home."

"Of course. I understand. But let's have some fun first, all right? Now go on and eat. Let's pretend we are on a picnic."

"I'm full. I don't want anything else to eat. Can I pick some flowers, please?"

"All right, but stay close. You must never go so far away from me that I can't see you. Do you understand? It's very important that you don't wander away. Stay right here where I can see you."

"Yes, Steffi," Jakup said, and he walked a few feet away from them where he began to pick a bouquet of wildflowers.

"Thank you," Pitor whispered to Steffi.

"Of course," she smiled. "I'm sorry I had to refer to you as Pitor and not as his father. I think it might be best that we do it this way for a little while. Let's give him a chance to get used to you."

"I agree with you."

Then Jakup returned and handed Steffi the flowers. "I picked these for you, Steffi."

She took them. "They are beautiful, Jakup." She bent down and kissed his forehead. "You are such a good boy," she said.

CHAPTER FORTY-THREE

Horst left the police station, then, with his head hung low, he walked home and packed a bag before he boarded a train to Poland. He'd heard about Auschwitz, and he knew it was a hotbed of disease, so he had never wanted to see it. However, he had no choice now. *If I am going to help Gretchen, I have to find this man called Pitor Barr, Konrad's impersonator. And so far, I have no other leads. Barr is going to look for the child, and the child is living with the Kommandant and his wife at the Auschwitz concentration camp. So, I must go.* He sighed.

It seemed to take Horst forever to get to Krakow, and from Krakow to the camp. He had heard about how they were burning bodies all day to dispose of them, so he knew as soon as he got off the bus in the town of Oswiecim that the fire burning in the distance was the crematorium, and the ashes were the remains of the dead. He shivered in disgust at the sickening thought that some, or probably most of the people whose ashes were all over him had been riddled with disease. *Can I catch anything from these ashes? I really hope that is not possible.* He wished he could leave and forget this place. But he forged on.

There was a distinctive and nauseating odor that grew stronger, causing bile to rise in his throat as he grew closer and closer to the entrance of the camp. It should have come as no surprise how horrible this place was. He'd heard a lot about what went on in these camps. Even though it wasn't openly discussed, there were whispered secrets that were shared. Still, nothing had prepared him for the terrible smell.

Horst walked up to the guard at the gate and introduced himself with a broad smile, then he said, "I'm here to see the Kommandant Reinhard Woolf."

The guard looked at him skeptically. Horst had no idea why, but this man was studying him. And for a moment, neither of them said a word. Then, because the guard was afraid to question a guest who was coming to see a superior officer, the guard just nodded. "He is not at work today. I am assuming he is at home. I will get you an escort to his house right away."

Within a few minutes, the gate opened as another guard walked over to Horst. "Heil Hitler," the guard said. "Follow me, please. I will take you to the home of the Kommandant."

They walked along the outskirts of the camp without speaking until they arrived at the house where Reinhard and Uta lived. But before the guard knocked at the door, he said, "I don't want to overstep my boundaries, however, I should probably tell you that Herr Kommandant has been missing from work for a few days. We asked his wife if she had any idea where he might have gone. But she doesn't know. In fact, no one is quite sure where he has gone."

"Missing?"

"Yes, he is missing. Also, a female prisoner, the Kommandant's house maid, is missing. I am not sure what all of this means, however, I thought you should know. You are about to meet Frau Woolf. I am certain that she is at home. However, you are going to find that she has been rather distraught over all of this."

"I see," Horst said.

"I just thought you should be aware of everything before you meet her."

"Thank you," Horst said. Then he knocked on the door.

A young woman opened the door. "What do you want?" she asked curtly.

Horst introduced himself. "I'm looking for Frau Woolf. Is that you?"

"Yes, it's me."

He nodded, seeing her standing there looking at him skeptically, he realized the situation looked very grave. *She is probably too distraught to talk to me.* But he'd come such a long way, and he needed to find Pitor Barr. So, making his voice as soft and gentle as possible, he asked Frau Woolf if he might come in and speak with her.

She didn't answer. She just opened the door and motioned for him to enter. Then she turned to the guard and said, "It's all right. Leave us."

The guard nodded and walked out. Uta closed the door behind him.

"Won't you sit down, please?" Uta asked, gesturing at the couch in the beautifully decorated living room.

"I'm sorry to do this to you right now. But I've come here to ask some rather uncomfortable questions," Horst admitted.

"Oh? Well, everything right now is feeling rather uncomfortable. My husband is missing. It seems he's taken our son and run off with a prisoner. Can you imagine my embarrassment? I can just hear what the other wives are saying," she shivered. She looked into his eyes. "So, go on, tell me what is it you want?"

Horst quickly explained the story. He told Uta what had happened between his wife, Gretchen, and her best friend, Heidi. Carefully he told Uta how Gretchen had accidentally, in a moment of passion and panic, stabbed Heidi and killed her. The shock on Uta's face made him careful as he continued telling the story. He knew he must not alienate

Uta. She might have the answers he so desperately needed. So, carefully, gingerly, he continued. Gently, he brought up the subject of Liam. "You see, my wife's best friend's husband, that tricky snake of a Jew who was posing as an SS officer, had developed an obsession with Liam."

"But why? Why Liam? That is very odd. How did he know Liam?"

"Well, that's what I wish I could avoid having to tell you."

"I don't understand."

"I believe this Jew was delusional. He saw Liam when my wife, who worked at the Lebensborn, brought him and a group of other children to the Eagle's Nest for a demonstration. From what he said, the Jew thought Liam looked just like his little brother who died. And so, he was determined to find the child. My wife would never have given him any information, but Heidi did. She gave him your address. I've come here because, now that he has been exposed as a liar and a fraud, the Jew disappeared. I might be wrong, but I think he might be on his way here looking for Liam. I think he might take him."

Her face went white as flour. "A Jew coming here to kidnap Liam?" she sucked in a deep breath. "You might be right. Liam, as well as my husband, and the female prisoner who kept our house and served as Liam's nanny, have all disappeared. I believed that Reinhard had gone mad. I thought he may have run away with this girl. The very thought that he would do such a vial and disgusting thing to embarrass me in front of all the other wives is just devastating."

"I can well imagine," Horst said, as sympathetically as he could manage.

"And now that you've mentioned it, when I asked the guard if he had any idea of what might have happened to Reinhard, the guard said that an Oberstrumführer came by the house for a meeting on the same day the three of them disappeared."

"So, it was him. He was posing as an Oberstrumführer. He has already been here," Horst said. "But, I can't imagine that your husband, the Kommandant, would have gone with the Jew willingly. He must have taken him prisoner. But why would he want him as a prisoner? Having the Kommandant with him would only slow him down," Horst said more to himself than to her. "It might even be worse."

"What do you mean, worse?" she asked. Horst had been lost in his own thoughts, but now he looked up at Uta Woolf, and he could see that she was trembling.

"Well, do you think your husband would have fought to protect his son?"

"I don't know," she said honestly. "He wasn't as fond of Liam as we had hoped he would be when we adopted the child. Reinhard was a busy and ambitious man. He had little interest in home and family."

"If your husband did put up a fight, he would have had to have shot and killed the Jew, or this Jew would have killed him. I know this because this Jew would not even need a gun, he is unusually strong and could easily have killed a man with his bare hands."

She shuddered. "I'm glad I wasn't at home," she whispered.

"Have you found any evidence of foul play? I don't mean to be crude, but have you found a body?"

"No, when I got home that afternoon, there was nothing disturbed in the house. I even checked the pool. No one was out there. I am ashamed to admit it, but just between us, I know you are searching for this Jew, but I really don't think the Jew had anything to do with my husband's disappearance. I have a horrible feeling that Reinhard ran away with the female prisoner, and they took Liam with them because she was quite fond of Liam. And he was fond of her. After all, she was his nanny."

"I don't know where to begin to look," Horst said, "but I am going to do my best to find them. I'll let you know of anything I discover."

She nodded. "I am so ashamed, so I haven't been able to bring myself to tell anyone here at the camp yet. I called in for Reinhard and made an excuse as to why he did not come into work. I told them that he had been called away on business. No one questioned me any further. We German's are a very small community here at Auschwitz. All my friends' husbands work at the camp together.

Once the word gets out, all the other wives will see me as a failure. They will laugh at me. I can't bear it. I don't know what made me tell you. I suppose there is something in your eyes that is telling me I can trust you. I hope I can."

"Of course you can. I think you should keep all this a secret for as long as possible," he said. *I am glad she will not tell anyone. Her ego and pride will help me by giving me time to find Barr before anyone else starts looking for him. I have a feeling the Jew must have murdered the Kommandant. Otherwise, what has happened to Reinhard Woolf? Unless she is right, this has nothing to do with Barr, and Woolf has run off with the Nanny. I don't know anything for sure, but this is my only lead, so I am no longer looking for one man. Now, I am searching for a man with a woman and a child.*

CHAPTER FORTY-FOUR

Jakup stayed close to Steffi. He watched Pitor fearfully, and even when both he and Steffi were exhausted, he still refused to let Pitor carry him. Steffi could see the hurt in Pitor's eyes whenever his son rejected his affection. But she didn't know how they might remedy this. All she could think of was that it would take time. The days passed, and the food that Steffi took from the house ran out. Then, one afternoon, when it was exceptionally hot outside, and the sun was relentlessly scorching their backs and heads, Pitor suggested they sit for a while. "I am thinking that during the heat of summer we should walk at night and sleep during the day. The weather is getting hotter and that is making the days much more difficult for everyone."

Steffi nodded.

"I will hunt—or go fishing when I can find a pond—in the early morning each day, while the two of you stay here to get some rest. Then, we can wake up in the evening and eat before we start walking again."

"Yes, I think that's a good idea. But if you are going to hunt for fish, I am afraid there will be a problem because we can't cook anything or there will be smoke," she said. "And I doubt Jakup will eat raw meat."

"I realize that. However, I have a solution. When I was living with the partisans, they taught me how to make a fire pit that would put out a very minimal amount of smoke. I am going to need very dry twigs. We can collect them in the evening as soon as we wake up. That way they will still be dry. If we do it during the day they won't work as well because the morning dew makes them wet."

"All right."

Then Pitor turned to Jakup and knelt down so that he was the same height. "Jakup," he said, "you must not eat anything you find in the forest without showing it to me first. No berries, no mushrooms, nothing. Do you understand, son?"

Jakup stared at Pitor, then he nodded.

"Good. We must be very careful because some of the things that grow here are not safe to eat. And you are very precious to me. I don't want anything to hurt you."

Jakup stared at Pitor distrustfully. Pitor smiled at Jakup, but Steffi could see that Pitor's lips were quivering. And she felt so bad for him.

"How far do you think the partisan's camp is from here?" she asked.

"Well, I can't say exactly. I met them outside of Warsaw, and at the time I was with them, their camp was heading west. The only problem is that because they are partisans, they are always moving around. They don't have a permanent place. The Nazis are always looking for them. So, this makes finding them difficult. I figure our best bet, for now anyway, is just to circle this area. The partisans are very aware of anyone who comes into their surroundings. They are always watching. So, I am hoping they will find us."

"Do you think they will remember you?"

"If the men who I knew are still alive, they will most certainly remember me," Pitor said.

She hadn't considered that his friends might no longer exist.

They could have been found by the Germans and killed. "What happens to us if we don't find them?"

"Nothing happens to us. We will find a way to survive. Since I can hunt and fish, we will eat, at least until the winter comes. Then we will have to find another way. But we have some time before that happens. For now, we can pick wild mushrooms and berries too. I'll show you what is safe to eat and what is not. And with God's help, this war will end soon. The American's are getting closer. They are here in Europe."

"Are you sure?"

"Yes, I am. When I was working for Hitler as Konrad Hoffmann, the other bodyguards whispered about a bloody battle in Normandy France."

"What if Germany wins the war?"

He shrugged. "We can only hope that they don't. But to be honest with you, I don't know what we will do if Germany wins. Hitler is a mad tyrant; he will not stop until he conquers the world and annihilates all the Jews." Pitor shook his head. "What a terrible thought, but I heard a lot of things when I was working as a bodyguard for the Führer. And some of the officers, although it was treason to say this, said that things have been looking bleak for the Germans since Hitler went after Russia. So, if Germany gets weakened on the Eastern and Western Fronts at the same time, there is a very good chance she will lose the war."

"We can only pray that you're right," Steffi said.

Jakup was tired of building castles with rocks he'd found. He was bored, and grew restless. He stood up and walked a few feet away from Steffi and Pitor, then, he took a stick and began to dig in the dirt for worms. "Jakup. Stop that please," Steffi said. She was nervous and annoyed at the sound of his stick scraping the hard earth. Besides that, he was getting dirt all over himself.

"It's all right. He is bored. Let him play," Pitor said gently.

"I wish you would stop calling me Jakup. I wish you would call me by my name. Why do you keep doing that?" Jakup asked Steffi.

"Because Jakup is your real name," she answered.

"So why did you call me Liam before, when we lived with my mother and father? Why didn't you just call me Jakup then? I don't understand any of this. I want to go home."

"Please, Jakup," she said, exasperated.

"Liam, my name is Liam. Tell me why you called me Liam before, but now you want to call me Jakup. What changed?"

"It's a long story. You are just going to have to trust me. I am doing what is best for you. What is safest for you. You know how much I love you and you know I would never do anything to hurt you."

Jakup nodded. "I know, but I just don't understand" he said, stomping his feet. Then he went back to playing in the dirt. There was a long silence.

Steffi whispered to Pitor, "Give him a chance. All this change is a lot for him to understand. He is just a little boy. And I can see why he is very confused right now."

"I know. I just wish he could remember me. Remember his mother, his home," Pitor sighed.

"Give him time. He will," Steffi reached over and rubbed Pitor's arm. He smiled at her, and her heart lit up like a tiny candle flame inside of her chest. She longed to tell him how much she had missed him, how she had thought about him all the time. And she wanted to say that she believed she might be in love with him. But she just smiled and remained silent.

The sound of birds singing filled the forest, and the fragrant smell of flowers and pine trees wafted through the air. Steffi closed her eyes for a moment. And her thoughts traveled back to her memories of the time she'd spent in Auschwitz. Even though they were sleeping outside now, and at the mercy of the elements, it was still a far better existence here in the forest, than it had been in that camp.

Then, without warning, Jakup began choking. He fell to the ground, unable to breathe. Within seconds, Pitor was on his feet. He ran to his son's side and knelt. He turned Jakup onto his stomach and began to push on his upper back. Steffi ran over to them both. Her hands covered her mouth, stifling a scream. Jakup was turning blue, but Pitor did not stop. He pushed harder. Tears were falling to the ground from Jakup's wide-open eyes. Steffi gasped. The child was struggling to breathe. And if his airways were not opened soon, he would die. Then, Pitor pushed even harder, and finally a nut like berry shot out of Jakup's mouth. Still gasping and coughing, Jakup began to breathe.

Minutes passed, which felt like an eternity. When he could speak, Jakup said, "I'm sorry, Pitor." The look on Jakup's face let Pitor know the child was terrified. "I know you said not to eat anything. But I thought that thing I ate was a cherry. But it wasn't, it was hard like a nut. Please, please don't hit me. Please," Jakup trembled.

Although Pitor was not aware of it, tears covered his cheeks. He shook his head, unable to speak. Then he reached for Jakup, who cowered in fear. But Pitor took the little boy in his arms and held him close. Then he whispered, "I would never hit you. You made a mistake. I am just glad you are all right. Please, don't do it again. Please don't eat anything without asking me first. Do you understand? Do you promise?"

Jakup nodded.

"And, please, Jakup, don't ever be afraid of me. I am your father, your papa. I love you."

Tears rained down Steffi's cheeks as she watched Jakup put his arms around Pitor's neck. *Everything is going to be all right between Pitor and his son,* she thought. *Jakup is still very young. He will forget living with the Nazis, and in time he will come to love Pitor the way Pitor deserves to be loved.*

CHAPTER FORTY-FIVE

Horst left Auschwitz with more questions than he had come with. As he walked through the barbed wire fence, he noticed a large pile of dead bodies that were little more than bones with dark, staring, accusing eyes. He shivered and turned away. Little did he know that beneath these corpses lay the body of the Kommandant, Reinhard Woolf. *This place is even more wretched than I originally imagined. Those corpses look like demons. And the smell here is overpowering. I don't have a good job right now, it's true. But even though the pay for working at one of these camps is better than what I currently earn, I wouldn't want to work here. Not because I care about these* Untermenschen, *these dirty Jews, and filthy gypsies, because I certainly don't. I feel towards them the same way as I feel towards poisonous spiders or snakes. But this place is hideous. From what I have heard, it's riddled with disease, and ashes are dropping on your head all day as they come flying out from the fires at the crematorium. Now that I have been here, I can see that these rumors I heard are true. These are ashes from the piles of skeletons whose bodies must be burned. I would never admit it, but the very thought of their ashes falling on me terrifies me. They might spread diseases. And just look at those eyes; they are*

black and unseeing, but I feel as if they are watching me. What if these Jews are demons? Their eyes wide open, dark, and horrible, they could haunt a man forever, he shivered.

After Horst's visit to the camp, he needed a drink. Beer was not going to be strong enough, so he walked to a local tavern and sat down at the bar. He ordered a schnapps and finished it with a single gulp. Then he ordered another.

Horst drank until he was so drunk he couldn't continue his search. And although he hated to waste money, he was so tired, he decided to get a hotel for the night. The cheapest hotel was a small place on the edge of town. Horst struggled up to his room. The furnishings were sparse, and the sheets on the bed looked like they could use a washing, but he was so tired, he fell onto the bed and was asleep in minutes, with all his clothes still on. Somewhere around two in the morning, still sleeping deeply, he began to dream. And in his dream, he saw their eyes. He couldn't tell if he was dreaming or if he was awake, but they were there and they were following him. Staring at him from every corner of the room, dark and accusing. He tried to run, but couldn't move. "I didn't do this to you," he screamed repeatedly.

"But you knew what your people were doing, and you didn't do anything to stop it. You don't care about the murder of innocent people. You only care about yourself." The corpses whispered.

"How could I stop it? You don't understand. I do what I am told. I am just following orders. We are *all* just following orders."

"And if you could have stopped it, would you have done so?" A woman with sunken eyes that looked like sparkling pieces of hot coal asked him.

"Go away, go away and leave me alone."

"Never, I will never leave you again. I will haunt you for the rest of your life. We all will." The woman motioned to a large crowd of skeletons who stood behind her, all of them staring at Horst with those same dark eyes.

Then, a river of blood poured from her lips and came flooding towards him. He felt himself drowning in it as it flowed higher and higher.

"Please, stop. Stop this..." he shouted.

Then he woke up screaming in a pool of his own sweat.

CHAPTER FORTY-SIX

The following day, to Pitor's surprise and delight, Jakup woke up at the same time as him. He walked over to his father and asked, "Can I go fishing with you?"

"Have you ever gone fishing?" Pitor asked.

"Never, but I would like to learn how."

"And...I would love to teach you. So, let's wake Steffi and let her know that you are going to go with me. That way she won't worry when she wakes up and you're gone."

"Good idea," Jakup smiled. Then he gently shook Steffi's shoulder until her eyes opened.

"Jakup, are you all right?" she asked.

"Yes, I am going to go with Pitor and learn how to fish," he said proudly, puffing out his chest. "Pitor said to wake you up and to tell you that we are going together so you wouldn't worry."

She saw Pitor watching Jakup, and when she saw how proud he was of his son, Steffi smiled. "All right. But be careful, you two."

"We will," Pitor said as Jakup walked over to him. Pitor took Jakup's hand and, for the first time, Jakup did not resist.

It was early morning, and the sun had not yet risen. The forest was quiet and cool before the heat of the day set in. Steffi watched them go. She smiled, then she turned on her side and fell back to sleep.

CHAPTER FORTY-SEVEN

Pitor and Jakup sat down beside a pond that was not too far away from where they had slept the previous night. Pitor patiently taught Jakup how to find and collect worms. Then, he made a makeshift fishing pole from a tree branch. Jakup watched intently as Pitor pulled a thread from the inside of his shirt, which he attached to the pole, creating a line. After he checked to make sure the thread was strong enough to hold a fish, he attached a worm to the line with the pin from an award that had belonged to Konrad.

"We're all ready to start," Pitor said as he carefully tossed the line into the water.

"What do we do now?" Jakup asked.

"Now we sit here quietly and wait for a fish to bite," Pitor smiled. "And while we wait, we can talk about anything you want to talk about. Or we don't have to talk at all."

Jakup smiled. "Is your rank higher than my father's?" Jakup asked. "My father was a Kommandant."

Pitor took a long breath. He had just broken through to Jakup, and he didn't want to say anything that would alienate the child, so he had to tread carefully. "That's a question that has two answers,"

Pitor said, patting Jakup's shoulder. *I must remember that he doesn't understand. I must be patient and explain everything carefully.* "I am not a Nazi, Jakup. I am a Jewish man. And you are my Jewish son. Someday, you will grow up to be a Jewish man too."

"But Jews are bad people. They are very dangerous. They steal children, it said so in *The Poisonous Mushroom*. I am afraid of them. Have you read that book? Steffi wouldn't read it to me. But my mother read it to me. And it said that I should be very careful of Jews. Then you stole me, just like the book said you would."

Pitor sighed, "I haven't read that book. But what that book told you is not true. I don't blame you for believing it, because you had no way of knowing any better. But now that you have met me, do you think I am a bad person?"

"You don't seem to be bad. But you did steal me from my parents, just like the book said you would. And I am afraid you are going to hurt me, like the book said you would. I am afraid you are going to kill me and drink my blood."

"I will never hurt you, Jakup. You see, I didn't steal you. When you were very little, you were stolen from your mother and me," Pitor touched Jakup's arm. "Your mother and I loved you very, very much. I am your real father, and Jakup is your real name. I would never kill you, and I would never drink blood, yours or anyone else's."

"Do you promise? Because my mother and father said never to trust Jews. They said that Jews were very dangerous, and that they are not really people. They are something called Untermenschen. And I must always be careful around them."

"I promise you we are real people." Pitor kept his composure, even though these words broke his heart. "And someday, when you are older, I will explain everything about your adopted parents to you in more detail. But for now, please, please, please, just trust me. I will take good care of you. I will protect you with my life. I promise you, Jakup." Then he looked into Jakup's eyes, so like his own, and he calmly and slowly repeated, "Your name is Jakup Barr, and I am Pitor Barr, your real father."

"Is Steffi my real mother?"

"No. Your mother died. Her name was Mila, and she loved you very much. She was a wonderful woman. The love and the light in my life." Pitor paused. *Oh, Mila, I wish you were here with me. To help me.* "But Steffi is a very good woman too, and she is a very good friend. She loves you very much."

"I know. She told me," Jakup said. Then he was quiet for a moment. "Why did my mother have to die?"

"Well, sometimes people die, Jakup. We don't want them to, but they do. And we must learn to find a way to live on this earth without them. When you get older, we will talk more about this. For now, just know that your mother loved you more than anything in the world."

"Even more than she loved you."

Pitor laughed. "Probably," he said. "We both were so happy the day you were born."

"You still remember the day I was born? I don't remember it at all," Jakup said.

"You were too little to remember," Pitor explained.

Jakup nodded. "I don't remember anything about being little."

"That's because you were too young to remember. But you're still a little boy."

"No, I am not," Jakup protested. "I'm almost six years old. I'm a big boy."

"Yes, I apologize. You're right. You are not a little boy, you are a big boy, son." Pitor tapped Jakup's shoulder, "And I am very proud of you."

"Will you let me hold the fishing pole?"

"All right. But I am going to help you, because when the fish eats the worm, it pulls on the line and then tries to pull away. And since it's your first time fishing, I want to help you bring it in."

"That's very sad for the fish."

"Yes, it is. But we must eat. I never hunt or fish for sport, son. I only take what we need to keep us alive."

Jakup nodded. "I want to learn how to do it."

"And I want to teach you so many wonderful things," Pitor said, his heart swelling with joy as he looked down at the top of his son's head filled with golden curls just like his own.

Pitor handed the pole to Jakup, who took it from him and held it tightly. Pitor smiled secretly as he looked at Jakup's face, which was very serious. Pitor knew that when a fish bit, it would jolt the little boy, and he didn't want Jakup to be scared, so he held the pole with him.

A few moments passed. "Next time you go hunting, can I go with you? I want to learn to fire a gun."

Pitor let out a long breath. "You're very young to go hunting."

"Why?"

"Because I will have to kill an animal. And it's not something pleasurable."

"You don't like it?"

"No, I don't like to kill anything. But I am forced to, because we must eat. So, I do what I have to, to keep us alive." He looked into Jakup's eyes, then he continued, "You see, son. I have a lot of respect for all of God's creatures. So, I never take a life without realizing how serious it is. And I am always grateful to have the food the animal provides for us."

Jakup was quiet for a moment, then he nodded. "I want to ask you something. But please don't hit me."

"I'll never hit you, Jakup. You can ask me anything."

"Remember that day when you first came?"

"Of course, I do."

Jakup paused. He was suddenly not as confident. "I saw you kill my other father," he said.

"Yes," Pitor replied.

"I never told anyone else this, but my other father was mean to me. He made me swear I would never tell anyone. He said he would make it worse for me if I did. But he hit me lots of times. He kicked me in the stomach, and he cursed at me too. He always cursed at me. And sometimes he cursed at my mother. She didn't tell me, but I heard him hitting her one night when I was supposed to be asleep," Jakup said.

"But you said you wanted to go home? Why?"

"I wanted to go home, because I was scared. I didn't know who you were, or why you were taking me. I was afraid. But my other father was not nice to me. He was only nice when other men who he worked with came to our house. Then he was very nice to my mother and me. He wanted them to think he was always like that. But he wasn't."

Pitor winced as if he'd been punched in the gut. "I'm sorry, son. I wish I could have come for you sooner."

Several long, silent moments passed. A black bird let out a loud caw above them. "You are my real father, aren't you?"

"Yes, Jakup. I am. You were stolen from your mother and me. I would never have given you up willingly. We both loved you very much. More than I can ever say." Pitor repeated again, hoping Jakup would understand.

They sat quietly side by side as the sun rose, its light scattering across the pond like tiny diamonds. Then, out of nowhere, Jakup looked up at Pitor. "I believe you," Jakup said, wrapping his arms around his father.

Then a piercing scream broke the peace of the morning. It came from the direction of where they'd spent the night. And Pitor knew that it was Steffi. Something was terribly wrong.

Jakup heard the scream and looked up at his father. "That sounded like Steffi."

"Yes, son. Follow me. Stay behind me. But stay close," Pitor said.

"What should I do with the pole?" Jakup asked, he was looking at Pitor. His little body was trembling.

"Leave it," Pitor said. He was already on his feet. "Come on son, hurry, we have to get to her as soon as possible."

CHAPTER FORTY-EIGHT

Steffi had fallen back asleep when Pitor and Jakup left. But she was awakened, as she always was, when the sun rose. She sat up and leaned her back against a tree. Mornings in the forest were beautiful, renewing. Although she realized that this was the summer, and once the winter came, the forest could be deadly. Trying not to think about how they would survive once the snow came, she sat patiently waiting for Jakup and Pitor to return. Closing her eyes, she listened to the different songs of the birds. And although living in the forest, even in the summer, could be dangerous, Steffi was happy. *It is a miracle. Pitor came back. There are so many miracles to be grateful for.* A smile twinkled in her eyes as she contemplated this. *God made so many things possible. I know it was God who arranged for me to be Jakup's nanny. God had to know my heart, and He knew I would love Pitor's little boy as if he were my own child.* Then Steffi sighed. *Pitor is not my husband, as I always dreamed that he might be, but that is all right; I am just glad to be close to him.* Sometimes, before she fell asleep at night, she would make believe in her mind that Pitor was her husband and Jakup was her child. Of course, she knew she could never tell him this. He would be so shocked if he knew how much she cared for him. He might even be appalled or offended. After all, he'd always told her he was still in love with his wife, and Steffi respected that. His love for Mila was undying, and even though she wished he could love her that way, Steffi found it to be one of his most beautiful traits.

The rays of the rising sun cast down tenderly onto the earth, illuminating the flowers, the leaves, the grass, warming her legs, her face, and her chest. Steffi closed her eyes to better feel the sun's warmth caressing her.

Then she heard a noise. An unfamiliar rustling very close beside her. *Jakup and Pitor must have returned,* she thought, as she lazily opened her eyes. A man, wearing a soldier's uniform, the brown uniform with the red on the lapel of a Russian soldier, was kneeling down and rifling through the bag of food, clothing, and other important things that Steffi had packed when she left Reinhard's house.

"Who are you and what do you want," she said, trying to sound brave, but silently cursing herself for not keeping a gun at her side.

"Food. Got any food?"

"No, no food. I'm sorry. Go away." Steffi said as assertively as she could manage, but her hands were shaking.

The man didn't look up. He continued tearing through the bag. He found the gun and ammunition, tucking them into his uniform pants. Then he took the rest of the bread and stuffed it into his shirt. He emptied the rest of the bag onto the ground and took the cheese. He was about to leave, but then he turned and looked at Steffi. "You certainly are a scrawny thing, aren't you?" he asked. "German too. I can tell. What are you doing out here, all alone in the forest?"

She glared at him. "That's none of your business," she tried to sound brave.

His face and uniform were dirty. She noticed that some of his teeth were black.

"You are a kraut. That's for sure. And if there is anything I hate, it's the krauts. Nazi bastards, all of you," he sneered. "Killed my brother. My best friend too."

"Get out of here," she said, trying to sound strong and menacing, but she knew she had no leverage. Her gun was in this man's possession. He had all the power. *Pitor, where are you?*

There was rage in the Russian's eyes. And looking more closely at him, she could see there was something akin to madness too. He grabbed her and tore her blouse open. "Been a long time since I had a woman. Like I said, you're a scrawny kraut. But you're better than nothing. And besides, I am going to make you pay for what your people did to me."

"No, oh no," she said as she tried to stand up to run away. But he tightened his grip on her before she could move, and pushed her back down to the ground. He pulled her towards him, and she tried to resist, but hit her head on a tree root. White hot pain shot through her. "Not this. Take whatever you want, but not this."

He laughed hysterically, and the madness she saw a glimpse of earlier grew stronger. Steffi struggled to get away, but his grip on her was tight. He slapped her hard across the face, "Stop trying to escape from me. I'm not going to kill you. I'll let you go when I am done with you."

That was when she let out a scream. She prayed Pitor heard her. And that when he returned to camp, he would be ready to encounter danger. *Please Pitor, come quickly and please be careful.*

CHAPTER FORTY-NINE

When Pitor and Jakup came running back to the place where they'd camped the night before, they saw Steffi laying on the ground with a large, ape of a man looming over her. Her nose and mouth were bleeding, and she was fighting as hard as she could to get away. Pitor didn't hesitate. He grabbed the man by the shoulders and lifted him up. Then he threw him to the ground. The Russian soldier was strong; he jumped to his feet and punched Pitor. But Pitor was unfazed by the assault. He was stronger, and when he pulled his arm back and punched the soldier in the chest, the Russian was stunned. He fell to the ground, unable to catch his breath. Pitor pulled his gun, and without a word he shot the man in the chest. Blood poured from the wound, but the soldier was still breathing. Not wanting to waste a single bullet, Pitor reached down and snapped the soldier's neck. Now the invader lay lifeless. Steffi sat up and wiped the blood from her nose and lips with the hem of her dress.

"Are you all right?" Pitor asked.

Steffi nodded. "He took the gun I stole from Reinhard. It's under his jacket. He has the food too."

Pitor nodded. He removed the gun and ammunition, then he took the soldier's gun as well. Pitor put the food back into the bag, and then Steffi collected all their things from the ground and put the bag back together. She took a long, deep breath. "Thank God you came in time," she whispered. For a moment, they both forgot about Jakup, but then Pitor turned around to see his son crying.

"Jakup," Pitor said. He ran over and reached for the little boy to take him into his arms. For a moment, Jakup stood wide eyed, staring at Pitor. Pitor was afraid that what Jakup had just seen him do to the soldier might have scared him. And it could have set back his trust in him. Pitor prayed not, because it had been so difficult to finally break through to his child. "I'm sorry if I scared you. I didn't mean to."

Jakup nodded. He allowed Pitor to take him into his arms. "I promised I would protect you, remember?"

There was a long silence. Pitor wished he knew what Jakup was thinking. But then Jakup said, "When I grow up, I want to be just like you." Jakup wrapped his arms around Pitor's neck.

Pitor felt tears well up in his eyes, and he hugged his little boy tighter.

CHAPTER FIFTY

The summer months passed quickly. Pitor wandered all around the area where he had once stayed amongst the partisans, hoping that he would find them again. However, he found no trace of them. And by the time the chilly winds of autumn began to blow, and the leaves of the trees in the forest began to change from lush green to rich burgundy, orange, and deep brown, Pitor realized they had walked for such a long time that he was not sure if they were in Poland anymore. Everywhere in the forest began to look the same, or at least, it appeared as if they had been there before. Sometimes it seemed to Pitor that they had traveled for miles. Other times he thought they might have walked in circles. But no matter where they were, Pitor knew that with the winter coming, it was imperative that they find shelter soon.

One night, as Jakup slept wrapped in Pitor's uniform jacket to ward off the cold, Pitor and Steffi sat up talking in whispers.

"I don't know if we have left Poland, or if we have been walking in circles," Pitor admitted. "The winter is almost here, and if we are to survive, we must do something quickly or we will freeze out here."

"I know," Steffi said, taking his hand. "I've thought about it myself. But I don't know what to do."

"Well, I have an idea. Since I still have this SS officer's uniform, I'll put it on, and we can go into town and stay for a night. That way we can find out where we are. Then we can leave and come back here to the forest. But we will stay on the edge, and I'll try to find a farm who needs a worker. There are a lot of women who are trying to run these farms all alone. Many of them have lost their husbands or fathers in the war. In exchange for my working on their farm, I will ask if we can stay in their barn. I will request some food, and perhaps even a little money."

"I can be of use too, if they need someone to cook and clean. I am capable," Steffi agreed. "Maybe we can find someone who will hire us as a family."

"That's what I am hoping. We will tell them that we are Polish farmers. We will say our farm burned down and we are in need of a place to live until we can get on our feet."

"The plan sounds good except that it is very dangerous for us to go into town. I am not sure where we are either, but if we are anywhere near Auschwitz, they are probably still searching for us. Don't you think so?" she asked.

"Well, that's probably true. But I don't know if we are still even in Poland. We might be in Germany. Anyway, it doesn't matter. Winter is coming, and so we have no choice. When we are in town, I will use another name. I will say that I am a German, from Nuremberg, and we can remove the badges on my uniform so that I am no longer an Oberstrumführer. I don't want to attract any attention. I want to appear to be just an average soldier. That way, whether we are in Germany or Poland, no one will think twice about a small family coming through their town."

She nodded, but he could tell that she was worried. Gently, he rubbed his thumb over the back of her hand. Then he said, "Steffi, I don't know what else to do. As far as I can see, we have no other options. The weather will kill us if we are still sleeping outside in the forest once the winter sets in. We must find shelter. And this is the only plan I could come up with."

"I suppose you're right," she said. "I think we should go to town and then get out as soon as we know where we are. That way, if we are in Germany, we can go to the farmers and say we are German farmers who lost our farm. If we are in Poland, we can be Polish farmers."

He nodded in agreement.

She went on, "and we are going to need to use different names. That will confuse Jakup again. I say it's probably best if you go into town without us. Jakup and I will stay here in the forest and wait for you."

"No," he protested, "not after what happened last time I left you alone. I won't put you or Jakup at risk like that again. Here is what we will do. I will check us into a hotel. Then you and Jakup will go to our room while I go and buy some food and find out what we need to know. That way, Jakup will not see anyone, and no one will see the three of us together. So, if by chance, the Nazis are searching for a man, woman and child, they will not notice a single soldier traveling alone."

She nodded. "That sounds much better," she said. "When do you want to do this?"

"Well, as soon as we can make our way into town. Thus far we have stayed as deep in the forest as possible. Now we must try to find our way to the outskirts," he said.

"I assume you want to start tomorrow?"

"Yes," he said. "So, go and get some rest. We will begin in the morning."

She got up and went over to cuddle with Jakup. In his sleep, he felt the familiar softness of her body and nuzzled into her.

In the morning, Steffi awoke and removed all the badges on Pitor's uniform jacket. Then, after a quick breakfast of some wild berries, they began their journey.

As they made their way in the direction that Pitor thought was the outskirts, they saw a large area of forest where German soldiers were at work cutting down trees and removing debris. "Do you think they are building a camp here?" Steffi whispered to Pitor.

"I don't know. But they are clearing the land for something. Let's stay far away from them so they don't see us," he said.

"Look at all those men," Jakup said.

"Shhh, we must be very quiet. Don't say a word, all right? We must be very quiet, so they don't hear us. We don't know what they are doing here. So, it's best not to draw their attention to us," Pitor said gently, as he lifted Jakup into his arms. "I am going to carry you for a little while."

"All right," Jakup whispered in Pitor's ear.

It looks as though they are clearing the land to possibly build something, Pitor observed. And even after they came to the end of the construction, Pitor remained cautious. They walked in silence for a long time. Then, as the sun was about to set, Pitor saw a town in the distance.

"We're here," Pitor said, more to himself than to anyone else, but he was still carrying Jakup, and Jakup heard him.

"Where?" Jakup asked.

"Another adventure, son," Pitor said, winking at Jakup. Jakup smiled and winked back. "Now part of this game is that you must not speak to anyone in town. All right. Just stay where I tell you to stay. Steffi will be with you. I will return as soon as I can. I won't be long."

"All right."

Pitor left Steffi and Jakup in an alleyway between two buildings. He was worried about leaving them alone, so he hurried to the local hotel. They took one look at his uniform and did not question him at all. He was given a room key and a room number by a skinny clerk with dark hair combed over his balding, shiny scalp.

Pitor returned with the key and escorted Steffi and Jakup upstairs to the room. He felt better now they were with him and not waiting in an alley. But then he saw the desk clerk eyeing him skeptically, and his blood ran cold.

Once they were all in the room, Pitor turned to Steffi, "I'm going to buy some food. I'll see what I can find out about where we are, and also about what is being built right outside of town in the forest."

She nodded. "While you're gone, Jakup and I will clean ourselves up, won't we Jakup?"

Jakup nodded. Then he looked a Pitor and said, "Hurry back."

CHAPTER FIFTY-ONE

The only thing Pitor found to be still open was a tavern. But they served food, and he ordered several sausages and potato salad. Then, while the food was being prepared, the bartender began talking to him while he waited.

"You must be one of the German's who are working on the roads and towers out there in the Kampinos forest."

"Oh, yes," Pitor agreed, *so that was what the large group of German soldiers I saw in the forest were building.*

"I've heard the forests are dangerous. From what everyone says there are a lot of rebels—they call themselves partisans, freedom fighters—out there in the forests. The Germans who come in here say these rebels are no good. They're very dangerous. They're like cockroaches, they're everywhere out there. The Germans have told me that they had to call in the Gestapo, and even the Luftwaffe, just to get rid of them. But from what I've heard, they haven't gotten rid of them. They're still here, causing problems for the good Germans who are trying to build something, wherever and whenever they can. Of course, what else would you expect from Jews, Soviets, and partisans. They're all troublemakers. That's for sure." The bartender scoffed.

"Are you ever afraid of the Gestapo?" Pitor asked.

"Me? No, never. I don't do anything wrong. The people they kill deserve to die. You see, I'm a friend to the Germans. I want to get rid of the filthy gypsies, the lousy Soviets, the fanatical freedom fighters, but most of all the good for nothing thieving Jews, just as much as you do."

"Good man," Pitor said, tongue in cheek. He was wearing his Nazi uniform, and he realized the bartender was pandering to him. "It's always good to have a friend like you in town."

"Well," the bartender hesitated, smiling, "I want you to know that I sure am a friend to the Nazis. Even before you folks came, I was sure tired of all the wealthy Jews strutting around acting like they are something special. I'm glad that you Germans are getting rid of them." He licked his lips, then smiled. "And, you krauts sure are smart. And...by the way, I use that word affectionately. Anyway, I heard that you fellas are building some new roads for tanks and watch towers and stuff. I think this project is going to be very good for our business here in town. And since I am the owner of this tavern," he said proudly, "I am pretty darn happy about it. "

"That's right. You are certainly correct." Pitor agreed. He needed to know where they were. Was this Poland? Was it Germany? He wanted to ask, but he dared not ask outright. That would give him away. If he asked, the bartender would know he was not a German officer. So, he asked gingerly, "by the way, how do you spell the name of this town. I'm writing to my girl at home. And you know how women are. She wants to know where I am. I'd hate to spell the name wrong."

"Sure. I'll write it down for you. It's spelled K.A.M.P.I.N.O.S. Kampinos Village, Poland.

"Good, thanks. I appreciate it. How far exactly is this from the German border just in case I can slip away and meet her for a night or two."

"I can't tell you for sure just how far you are from Germany, but it's several days on foot," the bartender said. Then someone from the kitchen called out, "Norbert, your order is ready."

Norbert, the bartender, walked back to the kitchen. Then he returned with the food Pitor had ordered. Pitor wrapped it up, and thanked the bartender again. Then he left and walked as quickly as he could, without drawing attention to himself. He was headed back to the room where Jakup and Steffi waited.

CHAPTER FIFTY-TWO

Steffi breathed a sigh of relief when Pitor opened the door to the hotel room. "I was worried. I am glad you're here and you're all right."

"Yes, I am here. I bought food."

"I'm hungry," Jakup said.

"Sit down, and we'll eat," Steffi told him.

The three of them sat down on the bed, and quickly gobbled up all the food Pitor bought. When they were finished, Jakup was very tired. His eyes began to close. This was not usual for him; he usually fought going to sleep, because he never wanted to miss anything. But tonight, the bed was so soft, and his belly was finally full. The little boy curled up with his head on a pillow for the first time in a long time, and he was asleep within minutes. Steffi walked over to him and put her hand on his head softly. "Poor little boy," she whispered, "he's been through so much." Careful not to wake him, she took off his shoes. Then she covered him with a blanket.

"Yes, he certainly has been through a lot," Pitor said. He shook his head. He hated to think about all that his son had suffered. Pitor sat down on one of the chairs and softly cleared his throat. Then in a quiet voice, he called Steffi over to sit beside him. "I want to talk to you," he said.

She gently kissed Jakup on the top of his head, then walked over to where Pitor waited. She sat down beside him and patted his hand. Pitor's lips trembled as he told Steffi everything he learned from the bartender that evening.

"I think this shirt and slacks that I have that belonged to the Kommandant are too good of quality to be convincing. No farmer would have clothes like these. So, in the morning, I will go to a secondhand shop and buy clothes that would be appropriate for a peasant farmer. Then, I am hoping we can find a farm just outside of town where we can get work and stay through the winter."

She nodded. "You say that all of that construction in the forest is because they are clearing land for roads?" She repeated what Pitor had told her.

"Yes, that's what the tavern owner told me," he said.

"We must be careful to avoid them."

"He also said that the Germans out in the forest have found and killed a lot of the partisans. So, I am afraid that is why we have not been able to find my friends. They must all be gone," he said sadly.

"You mean the freedom fighters who you stayed with in the forest?"

"Yes, I know how aware they were of everything going on around them. So, I believe that if they were alive, they would have found us. And now that the bartender told me the Nazis have been arresting and executing the partisans, I am sorry to say it, but I am sure that they are gone."

She was silent for a moment. "I'm sorry. I am so sorry about your friends," she said, rubbing his shoulder. "I wish I could say something that would help. But there is nothing to say. So many people who we have loved and cared for are dead. Young and old."

"I know."

"We are lucky, Pitor, we are lucky to be together and alive," she whispered.

"I suppose you're right. But it's hard to see it that way. Don't misunderstand me, I am glad to be here with you and my son, but I miss Mila. She was so young. So full of life. And she died so needlessly." He was quiet for a moment, looking down at his shoes. "And these men, these freedom fighters. They were not really soldiers at all. They were family men just trying to survive and get home to their loved ones. Their loved ones who were probably already dead," he shook his head. "You know, there was one fellow who had been a schoolteacher. Another one was a rabbi. One was a doctor. There was also a woman with us too. She had learned to use a gun and fight like a man. But she had once been a mother of three. Just an ordinary mother of three." He sighed, "Then, all of her young children were killed."

Steffi shook her head. "The Nazis are horrible. They have taken everything from us."

He sighed. "Not everything." He said, then he took a long, deep breath. "I still have Jakup." Then he turned to look at her and said, "And, I have you."

Hearing his words, her face lit up. "Me?"

"Yes, you are a good friend, Steffi. And you have come to mean a lot to me."

"Oh Pitor. Really?"

He nodded. "Yes, really."

She took his hand and held it tightly. "I have wanted to say this for a long time," she said softly, "but I didn't want you to feel obligated to say it back to me. I still don't want you to feel obligated. But... well...Pitor," she hesitated, then she looked down at their hands and said, "I know I will never replace Mila. I wouldn't even want to try. But I would be a good mother to Jakup. I would raise him as if he were my own child. And...and..." She looked away. "I love you, Pitor. I have loved you since that day I first saw you. The day you came to my farm. After you left, I never stopped thinking of you. In fact, when I found Jakup in the camp, I was glad to be there even though Auschwitz was hell, I was glad because I recognized Jakup from the picture you gave me. I knew he was your son. And God was good; He put me in a place where I could take care of Jakup. From the first day I became Jakup's nanny, I knew I would do whatever needed to be done to protect him from harm."

Pitor heard her words. But he was at a loss about what to say. He didn't know what he wanted or what he was feeling. So he stayed silent, but he squeezed her hand. A long time passed, then Pitor stood up and said, "I need to take some time to think."

She nodded, but he did not look at her. He walked towards the door of the hotel room. "Don't go, Pitor. Please. I don't expect anything from you. Just stay and I promise I won't ever say those things again," a tear ran down her cheek.

"It's all right, Steffi. I'm all right. I promise you I'll be back. I just need to walk and to think."

"But is it safe for you to walk through town? I would rather you just stay here."

"I'll be all right. I promise you. I'll wear the Nazi uniform jacket. No one will bother me."

Steffi was afraid for him to walk through town. The less exposure they had, the better. However, she knew she couldn't stop him. So, she leaned back in her chair and tried to take a deep breath as he quietly closed the door to the room. Steffi watched Jakup sleep, but she couldn't rest. Not only was she worried about Pitor's safety, but she was afraid she'd driven him away emotionally. *I am such a fool. Everything was going along just fine. I should never have said anything about being in love with him, but there is nothing I can do about it now. He knows how I feel. But what he doesn't realize is that I really don't expect anything from him. I am happy to just be with him.*

CHAPTER FIFTY-THREE

Pitor did not go far. He did not want to leave Jakup and Steffi alone in the hotel for too long. He walked for a short distance, just to put a little space between himself and the center of town. Then he sat down on the ground with his back against the side of a building and looked up at the sky. It was a clear night. The sky was a mixture of deep royal blue and inky black, covered with twinkling silver stars. In a soft voice, Pitor whispered, "Mila, I know you're out there somewhere and I know you are watching. Steffi is right. She cannot replace you. No one could ever replace you. You were, and you always will be my bashert. But, Steffi is a good woman, a wonderful friend. And Jakup needs a mother. She loves him. She loves me too," he hesitated for a moment, then he said, "I love her. It's not the same way that I love you. Nothing will ever compare to that. But, the truth is, in my own way, I do love her. And I am grateful to have her beside me. Please forgive me. I would never want to hurt you, but I hope you can understand. And so, I have come to ask you for your permission to marry her. I need a sign from you that this is all right. If I don't receive one, I won't ask her to marry me," he said.

For a few moments, Pitor sat staring up at the sky. He remembered the first time he had seen Mila. He remembered their first kiss, and then he thought of how she looked on the day they got married. His thoughts drifted to memories of her lovely face right after she gave birth, and the first time she held Jakup in her arms. His heart ached with longing for the past. Then, a shooting star lit up the sky so brightly that Pitor knew it was the sign he had been waiting for. His body shook with emotion. *She is here. She is with me.* Tears ran down his cheeks. "Thank you, Mila," he said, his voice filled with love. "You will always be the love of my life. But if you knew Steffi, I know you would like her," he whispered as the stars twinkled, smiling at him, and reinforcing the answer. Then he stood up and brushed the dirt from his pants. Pitor felt confident in his decision as he walked back to the hotel.

CHAPTER FIFTY-FOUR

When Pitor arrived back at the hotel, the room was dark except for the moonlight glimmering through the curtains. Steffi and Jakup slept curled up like two kittens in the bed. And seeing them together made Pitor's heart swell with love.

After sitting under the stars, Pitor had decided he was going to propose to Steffi. Although he wasn't sure that this was the right time to do it. They had to focus on surviving the winter. He had to put all his effort into finding a secure place for them to live through the winter months. In the spring, he would talk about marriage. So, the following morning, Pitor got up and went to the secondhand shop in the town and bought the clothes he needed. Then he dressed as a Polish farmer, and the three of them left the hotel and walked to the edge of the forest. This is where they found several farms. Pitor knocked on the door of each of the farmhouses begging for work. And because he would not leave Steffi and Jakup alone in the forest, he brought them with him. Not one of the farms was willing to offer him work, or a place to stay. No one offered food or help. It was not that they didn't want to, but they said the Germans took too much of their crops away from them, and they hardly had enough to provide for their own families. Pitor, Steffi, and Jakup walked for hours until Jakup became cranky and tired. He sat down on the ground and refused to keep going. "I'm tired," he said.

"He's been walking for a long time. Maybe we should stop for today," Steffi said.

But Pitor would not stop. He picked Jakup up and carried him. He knew that winter was just hiding around the corner, and he must find a place for them to stay before the cold chill made living outside dangerous.

It was dark by the time Pitor finally agreed to stop for the night. They retreated back deep into the forest, where the thick brush provided a cover of safety. Pitor laid his jacket down, and Steffi and Jakup lay down on the jacket on the hard ground and fell asleep wrapped into each other.

Pitor could not rest. He knew the farmers were not lying to him. It was no secret that the Germans took almost all their crops, and if they had the nerve to risk their lives to steal food from the Nazis, they certainly weren't going to share it with anyone outside of their own families.

When Steffi awoke the following morning, she found Pitor awake. He was sitting against the tree where she'd left him the night before. "Have you been up all night?" She asked, concerned.

He didn't answer her question. For a few moments, he was silent. Then he said, "We must do something soon. I cannot find any farmer willing to hire us. These farms are barely surviving, themselves. They can't share their food. And, with the winter coming we are in danger. Once it gets cold, I don't see how we can survive. We don't have enough warm clothing or blankets to get through the season living outside. And besides that, we don't have any food. We are very vulnerable. But Jakup is especially vulnerable because he is so young," Pitor said, shaking his head.

"We will find a way," she tried to reassure him. But even as she said the words, tears began to burn the back of her eyes.

"Yes, we will," he cleared his throat, "I have an idea."

He saw her face light up with hope. But he knew that once he told her his plan, she was going to be against it. It was very dangerous. He knew this, but he couldn't see any other way. So, he took her hand and held it for a moment. Then he glanced over at Jakup, who was still asleep. Soon the little boy would awaken. He would be hungry, and there was nothing for him to eat. *I will not fail my son. I will not fail this woman, who has put her faith in me. I will do what must be done for all of us.*

"The roads that the Germans are building are not far from here."

"I remember," she said.

"I am going to go there and ask for work. I will tell them that I am a Polish farmer and that I lost my farm in a fire. I will beg for work of any kind."

"No!" she said firmly. "No, you can't do that. What if the Germans that are there have been told to look out for you? What if they are hunting for you for posing as an SS officer? What if one of them recognizes you? You dare not do this. I won't let you."

He smiled at her gently, then brushed the hair that had fallen into her eyes with his fingers. "Steffi, I must do this. I know you are afraid. I am too. I am not playing the hero here. I am just trying to do what must be done to keep us all alive."

"What about us, Jakup and me? What will happen to us if they arrest you?"

"I don't know. But what I do know is that if I don't try this, we are going to freeze or starve to death."

"Pitor, oh Pitor," she sighed, "if they do hire you, where will Jakup and I go while you are working?"

"I don't know yet. We might get you a hotel room, or perhaps the wives and children of the workers have lodging provided for them on the grounds. At least I will have money from working, so you two can stay somewhere in town. Please don't worry. I will do whatever I need to do to protect you both."

Jakup stirred awake. "Papa, I'm hungry," he said.

"I know. I know," Pitor said, "I'm going to buy some food for you. I'll be back soon."

"How long?" Jakup asked.

"A little while."

"You don't have any more money left do you?" Steffi asked.

"No, but I will find food. First I am going to the construction site and I'm going to try to get work. Then I'll see if I can steal some food."

"Oh Pitor. I am so afraid."

"You must put your trust in me. Now, be careful and stay out of sight. I'll return as soon as I can. Please be careful. Keep the gun at your side at all times. You know how much I hate to leave you two alone in the forest. But right now, I must. So, be very aware of every sound around you, all right?"

She nodded. He stood up and shook the dry leaves off his pants. Tears began to flow down her face as she watched him. She quickly wiped them away with the bottom of her skirt. Pitor leaned over and kissed Jakup on the top of his head. Then he walked back over to where Steffi sat watching and clumsily touched her face. Then he winked and gave her a reassuring smile. She reached up and placed her fingers on her cheek where his hand had just been. Her eyes were glued to his broad shoulders and back as he walked away, leaving her and Jakup alone in the forest.

CHAPTER FIFTY-FIVE

The Nazis didn't seem suspicious at all when Pitor, with his blond hair and blue eyes, and dressed as a Polish farmer, walked into their camp in search of work. "Please," he said humbly, "I have come here because I need work. I am very strong, and I am willing to do anything that needs to be done."

The officer in charge of the project that day studied Pitor, nodding his head as he looked Pitor up and down. "You do look strong," he agreed. "And we could use the help. We would like to have the road finished as soon as possible. Göring is coming to see our progress the day after tomorrow. I think he would be interested in hiring you. Why don't you come back then and meet with him. I do believe he might just hire you for some of the more menial labor."

"Yes, of course. I will come and meet him." Pitor said, bowing his head. "Thank you. I am grateful for the opportunity."

After Pitor left the site, he wandered until he found a barn that was unlocked. He knew that Jakup and Steffi were waiting for him, and he wanted to get back to them as quickly as possible. But he reminded himself that if he were caught and arrested, they would be alone. And alone, they would never survive. So, he forced himself to be patient and waited until the sunset and it was dark outside. Then, he entered the barn, where he found some carrots and potatoes rotting in a large metal container. An old horse watched him from its stall as Pitor pocketed the vegetables. He knew they had belonged to the horse, and so he went over and petted the horse's face to thank him. When he did, he happened to look in the stall, where he saw a half rotten cabbage laying on the hay. Quickly, Pitor picked it up and stuffed it into his shirt. Then, in the darkness, he ran back to the area where he'd left Jakup and Steffi waiting.

They had not eaten since the previous morning. So even though the vegetables were soft and rotting, they were glad to have them, and they ate them raw. Even Jakup was so hungry that he didn't complain. Although he did say he had a stomachache before he fell asleep on the ground with Pitor's jacket under his head.

Once Jakup was sleeping, Steffi asked Pitor what happened when he went to the construction site.

"I met with the foreman of the job and so far, it is all very promising," he answered.

"I am still so afraid. When you were gone, my mind played terrible tricks on me. I was worried that you had been arrested. I was sure that they had been looking for you and…"

"I know. I was worried too. But it was all right. No one recognized me. And believe me, if I could think of any other way we might survive, I would."

"How did you get the food? Did they give it to you?"

He let out a bitter laugh. "Do you really think a Nazi would be that generous? They wouldn't even give rotting vegetables to a poor man. I found a barn that was unlocked, and I stole whatever food I could find inside."

She nodded. "If they hire you to work on this project, then you will be with them all the time." She began shaking her head. "Pitor, I don't care if we starve, I would feel safer if you were hiding in the forest with us. When you are there with them, anything can happen. At any time, they might receive a message that alerts them to who you are. And they won't care if you have been doing a good job. They won't care about anything but punishing you. They are Nazis, and Nazis are cruel. Those men are terrible people. I saw their cruelty firsthand when I was in the camp. And I promise you they would think nothing of killing you if they found out the truth about you."

"I know," he said, in as comforting a voice as he could manage. "I would like to stay in the forest and never go back there. But we can't. We are going to need food and shelter. So, all we can do is hope they never find out. If Göring decides to hire me, I'll stay with them and work on this site until spring comes. Then as soon as the weather breaks, we can try to make our way to Switzerland. It has not been taken over by the Germans, so if we can get there, we won't have to be afraid of being arrested."

"Can't we try to go now?"

"I would, but it's a long way, and winter is too close. We won't make it through the mountains in the winter. It would be impossible. So, for now, this is what we must do."

"I wish we would have tried to do that earlier."

"I would have if I had known that the partisans were gone. I was sure they would find us."

She nodded sadly.

Steffi didn't argue with him, but Pitor could see her face by the light of the full moon, and he knew by her expression that she didn't approve of his plan. He touched her face and smiled at her. "It will be all right. You'll see," he said.

But knowing how she felt, he decided not to tell her the secret that was worrying him deeply. He just patted her hand and said, "You are going to have to trust me."

CHAPTER FIFTY-SIX

Two days later, Pitor left Steffi and Jakup with a warning to be very careful. Then he began to make his way back to the construction site to meet with Göring. His head ached with worry. He had not been able to tell Steffi what was on his mind. He'd kept it a secret, because he knew that if she was aware he'd met Göring before, when he was posing as Konrad Hoffmann, she would have argued fiercely against him going on this interview. It had only been a quick meeting, just a few moments, and so Pitor was hoping that Göring would not remember him. He was leaning heavily on the fact that Göring was a fat, overindulgent, self-absorbed idiot and that he wasn't paying much attention when he was introduced to a bodyguard who ranked far beneath him. Even so, Pitor's mouth was as dry as sandpaper, and his heart was racing. *What I am about to do is so dangerous*, he thought. Sweat beaded on his brow and caused circular stains in the armpits of his shirt. But for the last two days he'd racked his brain trying to think of any other possible way they might survive the winter. And he couldn't come up with anything. They would need shelter and food. Either the work site would provide this, or they would need the money he earned to pay for it. So, either way, he must take this risk.

As Pitor approached the construction site, he saw Göring standing outside watching the men work. Göring was wearing a heavy wool coat even though it was not freezing outside yet. It was chilly, but nothing like it would be next month and the months following. Göring held a bottle of beer in his hand as he stood talking to one of the supervisors. Gingerly, as a peasant farmer would, Pitor approached the two men.

Göring saw him and frowned. "What do you want?" he asked.

"Please," Pitor said in Polish, looking down at the ground as he spoke. "I am needing a job. I was a farmer, but my farm burned down and now I am desperate for work. I am very strong, and I am more than willing, and capable of doing anything you ask. You see, I have a wife and child to care for."

"I don't care about your wife or your child. But you do look strong," Göring studied him. Pitor glanced up to look into Göring's face quickly. He was searching to see if Göring showed any sign of remembering him, but he saw no recognition in Göring's eyes. Finally, Göring said, "Yes, you do look strong. And we could use another hand. I won't pay you much. But your wife and child can stay with the other families of the workers in the makeshift barracks. And you will have food."

"Thank you. Thank you for this opportunity, sir," Pitor said.

"You will refer to me as *Oberbefehlshaber der Luftwaffe*. Do you understand?"

"Yes, Oberbefehlshaber der Luftwaffe," Pitor answered.

"You can start work tomorrow. Be here before dawn. We start working when the sun comes up."

Pitor nodded.

"Go now."

Pitor left quickly. He tried to find another barn that was unlocked, but he was unable to find one, so he headed back to Steffi and Jakup.

CHAPTER FIFTY-SEVEN

"We are going to be moving into a complex with other families," Steffi explained to Jakup.

"So, I will have other children to play with?"

"Well, no. I'm sorry, but you must not talk to or play with any of the others. You must always stay close to me. No one must know anything about us."

"But why?"

"Because it is what we must do to stay safe. Please just listen to me, all right? Please, Jakup just do as I say."

He nodded.

"Now, I am going to have to give you a new name. A pretend name that you will use if anyone at this complex asks you your name. All right?"

"Another name?" he said sullenly.

"Yes, your name is Florian."

"Florian," he repeated.

Steffi's heart broke as she looked into Jakup's wide eyes. "I know that all of this is so confusing for you," she said gently.

The little boy nodded. "I don't want another new name. Not again," he said. "And I wish I could play with the other children. This doesn't sound like fun at all."

"I know that it is hard on you, but try to think of it as a game," she smiled.

"I don't think it's a game. I don't like it," he said. "First my name was Liam, then it was Jakup Barr and now you say I am to tell everyone that my name is Florian."

"I know." She took Jakup's chin in her hand and then looked directly into his eyes. "Your real name is Jakup Barr. Your papa's real name is Pitor Barr, but for now we will call him Albin, and, you know that in my heart I will always be your Steffi, but I will go by the name of Tomsia. The people in this complex must never know that our surname is Barr. We are going to say that our surname is Marek. Can you remember all of this?"

"I think so," Jakup repeated what she'd said to him.

"That's good. You are a smart boy, and you are doing very well." She acknowledged his retention of the names. "I'm so glad you are such a good boy."

He smiled at her sadly. "But if I can't play with the other children, then I wish we could just go on the way we were living. I wish we could just keep living in the forest. Just the three of us."

"I know. Me too. But winter is coming, and we need shelter. So, we are going to be living in a place where we will be surrounded by Germans who we can't trust. So, we must be sure that they think our name is Marek and that we are a family of Polish farmers."

"Why do we have to stay with them if we can't trust them?" Jakup looked at her, his eyes questioning. "Couldn't we find another place like that hotel where we stayed for a night?"

"When we stayed in the hotel it cost money, and we don't have enough to keep us there for the whole winter. It is much too cold in the winter to stay in the forest. Food will become scarce when it gets cold outside and we will need to have shelter so we can stay warm.

Just stay close to me and don't make friends with the other children and speak as little as possible. Can you do that?"

He nodded. "Once we move in with the other families, can I still talk to you and papa about everything I feel?"

"Only when we are alone. Never tell anyone else what you are thinking. All right?"

"Yes. I promise," Jakup said.

"It's very important Jakup. You must never forget that you can't trust any of the people we meet in the complex. All right?"

He nodded. And his eyes looked so old in his young face it hurt her heart to look into them.

Steffi was glad that when she was growing up, the neighbors who lived at the farm next door were Polish. Because she had become friends with their daughter, who was a year older than herself, she had learned to speak Polish quite well. And she had even perfected the accent. So, posing as a Polish farm wife would not be difficult.

The following day, after Pitor finished work at the site, he returned to the forest to collect Steffi and Jakup. While the three of them walked towards the barracks where the rest of families of the workers lived, Pitor explained again to Jakup that he must not talk openly to anyone. And he told Steffi that it was essential that she make herself useful. She didn't want to sit around and complain like some of the other wives. If she were busy, the German's might not consider throwing them out.

Steffi helped to cook and to keep the barracks clean. A group of German wives were in charge of the kitchen that served the officers. She offered to help them, and they accepted her help, but because they thought she was Polish and not one of them, they gave her the more difficult tasks. Steffi was made to lift heavy boxes and peel potatoes until her hands bled. But even as she toiled all day, she kept a close watch on Jakup, never letting him out of her sight.

The wives of the Germans who worked on the construction were cold and unfriendly to Steffi because she was not one of them. And although she felt their assumption of superiority, she was glad that they and their children left her and Jakup alone. It was a relief not to have to answer any questions they might ask. And although it was dangerous to be at the complex amongst the enemy, she and Pitor agreed that at least there was food to eat each evening.

CHAPTER FIFTY-EIGHT

One afternoon as Pitor lifted heavy boulders and large bricks onto his shoulders and carried them over to the construction site, he overheard two Nazi officers talking.

"These roads are going to make it easier to locate and take out the partisan groups," one of them said proudly.

"Of course. The Führer's vision reaches even into the forests. Nothing escapes German efficiency," the other replied.

Pitor was careful to hide any expressions of disgust that might have shown on his face. He kept his head down and did not draw any attention to himself as he continued his work.

CHAPTER FIFTY-NINE

Gretchen was miserable in jail. Her trial for murder was set to begin very soon, and Horst was beside himself with worry. If she were convicted, she might be sent to one of those horrible camps. When he went searching for Pitor Barr, he'd seen what Auschwitz was like, and he couldn't bear to think of her caged up in such a place. *I must find that lousy Jew and turn him in. It is the only possible way I might be able to convince the authorities to let Gretchen out. I will tell them that she was in shock, that her best friend had been soiled by sleeping with a Jew, and that she acted irrationally. They will believe me when they have that Jew in custody and they can question him about the wicked web he spun. But I have no idea where he is. I can only assume he has found a group of partisans and has joined them.*

Horst had lost everything he held dear when Gretchen was arrested, and he blamed Pitor for all of it. Without Gretchen's salary, he would no longer be able to afford his apartment. But it didn't matter, because he had not worked since Gretchen's arrest, so he'd lost his job too. He'd spent quite a bit of their savings, first protecting himself by paying the Polish man to convince the Nazis that Liam was their child, and then he'd had to pay for a train ticket to Poland, trying to find Pitor. Now, the money that he and Gretchen had saved was nearly all gone.

When Horst left Auschwitz, he didn't return home. He couldn't go back, not without Pitor as his prisoner. If he did, he would have nothing to use as leverage to free his wife, and without Gretchen, Horst felt he had no reason to live at all. So, he took whatever money he had left and bought whatever food he could afford. Then, Horst disappeared into the forest, wandering and searching for Pitor. Horst knew the Gestapo wouldn't take pity on Gretchen. They never took pity on anyone. He'd heard of other Nazi Party members who'd broken a law and were punished severely. *Especially because my Gretchen killed a good German woman,* Horst thought. But Horst was hoping they might be grateful to him, a man who had found a Jew that had dared to put himself in a position where he could endanger the Führer. *This Pitor Barr, was a very special Jew. He was one in a million. He was a Jew who had found a way to trick them all and become a bodyguard for the Führer.* Horst shivered when he thought of Barr, a Jew in charge of the safety of the most important man in Germany. *This is an unforgivable offence.*

The forests were dangerous and unkind to Horst. He had never enjoyed nature. And since he'd grown up in the city, and his father was not a hunter or fisherman, he'd never learned to fend for himself. Once when he was twelve, he'd gone fishing with a few of his cousins, but he had not caught anything and so he found the entire outing to be a bore and never attempted to fish again. Horst had learned in the Hitler Youth that many of the things that were found growing in the forest were poisonous if consumed. But he had not paid much attention when his troop leaders were giving the lesson, so he had no idea which were edible, and which were not. He feared the wolves and the owls, so he stayed on the edge of the woods and entered only briefly, never going in too deep. His uniform enabled him to extort food and money from frightened farmers, whose farms he passed along the way. And he used the money that he stole for cheap hotel rooms where he stopped to clean up in each town he passed. Horst carried a photograph with him that had been taken when Pitor had received his promotion at the Eagle's Nest. He showed it to everyone he came in contact with, asking if they recognized the man in the picture. But thus far, no one had seen Pitor Barr, the man who had posed as Konrad Hoffmann. And so, Horst continued on what seemed like an impossible journey. As Horst moved through the forest, he was almost caught by a group of partisans, but he hid before they saw him, and stayed hidden all night until they moved on. Then he followed them back to their camp, where he searched for Pitor, but he didn't find him. Another time, he heard the voices of two German soldiers, both of them deserters. He watched them as he hid behind a bunch of thick bushes. The woods were full of danger. If the partisans or the deserters had seen him, he was certain, they would have killed him. Horst longed to return home, but his home was gone. And his life would never be the same without his wife. He had come to lean on Gretchen for everything, and he had to find a way to free her. So, he continued his search.

By the time Horst had made his way to the small village of Kampinos, he was distraught and almost ready to give up. But when he checked into the local hotel and showed the photo of Pitor Barr to the skinny desk clerk asking if he'd ever seen this man before, the clerk nodded his head and responded, "Actually, yes, I remember this man. I saw him. He was here a few months ago."

Horst felt as if he had been injected with a shot of hope. And for the first time in a long time, he felt alive. "Did he stay here?"

"Yes, actually, he did."

"What can you tell me about him?"

"Only that when he came in, he was wearing the uniform of an SS officer like he is in this photograph," the desk clerk said, "however, this is rather strange, but when he left, he had a woman and child with him, and he was not wearing his uniform. He was dressed in the clothes of a Polish peasant farmer. I must admit, I found that to be rather odd."

"Do you know if he went anywhere else here in town? Do you know if he had contact with anyone else?"

"I can't say. But I do remember that I saw him carry food into the hotel. And since the only place open at the time of night when he brought the food was the local tavern, I would assume he got it there."

"Well, that's good to know. You've been very helpful. Thank you," Horst said.

The clerk handed Horst his room key. "Why are you asking all of these questions?" the clerk asked.

Horst didn't want to tell anyone about his plans. *I can't risk someone else finding Pitor Barr and turning him in before I do. After all, there is a reward for Barr's capture. I am sure that if this desk clerk is able to find Barr, he will try to claim it for himself. Barr is my only chance to free Gretchen, and I have been working so hard to find him.* So, Horst smiled at the desk clerk and said, "Oh, the man in this photograph happens to be an old friend of mine. I heard he was coming here to go hunting. I am sure that is why he changed out of his uniform into what appeared to be the clothes of a farmer. He must have been going hunting. I hear that it's good in these forests."

"Yes, you're probably right. Hunting used to be very good here. But the new roads and watch towers that the Germans are currently building in the forest right outside of town have scared away a lot of the animals. Have you heard about the new extra wide roads for the tanks?"

"Yes, of course I've heard all about it," Horst said, but he didn't know anything about it.

"I believe Hermann Göring is the one in charge of all of it. At least that's what I've heard. Although the Germans are building roads, everyone here in town thinks this will be very good for the local businesses. It will allow more Germans to travel through our town, and hopefully even stay at the hotels. We believe that people will stop at our restaurants and taverns, and bring lots of money to our town."

"Oh yes, I am quite sure it will," Horst said. Then he took the key to his room, put it in his pocket and thanked the clerk for his help. "I think I am going to go out and get some dinner," Horst said, smiling. "Where is the local tavern you mentioned?"

"Just a few steps from here. When you get outside, turn right and walk for a bit. You can't miss it."

"Is the food good?"

"Yes, very."

"Good," Horst said, and he gave the desk clerk a smile.

The desk clerk nodded and returned the smile.

Horst took a long deep breath as soon as he walked out of the hotel. Immediately he began to head down the street toward the local tavern. He was famished and he did need to eat something, but more importantly he wanted to speak with the bartender to see if he could find out anything more about what Pitor might have said when he was in town. *Perhaps Pitor had a few drinks and felt comfortable enough to give the bartender some clues as to where he was going.*

CHAPTER SIXTY

Horst made his way to the local tavern that he had been told Pitor Barr visited. He sat down at the bar and ordered. "This is a nice place," Horst said, as the bartender brought him a dark beer.

"Thank you. I am the owner," the bartender said proudly.

"Beer is very good too," Horst said as he took a sip.

"I brew it myself."

"Really?" Horst found the bartender to be friendly and very talkative. Horst took a folded up picture from the breast of his jacket and showed it to the bartender. "Do you recognize the man in this photograph?" Horst pointed to Pitor.

"Yes. He was here one night. He is working on the new roads and watch towers that they are building in the forest."

"What do you know about the construction?"

He told Horst everything he knew about the site.

"So, you are telling me that he is working in construction?" Horst reiterated what the bartender told him, almost in shock. *Oh how the mighty have fallen, a man who was once so high and mighty is now working a construction job.*

"I can't say for sure. It was a while back that he came in. He may have left by now. But at the time, I believe that he was working there."

"Tell me a little about the man who came in here. Can you? Tell me whatever you can remember."

"Well..." the bartender said, "the fellow who came into this bar was a tall, healthy, strong German. He wore the uniform of an officer. I must admit he was quite Aryan. Not that I am concerned with such a thing as another man's looks." He smiled at Horst strangely. *Well, he disgusts me, but who cares? My goal is to find Barr, that dirty Jew, and use him to free my wife. My food and money are almost gone, and Gretchen is about to go to trial. So, the sooner I find Barr and bring him back to face justice, the better my chances will be of saving my wife.*

CHAPTER SIXTY-ONE

The men who worked at the construction site were unkind to each other, especially to the weaker ones, or the ones who were not German. They teased and jeered at them. But because of Pitor's size and strength, no one bothered him. They did not tease him, but they also did not invite him to sit with them when they sat down to eat their midday meal, but Pitor didn't care. He didn't want or need their friendship. It was better this way. Pitor kept to himself, so he did not have to worry about answering any questions or keeping any lies straight. The Germans who were working had their own group, and there was no room for a Polish farmer, even if he had uncanny strength, which made him a valuable asset.

The day's work ended at sundown, and after, Pitor joined Steffi and Jakup in the small room where they shared a bed. Although there was no intimate contact between Pitor and Steffi, there was a warm feeling of family that circulated between the three of them. Sometimes Pitor would recall the conversation he'd had with Mila that night when he spoke with her as he sat under the stars. And he was certain that she had answered him, and that she approved of a marriage between himself and Steffi. He felt confident that she would have wanted Jakup to have a mother. Over the course of the last few months, as they had wandered the forests together, Pitor found himself developing feelings for Steffi, the quiet woman who gave all of herself to him and his son without question, and never asked anything in return. And although Steffi would never take Mila's place—no one ever could—he found that in his own way, he loved her. *I never thought that love could happen twice in a lifetime. I grew up believing that a person had one bashert, and once that person was gone, the other would never love again. However, Steffi has made me feel different,* he thought one night as she lay sleeping beside him, her soft breath flowing slowly and evenly. *Tomorrow,* he decided, *tomorrow will be the day that I will ask her to be my wife. And if she agrees, we will marry the only way that we can. Since we cannot have a civil ceremony because neither of us are using our real names, and there are no religious leaders here that we can ask to marry us, we will stand outside and in a private ceremony we will declare our undying devotion to each other forever.*

CHAPTER SIXTY-TWO

It was late when Horst left the bar, but he felt better after his conversation with the bartender. Now he was one step closer to finding Pitor. He chose not to venture into the forest right away, because it was night and he preferred to wait until morning to go to the construction site. The streets were dark and quiet as he made his way back to his room at the hotel. And that night, he slept more soundly than he had since Gretchen was arrested. Finally, he could see a light at the end of the tunnel.

It was very early the following morning when Horst was awakened due to a full bladder. He would have preferred to stay in bed, but the nagging need to urinate forced him to get up. *Damn all that beer,* he thought as he walked down the hall to the bathroom. After he took a quick shower to wake himself up, Horst went back to his room and put on his uniform. Horst went downstairs to ask the desk clerk for directions to the building site. When he got to the front desk, he was ignored by two women standing behind the desk, one who appeared to be in a maid's uniform and another woman who was the day clerk.

Horst interrupted their conversation. "I am looking for the man who was working here last night. Do you know when he will be back?" Horst asked.

"Of course, you're talking about Felix, but he won't be back until four o'clock tomorrow afternoon. He's off today," the woman said with a smile. Her lips were full and painted with bright red lipstick. Horst turned around for a moment. He felt as if he were a burden, and he was feeling insecure. *Everything had been going so well, and now I have to wait another day. Or maybe I should just ask her. Maybe one of them would know exactly where the site is.*

"Excuse me." Horst interrupted the women again. "I hate to bother you again."

Both women looked at him curiously. "How can I help you?" the desk clerk asked politely.

"There is a site in the forest where the Germans are constructing new roads and watchtowers. Do you happen to know where it is?"

The girl studied him. Her eyes traveled up and down his body. "You're a German, yes?"

"Of course, I am" he said.

Then she smiled. "Of course, I can tell you," she said, smiling. "Everyone here in town knows where it is."

Can you give me directions to get there?"

"Sure."

CHAPTER SIXTY-THREE

Beads of nervous sweat ran down Horst's armpits as he walked towards the construction site. He had seen firsthand just how powerful Pitor could be. Several times he'd seen Barr lift and carry heavy loads effortlessly, without even straining. Horst felt his courage waning. He wanted to weep because he had no choice but to face this man. A shiver passed through him as he walked through the forest in the direction of the site. For a moment, he closed his eyes as the sun beat down on his head, and he recalled a time when he'd attended a party with Gretchen where he'd overheard Johann Rattenhuber, who was the head of Hitler's bodyguards, talking to Joseph Goebbels. Of course, Horst was not important enough to speak to either of them. He was nothing more than a guard, so he didn't utter a single word when he heard Rattenhuber tell Goebbels that Konrad Hoffmann had the uncanny strength of a perfect Aryan man. At the time, Horst had been terribly jealous. Not only did Hoffmann have a wonderful, well-paid career, but he was admired and respected. And even then, Horst knew Hoffmann was a fake. He opened his eyes and let out a laugh. He was so taken with the absurdity of it all. Somewhere in the distance, a bird mocked his laughter, and the sound reminded him he must be quiet. *The last thing I need right now is to be found by some partisans or some deserters. I have a gun, but they might have the element of surprise. It's best to be as quiet as I can be,* he thought, then he recalled how Rattenhuber had raved not only to Goebbels, but to Eva Braun. *Beautiful Eva Braun, she too had believed that Hoffmann was a boy wonder. And,* Horst thought, *all along I was the only one who could sense that Hoffmann was a fake. I felt it in my bones. Hitler thinks Rattenhuber is such a good judge of character. It's rather funny that he could be fooled by a Jew.*

It would have been easier to go to the site and speak directly to Göring. He could tell him all about Barr. But Horst was concerned that if he did, he would not be given credit for his efforts, and that would mean he would have no leverage to have Gretchen released. *No, I must wait until I have the opportunity to capture Barr. Then I must take him back to Munich with me at gunpoint. The only way I can do this is if I hide and wait until I can find him alone. It would be so much easier to just shoot him. He is such a dangerous, strong man. I am taking a real risk in taking him prisoner. But if I kill him, I will have no proof of who he is. I need him to confess. Once he admits to being a Jew, the authorities will understand why Gretchen went out of her mind and accidentally killed her best friend.*

Horst stayed outside in the forest that night. He couldn't sleep at all; every hoot from an owl or howl of a wolf set his heart racing with fear. But he stayed hidden in the woods and waited until morning. He could not be sure that Barr was working at the construction site. The bartender said that Barr had been working there a while ago. However, that didn't mean he was still there. Horst was terrified of what was to come next, and so he half hoped that he would not find Barr. But he knew he must try.

CHAPTER SIXTY-FOUR

That night, as Pitor and Steffi lay in the tiny cot that had been provided, watching Jakup sleep between them, Pitor whispered, "Steffi, I have something to ask you."

"Oh? What is it?" She said, hoisting her head up on her hand as she bent her elbow.

"I know that in our current circumstances this might sound petty. Even silly. But it means a lot to me."

"Please, ask whatever you want. You know that nothing you ask me is ever petty or silly," she said softly.

"Well..." He hesitated. "Over the last several months I've come to have feelings for you. Special feelings." He heard her breath catch in her throat. A silent moment passed, then he continued speaking. "I suppose what I am trying to say, is that I think I love you."

She let out a whimper. "Oh Pitor," she said. "You don't know how much I have hoped and prayed that someday you might say that to me. I never thought it would come true. I never believed it was possible."

"Steffi, you are beautiful on the inside and out. You are a wonderful companion, and a terrific mother," he said, "and, well..."

he hesitated. "I want you to be my wife and if you are willing, I want you to be a mother to my son."

"Oh Pitor, yes. I love Jakup as if he were mine. Pitor..." She hesitated, and he heard her draw a breath. "I've loved you since the first time I saw you. In fact, even when I was in the camp, the only thing that kept me alive, until I found Jakup, was the hope of seeing you again."

He felt a tear filled with emotion run down his cheek, and he was glad that the room was dark. "So...then...you'll be my wife?"

"Yes."

He leaned over and kissed her. She melted. "We can't make love," she whispered. "We'll wake Jakup."

"I know," he said, "but soon I will think of a way that we can be together."

"How can we get married? Everyone here thinks we are already married?"

"We'll marry ourselves. We'll go out under the stars and declare our love for each other so that God can hear us." He said, "Will you go with me?"

"Do you want to go now? Do you think it's all right to leave Jakup alone here?"

"Yes, we can leave Jakup for just a few minutes." Pitor, careful not to wake Jakup, stood up next to the bed. "He's asleep and everyone else is too. He'll be safe. We'll come right back. Will you go with me?" Pitor reached his hand out to Steffi, and she placed her hand in his.

"Yes."

CHAPTER SIXTY-FIVE

They walked out into the brisk night air. The inky blue-black sky was lit by a thousand stars as they made their way away from the camp into the forest.

Once they were alone, Pitor turned to face Steffi, then in a serious voice he said, "I, Pitor Barr, vow to be your faithful and lawfully wedded husband for the rest of my life. And as God is my witness, I will love and cherish you forever."

Tears of joy ran down Steffi's cheeks as she repeated Pitor's vow. There was a brief silence once she'd finished. Then he took her into his arms and held her close to him for a long time. Their hearts beat together as Pitor took off his shirt and, despite the cold, he laid it down on the ground. Then he helped Steffi to lie down on his shirt, and he began to kiss her.

"Papa? Steffi? Papa where are you?" It was Jakup. He was calling out from somewhere close by.

"It sounds like he woke up and found us just in time," Pitor said, then he and Steffi both laughed.

"We're over here," Pitor called out to his son as he got up and made his way to where Jakup stood shivering.

"I woke up and I was scared because you were both gone," Jakup said.

"It's all right," Pitor said as he took Jakup in his arms, and together they walked back to where Steffi was waiting.

Steffi picked Pitor's shirt up off the ground and wrapped the little boy in it. "It's cold out here. You must be freezing," she said.

Jakup nodded. "When I woke up and you were both gone, I thought you had left me here all alone."

"Never, we would never leave you," Steffi said as she held Jakup close to her.

"Do you promise?"

"Yes, I promise," she said.

"And I still remember that you once told me that you will never break a promise to me," Jakup said.

"That's right. And it's still true." She smiled at him. "I will never break a promise to you."

CHAPTER SIXTY-SIX

The sound of Jakup's desperate calls as he searched for his father and Steffi had broken through the darkness, reaching the ears of Horst, who had been hiding only several feet away. He wasn't sure who the child was or why he was calling for his father, but his nerves were on high alert. Quickly, Horst grabbed his gun. The voice was definitely the voice of a child, and this made Horst wonder if it could be the little boy who he'd taken from Pitor so long ago. The child he had stolen from the Warsaw Ghetto. If he could only go back to that day, he would never have taken the child. It had not saved his job. He'd still been demoted and never rose in the party again. But there was no way to change the past. So, he sucked in a breath and, remaining hidden in the shadows, Horst followed the noise of human voices until he saw him. His body trembled when he saw it was Barr. He'd been right; the child was the same one he'd taken from the ghetto. And they were with a woman, a blonde woman he didn't recognize. Horst raised his gun and pointed it at Pitor. He didn't plan to shoot. He was only planning to arrest Pitor and then take him to Munich alive. But the woman spotted Horst. Their eyes met. She cried out, "Pitor look out!" That was when Pitor turned around and his gaze fell upon Horst. Horst felt his blood run cold. Pitor was coming towards him fast. He panicked and pulled the trigger, but not before the woman stepped in front of Pitor. She took the bullet that was meant for him. She was so small and slight that she fell without making a sound. Horst saw the look in Pitor's eyes, and he knew he should run, but his feet were frozen. He couldn't move. And within seconds, Pitor was upon him. His strong hands wrapped like a boa constrictor around Horst's neck, squeezing the life out of him. Jakup was weeping as he knelt beside Steffi. Both Jakup and Steffi were covered in blood. Horst was terrified. He felt his eyes bulging out of his head, and he wanted to scream, but he couldn't breathe. Pain seized him, and tears ran down his face. His eyes were closing. They were so heavy he could not keep them open. In his mind, he saw demons, horrible, terrifying demons. And he felt himself free falling into an abyss. Horst was shivering. It was so cold. He would have begged for his life, but he couldn't speak; the hand around his throat was preventing it. Pitor squeezed harder until Horst's heart stopped beating, his breath was gone and although he was dead his eyes were filled with bright red blood and wide open.

Once Pitor knew Horst was dead, he ran to kneel at Steffi's side. He put his hand under her head and held her close to him. "Please Steffi, please don't die. I can't lose you. I can't."

Jakup was hysterical and holding on to Pitor's leg. "She promised she'd never leave me," he cried.

"I will never leave you," Steffi whispered to Jakup. "Even if you can't see me anymore, I will always be with you."

"No, Steffi. No," Pitor said, "You can't die. Please don't go."

Then there was a rustling in the trees, and a man appeared. "Pitor Barr?" The man said.

Jakup was shaking with fear.

Pitor looked up. He recognized the man right away. It was Alex, a Polish man who had been one of the partisans who Pitor knew from the time he'd stayed with them right after Mila died. Pitor glanced down at Steffi; her eyes were closing. *I can't bear to go through this again,* he thought. "Can you help us? Please." Pitor begged.

"Yes, of course, let me help you carry her. There is a doctor at our campsite. It's not far from here. We can take her there."

"I can carry her," Pitor said, then he turned to Steffi who was still conscious, "It's all right, Steffi. You're going to be all right," Pitor said, then he glanced over at Jakup as he lifted Steffi in his arms. "Stay close to my side. I can't hold your hand so hold on to me as we walk, all right?"

"Yes, Papa," Jakup agreed, his small hand trembling as he held tight to his father's pants leg.

CHAPTER SIXTY-SEVEN

The entrance to the partisan's campsite had been moved since Pitor had stayed with them. It was now well hidden by trees and brush. But it was not far from the construction site. Jakup tripped and fell twice during the walk, but he did not cry or complain. Even though he was just a child, he knew that there was no time to stop and nurture him. Steffi was in desperate need of help, and every second counted.

When they entered the small campsite, everyone looked up. "For those of you who don't know him, this is Pitor Barr. He is my friend. His woman needs help. Shmul, can you help her?" Alex asked.

"Yes," a man in his late twenties, with dark hair and thick glasses, who Pitor did not recognize, approached them. "I'm Shmul," he said to Pitor. "I was a doctor in Germany."

"My wife has been shot. She needs immediate attention. Please, help her," Pitor said.

Shmul nodded. "Let me have a look."

Jakup watched closely and wept softly as Shmul uncovered Steffi's chest. She was covered in blood.

"It's good news," Shmul said finally. "The bullet missed her heart. But she is losing a lot of blood so, I'm going to remove the bullet right away. Maybe it would be a good idea for the child not to watch this."

"Come with me," Pitor said, taking Jakup's hand.

"No, I won't leave Steffi. She always held my hand when I was scared. She's scared now, and I am going to stay and hold her hand."

Shmul was busy washing his hands with a bucket of water and a small bar of stolen soap that stood under a tree.

Shmul returned ready to begin.

"The doctor is going to do something that is going to be unpleasant for you to see. There will be blood involved," Pitor said gently.

"I don't care. I want to be with Steffi," Jakup demanded.

"Is it all right?" Pitor asked Shmul.

"Yes, but he must be quiet. And he cannot cry or scream," he said, then he turned to Jakup and asked, "Can you do that? Because if you scream or cry you will bring the German's right here to us and all of us, including your family could be killed."

"I will be good, and I will be quiet," Jakup said. It hurt Pitor's heart to hear his son sounding so adult. *My poor Jakup has never had the opportunity to be a carefree child.* Pitor thought.

Shmul set half a bottle of schnapps beside him. Then he lit a match and put the blade of a sharp knife through the fire. After the knife was sterilized, he took a moment to let it cool, and then he began his work. He made a small, careful incision in Steffi's shoulder and began to remove the bullet. Steffi's eyes grew wide with pain as she looked around her, wild and disoriented. Then she began to thrash and panic until she saw that Pitor and Jakup were at her side. Shmul held up the schnapps bottle, then in a gentle voice he instructed her to take a long swig of the schnapps. She did as he told her to do, but she gagged and almost vomited it up. But she kept it down, and it helped to take the edge off the terrible pain.

Once the bullet was removed, Shmul reminded Steffi that she

must not scream. "Here, bite on this," he said as he gave her a worn blanket. "I have to cauterize the wound."

She nodded. Then with trembling hands she held the blanket in her mouth.

Shmul poured some schnapps on the open cut, and Steffi flinched. But when he burned the wound, she fainted.

Pitor looked at the doctor with fear in his eyes. "Is she still alive?" he asked.

"Yes. She passed out from the pain," Shmul said, as he stitched the cut with a needle and string that he kept in a makeshift doctor kit. "It's better for her this way." Once he finished closing the wound, he said, "Now, all we can do is let her sleep. She needs to rest. God willing she'll make it. We must pray that infection doesn't set in. That is our greatest concern right now."

Shmul showed Pitor how to keep Steffi's incision clean. And each day for the next two days, with Jakup at his side, Pitor made sure to keep the wound clean and change the bandages. But Steffi did not regain consciousness. By the second day, Pitor was distraught. "Will she ever come back to us?" he begged Shmul for an answer. "I'm afraid this was too much for her. I wish she hadn't stepped in front of me. I wish she'd let me take the bullet. I'm stronger. I could have handled it better."

Shmul checked Steffi's wound and found no sign of infection. Then he checked her vital signs and assured Pitor that she was still alive.

Pitor held her hand to his lips and begged her to come back to them.

Then, on the morning of the third day, Steffi slowly opened her eyes. She glanced around confused, until she saw Pitor and Jakup. "Pitor, Jakup." She said, her voice soft, barely a croak. "Where are we?" She tried to sit up, but when she did, she winced in pain and lay back down.

Pitor, who had been sitting beside her, gently took her into his arms. He held her close to his chest, and tears ran down his cheeks.

"You're alive." He said, and then he began to laugh and cry at the same time. Holding her and kissing her eyes, her cheeks, her lips. Jakup, not knowing what to do, began to cry too.

"Where are we, Pitor?" Steffi asked.

"We are safe," Pitor whispered. "The partisans have found us. We are in their camp."

"My shoulder hurts very badly," she murmured.

"You were shot. There is a Jewish doctor here living amongst the partisans. He is helping you. You will be all right." Then he asked, "Are you hungry?"

"Yes, very." She nodded.

Shmul, who had been standing on the side watching, said, "Hunger is a very good sign. There is a pot of soup cooking on the fire. Give her some."

CHAPTER SIXTY-EIGHT

When Horst did not return, Gretchen thought he'd run away and left her to face the consequences of her actions alone. She cursed him. But the war was almost over, and the Germans knew they were losing. They had more important things to worry about than a woman who had accidentally murdered her friend in a moment of insanity. And so, Gretchen was released. The police, the SS, the Gestapo, the guards at the camps and everyone in the Nazi Party began to panic. Hitler married his longtime girlfriend, Eva Braun. Then, along with Goebbels, and Goebbels' wife and six children, they all went down into Hitler's private bunker. First, they killed Hitler's loyal German Shepard. Eva was next; she willingly died for her love of the Führer. Then it was Hitler's turn. It is said—although it is not certain—that Hitler committed suicide. The following day, Joseph and Magda Goebbels murdered all six of their young children with cyanide capsules, and then they took their own lives.

Without their leader, the Germans knew that they were finished. They also knew that when the Allies arrived, they would see the terrible things that the Nazis had done. So, as quickly as they could, the Nazis destroyed the evidence of their crimes. They murdered as many of the innocent prisoners who were left as possible. And then, like the cowards that they were, they ran away before the Allied troops arrived.

EPILOGUE

Many of Pitor's old friends, who he had grown close to when he lived with the partisans, were now gone. Alex explained that some of them died from sickness, while others were killed by the Nazis during missions. Pitor was at a loss for words. He could not respond. He only shook his head. It sickened him to think of the needless deaths of so many good people. But there was no point in trying to understand all that had happened. The only explanation was that the Nazis were sick and cruel. It was a true travesty that they had taken so many valuable lives. They had stolen the gifts and talents of these people from the rest of the world. Sometimes, when he was alone and unable to sleep, Pitor wondered about what kinds of wonderful contributions those who had been murdered might have made to mankind, if their lives had not been taken from them.

Steffi recovered slowly. And once she was strong enough to work, she became Shmul's helper. She tended to anyone who became sick and assisted Shmul when he had to perform surgery. Pitor left early each morning, going out each day to hunt and fish.

A young Jewish girl who had escaped from a moving transport joined the partisans late that year. She was a solitary girl who hardly spoke to anyone. And each day she went out walking alone. One afternoon, as a cold winter storm began to descend upon Poland, she returned with a small wolf cub that she'd found in the forest. When Jakup saw the little gray wolf, his eyes opened wide. "Can I pet him?" he asked the girl.

"You can have him, if you'd like, he's all alone in this world, like me," she said sadly. "But I can't stay here with him. I have to try and get home. I have to try to find my sister."

Jakup turned to his parents, "Please, please, can I keep him?" Jakup begged.

Pitor nodded. "Yes, you can keep him."

And for the first time since Steffi was shot, Jakup smiled.

On an exceptionally frigid day in February, two of the partisans went out trying to hunt. They found a man lying on his back in the forest. His hair and eyelashes were frozen, and he was almost at death's door. They brought him back to camp; he was parched and half starved. But by some miracle he survived. His name was Hymie, and once he regained his strength, he told them he had been a rabbi in Poland who had escaped from one of the concentration camps.

That spring, despite the Nazis, the earth began to renew herself, the trees began to grow leaves, and flowers began to bloom. And in a small ceremony among their partisan friends, Hymie, the rabbi, married Pitor and Steffi.

Meanwhile, the partisans got word that the Germans were losing the war. Even so, they continued to carry out dangerous missions of resistance against the Nazis. And although a few were killed in the process, by some miracle the camp remained hidden until the war finally ended.

Once the war was over, the brave freedom fighters separated and made their way to their respective homes in search of any family that they might find still alive. Pitor and Steffi had no family left and nowhere to return to.

Shmul, who had become like a brother to Pitor and Steffi, had told them about a displaced persons camp where they could get help until they decided what to do next. "I have an idea," he said to Pitor and Steffi. "I have a cousin who lives in America. While we wait at the displaced persons camp, I will send him a letter and ask him if he will sponsor us to move to America. I have never met him, but my father always liked him. He said he was a very successful businessman, very wealthy, kind and also very generous."

"America." Pitor said, nodding his head. Then he repeated the word again, "America. Yes! That's where we want to go."

"But we don't know anyone there. And even if Shmul's cousin agrees to sponsor us, we can't expect him to take care of us. How will we make a living? How can we survive? I don't speak English, do you?" Steffi asked.

"I speak a little English," Pitor admitted. "And I am a fast learner. Besides that, I am a butcher by trade. And I am a good one. So, I will find work for a butcher shop."

And so, they went to stay at a displaced persons camp. True to his word, Shmul sent a letter to his cousin. Months passed with no response. Just as Pitor was losing hope, like a miracle, a letter arrived from America inviting Shmul and his partisan family to come to Chicago.

Soon Shmul, Steffi, Pitor, and Jakup would board a ship to New York. From there they would take a train to Chicago.

And when they first arrived, Shmul's cousin insisted they stay with him and his wife. Since the cousin had never had children of his own, he and his wife were immediately smitten with Jakup. They were all made to feel welcome, even Jakup's wolf pup, who was now a full grown, but well-behaved wolf, and for this Pitor was grateful. But Pitor wanted to work. He would not live under another man's roof and eat his food without making some form of payment. He went out searching for a job but had a difficult time. His English was broken. So Shmul's cousin found Pitor a job at a butcher shop where everyone spoke Yiddish. It was in a primarily Jewish neighborhood on the west side of Chicago, where many other Holocaust survivors were trying to make a new start.

Steffi got a job cleaning houses, and she and Pitor worked very hard and saved every penny they could. Finally, five years later, they opened a small café with its own bakery and butcher shop. Every meal was homemade, and people came from all around the Chicago area to enjoy the Jewish, European cuisine. But the most unique thing about the little café was its name. They called it 'A Million Miracles.' A *mezuza* was placed proudly above the door so the patrons knew that the establishment was owned by Jews. And handwritten on the front of the menu it said:

This restaurant is called A Million Miracles, *because it took a million miracles for us to survive the Holocaust and make it here to America to bring you this wholesome and delicious food. We, the Barr family, truly hope you enjoy it!*

A NOTE FROM THE AUTHOR

Dear All,

    I always enjoy hearing from my readers, and your thoughts about my work are very important to me. If you enjoyed my novel, please consider telling your friends and posting a short review on Amazon. Word of mouth is an author's best friend.

Also, it would be my honor to have you join my mailing list. As my gift to you for joining, you will receive 3 **free** short stories and my USA Today award-winning novella! To sign up, just go to my website at... www.RobertaKagan.com

                I send blessings to each and every one of you,
                                      Roberta

Email: roberta@robertakagan.com

ABOUT THE AUTHOR

I wanted to take a moment to introduce myself. My name is Roberta, and I am an author of Historical Fiction, mainly based on World War 2 and the Holocaust. While I never discount the horrors of the Holocaust and the Nazis, my novels are constantly inspired by love, kindness, and the small special moments that make life worth living.

I always knew I wanted to reach people through art when I was younger. I just always thought I would be an actress. That dream died in my late 20's, after many attempts and failures. For the next several years, I tried so many different professions. I worked as a hairstylist and a wedding coordinator, amongst many other jobs. But I was never satisfied. Finally, in my 50's, I worked for a hospital on the PBX board. Every day I would drive to work, I would dread clocking in. I would count the hours until I clocked out. And, the next day, I would do it all over again. I couldn't see a way out, but I prayed, and I prayed, and then I prayed some more. Until one morning at 4 am, I woke up with a voice in my head, and you might know that voice as Detrick. He told me to write his story, and together we sat at the computer; we wrote the novel that is now known as All My Love, Detrick. I now have over 30 books published, and I have had the honor of being a USA Today Best-Selling Author. I have met such incredible people in this industry, and I am so blessed to be meeting you.

I tell this story a lot. And a lot of people think I am crazy, but it is true. I always found solace in books growing up but didn't start writing until I was in my late 50s. I try to tell this story to as many people as possible to inspire them. No matter where you are in your life, remember there is always a flicker of light no matter how dark it seems.

I send you many blessings, and I hope you enjoy my novels. They are all written with love.

Roberta

MORE BOOKS BY ROBERTA KAGAN
AVAILABLE ON AMAZON

A Million Miracles Series
I'll Never Cry Again

Searching for Jakup

A Million Miracles

Margot's Secret Series
The Secret They Hid

An Innocent Child

Margot's Secret

The Lies We Told

The Blood Sisters Series
The Pact

My Sister's Betrayal

When Forever Ends

The Auschwitz Twins Series
The Children's Dream

Mengele's Apprentice

The Auschwitz Twins

Jews, The Third Reich, and a Web of Secrets
My Son's Secret

The Stolen Child

A Web of Secrets

A Jewish Family Saga

Not In America

They Never Saw It Coming

When The Dust Settled

The Syndrome That Saved Us

A Holocaust Story Series

The Smallest Crack

The Darkest Canyon

Millions Of Pebbles

Sarah and Solomon

All My Love, Detrick Series

All My Love, Detrick

You Are My Sunshine

The Promised Land

To Be An Israeli

Forever My Homeland

Michal's Destiny Series

Michal's Destiny

A Family Shattered

Watch Over My Child

Another Breath, Another Sunrise

Eidel's Story Series

And... Who Is The Real Mother?

Secrets Revealed

New Life, New Land

Another Generation

The Wrath of Eden Series

The Wrath Of Eden

The Angels Song

Stand Alone Novels

One Last Hope

A Flicker Of Light

The Heart Of A Gypsy

Made in the USA
Middletown, DE
17 December 2025

25236669R00167